SHAKEN NOT PURRED

Enjoy!

Kelle Z. Riley

SHAKEN NOT PURRED

Undercover Cat Series, Book 2

KELLE Z RILEY

This is a work of fiction. Names, characters, places and incidents are products of the author's imagination or are used fictitiously and are not to be construed as real. Any resemblance to actual events, locales, organizations, or persons, living or dead, is entirely coincidental.

Published by
Curtis Brown Unlimited.
Ten Astor Place
New York, NY 10003

Cover Artist: Jaycee DeLorenzo, Sweet 'N Spicy Designs

To Bob and Sue Zeiher,
my big brother and his loving wife.
Your wonderful, wild adventures inspired me to dream big,
and reminded me that happiness is always within reach!

ACKNOWLEDGEMENTS

This work would not be possible without the help of many. Thanks go to:

- My agent, Laura Blake Peterson, of Curtis Brown Ltd., for her unfailing support; you've been a faithful partner during this journey.
- The dedicated staff at CB Ltd., for their tireless work.
- Mystery author, Denise Swanson, for continued support and inspiration in this crazy business.
- My writer community—CARA; Windy City RWA, GRW, TGN, CWG. If you can figure out the alphabet soup, you know who you are! Your encouragement, advice, critiques and support keep me motivated, sane and humble.
- My science colleagues from *The* Ohio State University, Indiana University, University of Cincinnati, The Garratt-Callahan Company, AkzoNobel Surface Chemistry and Nalco Chemical Company. Your quirks, mannerisms, and dedication to science helped bring my characters to life.

Most of all to my beloved husband and "spouse assistant", Tom Riley. Having you by my side makes it worthwhile—and much more fun!

CHAPTER 1

Being a spy wasn't all it was cracked up to be in the movies.

What had she gotten herself into? She was a chemist, not a spy. At least, that's what her diplomas said.

Bree stepped from the podium, hands shaking. Petrochemical engineers swarmed her, shouting questions.

"Can you show us what chemical binders you used to add stability?" The voice rose above the others and Bree turned to the speaker.

"I'd love to..." she gave a tiny, deliberate shrug, "...but my attorney won't let me."

"Damn patent attorneys." The crowd chuckled in response.

Bree's hands steadied. The diversion thinned the crowd and staunched the flow of questions. Good thing, since Bree was posing as an expert in a field she barely knew, presenting data on a fictional product, hoping to catch the interest of a suspected international terrorist. Her presentation was nothing more than a baited hook.

Outside, Texas summer heat baked the sidewalks and withered the grass. Inside, Bree shivered—whether from fear or the chilled hotel air, she didn't know.

1

"Good job." Matthew Tugood's voice sounded in her head via her hidden earpiece. She fought the urge to reply and focused on the crowds headed to the exhibit hall. "He's here," Tugood said, voice low and calm. "At your nine o'clock."

Bree swiveled to the right.

"Nine, Bree. Not three. Remember, under that blonde wig, you're still a brainy brunette."

She looked left and immediately encountered the outstretched hand of a tall Asian man with thick, dark hair. The target they had code named Zed. "Intriguing paper." His slightly accented English sounded as if he was Chinese or perhaps Korean. "Ice that burns is a paradox. I've always considered gas hydrates too unstable for practical use. But your work makes them seem less, shall we say, dangerous."

Her skin prickled at his smooth words. Sweat slickened her hand as she shook his, her eyes never leaving his hooded gaze. Was he testing her? Challenging her?

"Thank him." Tugood's voice hissed through the headset.

Bree managed a terse reply.

"You seem nervous," Zed said with a smile. "Is this your first paper at the SPE conference?"

Bree nodded, grateful he blamed her nerves on the talk. "I just joined the Society for Petroleum Engineers." She tugged her hand from his grasp.

"You did a good job. I'd like to discuss your research further, if you have time." He produced a business card. "My name is Lei Chan."

She studied the card. "Nice to meet you, Dr. Chan." Bree handed over one of her fake business cards. "I'm—" she paused, mentally reminding herself of her cover identity, "Catherine Holmes."

"Dr. Catherine Holmes," he said, consulting her card. "Impressive. But I've never heard of *Energy Unlimited*."

"We're a startup company."

"I see. Are you headed to the exhibit hall?" He steered her toward the crowded vendor area while asking questions about her research.

In her other ear, Tugood fed her a constant stream of information to pique Zed's interest. Bree struggled to keep her face impassive, her conversations straight, and her cover ID intact. All while trying to interpret Dr. Chan's questions, gestures, and facial expressions in light of what Tugood had told her about him.

By the time they reached the exhibit hall with its sumptuous lunch buffet, her brain felt as thick and gooey as freshly poured asphalt. A headache pounded behind her eyes—and in her eyes. Wearing green contact lenses to disguise her boring brown color had been a mistake. Under the blonde wig, her scalp prickled with an itch she didn't dare scratch.

When Dr. Chan greeted another colleague and moved away, Bree panicked. Tugood needed her to gain Zed's trust. "Dr. Chan…Wait." She scurried after the pair. "Wouldn't you like to arrange a time to…"

Zed halted and turned back to her. "I'll be in touch, Dr. Holmes." His lips twisted into the tiniest of smiles. "Soon."

"Let him go, Bree." *Was that disappointment she heard in Matthew's voice? Resignation? Or was it her imagination?*

She snagged a can of Diet Coke from one of the buffet's coolers and downed half in quick gulps, hoping to clear her brain.

Her first undercover mission for the Sci-Spy organization presented more problems than a freshman chemistry book.

Most of which centered on the damn earpiece. And the irritating voice it transmitted.

Over the last hours, Tugood's once soothing baritone had morphed into an annoying, mosquito-like drone, constantly with her and rarely wanted.

Worse yet, the earpiece itched.

Bree tried to nonchalantly rub the irritation away. Only to be subjected to a different irritant.

"Stop that." Matthew Tugood's strident tones reverberated inside her head. "Touching your ear interferes with my ability to hear. And it draws attention to the earpiece."

Bree buried her head in her conference program to hide her response. "I'm a PhD chemist, not an idiot," she snapped, resisting the urge to say more. It would do no good and only get her another lecture on undercover protocol.

"Stay sharp, Dr. Watson."

It's Mayfield-Watson. Bree gritted her teeth and lowered the program. *Or Dr. Catherine Holmes.* The thought of her cover identity caused her headache to throb more fiercely.

She scanned the room, ignoring her Sci-Spy colleague, Milt Shoemaker, who lurked nearby. Tall and slender to the point of being gangly, "Shoe" literally disappeared into his cover the minute he donned the maintenance worker uniform. Without straightening from his stooped, hangdog posture, he lifted his head and gave her a covert thumbs-up. She'd made contact with her target and hadn't required backup intervention.

Now, Bree had a more pressing problem. Thanks to two cups of coffee and a can and a half of Diet Coke, she desperately needed a bathroom. And privacy.

She craned her neck to look past the vendor booths advertising everything from chemical additives to oil drilling equipment. Objective number one was in sight.

She headed to the ladies' room, wondering how to achieve objective number two. Privacy.

Her pendant necklace, plastic rimmed glasses, and briefcase all contained hidden cameras.

She flipped the necklace over, slipped her glasses into their case, and draped her suit jacket over the briefcase, effectively blinding Tugood and team.

"What are you doing?" His voice held a trace of annoyance.

"I need to use the bathroom."

"So go."

"Turn your surveillance off." Bree rubbed her ear, wondering if stuffing a tissue in it would deafen him.

"How can I keep you safe if I can't see or hear what's going on?"

"Five minutes, Matthew. Please." She hated the whine in her voice, but a full bladder did that sort of thing to a woman.

A heavy sigh sounded in her ear. "Two minutes. Then, ready or not, the sound is back on. If your cameras aren't letting me see what's happening, I'll have Shoe set off the sprinkler system and force an evacuation. Got it?"

"Three minutes," Bree countered.

"One minute, fifty seconds and counting." A click followed Matthew's warning.

Bree hustled into the bathroom, amazed at the weight that lifted from her shoulders the moment Matthew no longer followed her every move.

Dammit. James Bond didn't have to put up with this kind of crap.

Being a spy was *so* not like in the movies.

CHAPTER 2

SCI-SPY TEAM HEADQUARTERS

Morning light bounced off the white exterior of the corporate complex, blinding Bree as she trudged across the parking lot. She shaded her eyes, scanning the new signage. Science Professionals for Hire – Sci-PHi.

"Looks like the old building got a facelift while we were away," Shoe said as he came up beside her. "And no geese." He glanced down, his features softening as he searched her face. "How's it feel being back at the day job after our first mission?"

"Like I'm still undercover—except I'm wearing normal clothes." She gestured to her casual slacks and flats. "I don't understand why Tugood and his partner bought our *entire* research company. Why not just hire the few of us for the undercover work they do?"

"Like he said, a temporary science staffing business is a great cover and good way to keep track of chemical technology without raising suspicions. And the proceeds fund our covert activities."

"Yes, but do you believe that?"

Shoe shrugged as they walked the building. "Personally, I think he didn't want all the researchers to lose their jobs after the unfortunate events last spring."

Unfortunate events. Not the way most people would describe murder and fraud. But Milt Shoemaker wasn't most people. He was like her: a spy posing as a chemist. Or was it a chemist posing as a spy? Perhaps, something in between. One of five in the entire company.

"Maybe. But it means more people I have to lie to about what we're doing." Bree unlatched the door using her key card. "I hate lying to my family and friends," she grumbled.

"Then don't have friends."

Bree glanced at his now tight-lipped expression. She swallowed the urge to ask about his family and went about her day, preparing for the dreaded Monday morning staff meeting.

She arrived in the conference room a few minutes before nine, coffee in hand, and slid into a seat beside her friend Kiki. "Are you okay?" Kiki whispered as she nodded to the empty place at the head of the table. The motherly concern in her voice contrasted sharply with her spiked hair and youthful attitude, hinting at the decade that separated them in age.

Bree nodded. "I'm fine. I can deal with the *new* boss."

Kiki shook her head. "You can't be okay with him getting the promotion you deserve. He was barely competent when he was your technician. He's out of his league as your boss."

"I'm *fine*," Bree repeated. Troy was a pain in the—He was a pain. Period. In every way possible. But Bree couldn't let Kiki know the reasons behind Troy's promotion, no matter how much her friend worried about her.

When Troy strode into the room with his assistant Norah Kingston trailing behind, Bree slumped in her seat. As he settled in at the head of the table, Norah crammed a handful of gum in her mouth and chewed noisily. Today, her goth attire consisted of purple leggings, a short black

7

skirt, and layers of purple-on-black tee shirts. Her neck, wrists, and ears were festooned with chains featuring skulls and bones. She blew a bubble. Purple, of course.

"Since when did Norah start chewing gum?" Bree asked Kiki.

"Since she learned it annoys Troy."

"I'll get her a jumbo pack next time I'm at Costco." Bree sent Kiki a grin.

The worst part of being a spy—far worse than itchy earpieces, lack of privacy, and risk of exposure—was not being able to share any of it with Kiki. Or her family. Or anyone who hadn't been recruited to work undercover.

"Everyone, I need your attention." Troy rapped his knuckles on the table, causing Bree's coffee to slosh over the rim of her cup. Bree swiped at the spill with her napkin and clenched her teeth to keep from snapping at Troy.

The noise in the room didn't decline. "People," Troy tried again to get them to quiet down, "pay attention."

Silence followed. Broken immediately by Norah popping a large purple bubble. Troy flinched.

"Some of you," he continued irritably, "have not yet requisitioned your new business cards." Troy glared at Bree. Behind his back, Norah mouthed "sorry" before blowing—and popping—another bubble.

Troy flinched again, his jaw tightening. "CIC has been sold and the staff reassigned. We're now Science Professionals for Hire. Sci-PHi. Bree, do you give your consulting clients old CIC cards?"

"No," Bree muttered. *I give them a card that says I'm Dr. Catharine Holmes.* "I'll order my cards." *And add them to the stack of fake identities that clutter my wallet.*

Before Troy could say more, Norah popped another bubble.

"Dammit, Norah, stop that." Troy whirled on the girl, only to receive an insolent shrug for his reprimand.

"We could all use a lot more professionalism around here." He turned to the rest of the department. "Kiki, how's the new forensics lab integration progressing?"

Kiki took her time, downing a swallow of coffee and waiting for the atmosphere in the room to settle before speaking. "I've worked with Nate Rayburn and his analytical lab techs to get them trained to handle the police lab overflow. The bulk of the labor is processing rape kits, but we're almost up to speed on everything we need to know."

"Good. The police contract is a big one. Steady lab work. I'm glad it's on schedule." He turned to the other department members. "Those of you not training on forensics techniques will continue working with clients who require 3rd party verification and other contract jobs. We're not a research company anymore." He shot another glare at Bree.

"What about our consulting clients?" Milt stretched, leaning back until his chair balanced on two legs. "Where do they fit in?"

"You should know," Troy replied, letting irritation slip into his tone. "The consulting clients are scheduled and run through the Special Projects Division. You're always off installing pumps and chemical feed stations and whatnot. And Bree spends most of her time doing god-knows-what for god-knows-who."

"So," Milt continued, "Mr. Tugood's division."

"Yes. Matthew Tugood's Special Projects Division. But you both still report to me. And speaking of special projects, Bree, the energy company you consult with sent a letter of commendation." He waved a paper in front of her before tucking it away. "Would you care to share the highlights with the rest of the team?"

Bree gave him an apologetic half smile. "I presented a paper on the endless energy gas hydrate project. I can't say more without violating the non-disclosure agreements."

Silence—and blank stares—met her pronouncement. Bree shrugged it off, glad no one asked questions. The fictitious research about potential explosives had served its purpose—capturing the attention of Zed. Now, she had to reel him in and hope he led her to other members of his terrorist organization.

"Endless, unlimited energy," Troy muttered, breaking the silence. "Sounds like a perpetual motion machine, if you ask me. I think the Special Projects Division went out on a limb with this one. I hope you don't get burned, Bree."

"So do I." A trickle of dread slithered down her spine. Being tainted professionally wasn't the problem. Fear of being burned in the spy world—of having her cover blown during a mission—kept her awake at night more than she cared to admit.

Milt banged his chair down with a sharp crack. "Dr. Mayfield-Watson is the most competent scientist I know. She won't get burned."

Tension seeped from Bree's shoulders when she heard Milt's encouragement. After years as an unappreciated jack-of-all trades, Milt was thriving in the new Sci-Spy organization. His ability to disappear into his cover—something Matthew claimed Bree also had—impressed Tugood and inspired Bree.

Troy grunted and glared at Milt before reminding everyone to record their billable hours and turn in their monthly reports. He adjourned the meeting, but waited for Bree as she made her way out of the conference room.

"The Director of Special Projects appears to have taken quite an interest in you. He's asked you to meet with him.

Again." Troy's eyes narrowed to glittering slits. "Don't you think as your manager, I should be involved in these meetings?"

Bree ignored his petulant tone and ineffective glare. "It's just a review."

"A review of the work your non-disclosure agreement won't allow you to talk to me about?"

The edge in Troy's voice made the hairs on Bree's neck stand. Until today, he hadn't taken much interest in her projects. The all-purpose excuse of working at the fictional client company covered her absences from the labs. If he started micromanaging her, it could compromise her undercover work.

"Personally, I don't think it has anything to do with agreements or special projects." Troy stopped walking and turned to her. "I've seen the way Matthew Tugood looks at you. Like you're a piece of candy and he's craving a sugar fix. The question is, does he want you in his bed or taking over my office running the FAR department? Or maybe both."

"That's uncalled for." Bree stared at Troy until he opened his mouth again, then deliberately cut him off. "Tugood coordinates senior scientists working with consulting clients, nothing more. He doesn't want to replace you." *And he definitely doesn't want me in his... his intimate circle.*

Bree ignored the flash of warmth that surged through her at the thought of seeing Tugood in more intimate circumstances.

He's off limits. She mentally ticked off the reasons. One—he was her handler in covert operations. Two—he was the secret owner of her new company. And three—he was, as his name implied, too good to be true.

Sexy super-spies like Matthew Tugood might use scientists like her for their own purposes, but Bree knew better than to think he'd fall for a well-endowed (okay, overweight), soft-around-the-edges, dreamy-eyed geek. Especially one so plain and unremarkable that she could disappear into a cover without any effort.

The more she reminded herself of that, the less likely she'd be to get burned. Not as a scientist. Nor as a spy. But as a woman who dared to put her heart on the line.

CHAPTER 3

B ree hustled along the second-floor walkway connecting the research and business sides of the complex. The business hub, once bustling with marketing, legal, and support professionals, now consisted of a few offices for the owners' team that handled official company business.

Unofficially, Sci-PHi was a front company for the espionage activities of Matthew Tugood and his former partner, Gary Dolinski. Tugood handled spy missions through his Special Projects Division. Dolinski—she assumed—financed the operations using cash from his sprawling conglomerate of companies.

Bree steadied herself with a deep breath and knocked on Tugood's door. He opened it and gave her a warm smile before ushering her in.

What Tugood's office lacked in space, it made up for in security. The walls consisted of soundproof, and presumably, bulletproof material. They closed the main door and walked to a bookcase. Bree ducked under Matthew's arm and tugged on a worn copy of Webster's Dictionary. The shelves swung open, revealing a hidden elevator. Bree stepped inside.

"How did the staff meeting go with Troy?"

Bree shrugged. "The usual pompous-ass behavior."

"Are you sorry we picked him for the role of department head? We could have promoted Kiki instead."

Bree's gut cramped at the thought of even more lying to her best friend. "No, Troy is easier for us to manipulate and control." She sighed. "Today he was just miffed about not being invited to my meetings with you. He thinks you might want to promote me to his position."

Matthew followed Bree into the elevator and the bookcase door closed behind them. The already small space shrunk to something barely larger than a test tube. A pheromone-filled test tube. As always, being near Matthew caused Bree's pulse to speed up and her senses to go on alert. She inhaled the faint whiff of soap radiating from his clean-shaven jaw.

"So, is that all? He's worried about his job?"

Bree swallowed. "No." The heat from Matthew's body wrapped around her, as potent as a physical caress. "He also thinks you want me for your lover. It's ridiculous."

"No, it's not," Matthew replied slowly. He leaned against the elevator wall, pushing farther into her space. Close enough for her to watch his eyes darken from a stormy-sky gray to deep charcoal. Her heart pounded faster and she sucked in a breath saturated with his scent. His essence. "I think being lovers would make a great cover."

The elevator lurched to a stop. Bree pushed past Matthew to open the door. "Get over yourself, Tugood." She fought the lightheadedness that her sudden movement caused. "Even if someone would buy that story, I doubt I could pull it off."

"Posing as my girlfriend would strain your acting abilities?" The grin he flashed her reeked of mischief. "I think you were very convincing just now in the elevator."

Bree didn't respond. Instead, she walked to the wall of computer monitors that dominated the Sci-Spy Tech-Ops

Center. Once the executive suite, the rooms now looked like something straight out of a superhero comic book. Bree scanned the security feeds from around the complex, images of the bat cave swirling in her mind.

"I assume you called me in to discuss the next steps with Zed."

"The next step is to let him contact you. Once he trusts you, we'll move forward. We're running a long-term game here, Bree. Uncovering Zed's network and plans may take months. When he contacts you, let me know. Otherwise, do nothing."

"Why is the Zed mission so important to you?" Bree watched as Matthew's lips compressed into a thin, hard line. Seconds ticked by. Eventually, he spoke.

"A little over two years ago, an oil drilling platform exploded in the North Sea. Do you remember?"

She shook her head. "No. I was focused on water and mining projects, not oil."

"The incident was hushed up, and except for a few environmentalists wagging fingers, it didn't make much news." He stared at her, eyes narrowing. "By design."

"Do you mean our government hushed it up?" Bree wrinkled her brow. "Or the oil company?" She opened a search window on one of the computers before directing her attention to him.

Matthew paced the width of the room, his steps edgy with suppressed energy. "I was on that oil platform—posing as a chemist. Employed by the company Zed worked for. He visited the site less than twelve hours before the explosion." He stopped, frozen in thought.

"And?"

"If I hadn't eaten bad sushi and needed to be airlifted off the platform, I would have been on it when it exploded."

"The explosion could have been an accident. A coincidence."

"It was a weapons test." His flat tone left no room for argument.

A chill raced up Bree's spine. She'd been currying the interest of a mastermind of *weapons testing.* Not some low-level operative. She turned to the computer screen where her search yielded a handful of photos and news articles about the incident. Weapons testing.

Matthew could have died in the explosion. One he believed was set by Zed. It explained a lot.

"The day after the explosion I burned my old identity. I cleaned what I could out of the labs, resigned, and disappeared before Zed could make another move to stop my investigation."

Matthew's voice washed over her. She didn't need to look at him to detect the pain and anger behind his words. "However long it takes, however many blind alleys I have to go into, I will find him and dismantle his organization. That's all you need to know for now."

Silence—and the hum of computer monitors—filled the room. Bree closed the search window and drew a few cleansing breaths while pushing the new information to the back of her mind. "So, if you don't want to meet with me to talk about Zed, why am I here?"

She turned to find Matthew leaning against the polished wood of an executive desk. Something in his stance set her nerves on edge—and not in a pleasant way.

Instead of answering, Matthew walked over to the refrigerator and pulled out a can of Diet Coke. She ignored the brush of his fingers as he handed it to her and focused on the rigid set of his shoulders.

The teasing Matthew of this morning was gone. So, too, was the anguished Matthew of a few minutes ago. The man who faced her was sculpted of muscle, steel, and determination. No softness, no humanity anywhere.

Her heart dropped to the pit of her stomach and she braced herself for his next words.

"One of my government clients contacted me with a new mission. What do you know about running a meth lab?"

Two days later, Bree sat across from Paul Bender in a tiny office at a private local college, wondering if she should have let the Sci-Spy makeup artist stencil a tattoo on her after all.

Paul's heavily lined, sun-weathered face belonged to someone in his 80s, not his 60s. The faded ink—maybe a snake?—crawling from under his conservative collar to disappear into his ash-gray mullet definitely should have stayed in the 1970s.

Bree shifted in her seat and tried to remember what she'd read in the dossier on Paul. Brilliant organic chemist. Founded the company *Naturalistics* with his wife nearly two decades ago. Politically liberal, but fiscally conservative, if his stock holdings and bank records could be trusted. Vegan since 1992.

Not much to go on.

Meanwhile, Paul scanned the papers she'd given him. She couldn't cross her fingers for luck, so she crossed her toes instead and hoped Tugood's cover story for her held up.

"Looks like your university and this temporary agency worked everything out through my secretary." Paul punched in a few numbers on his speakerphone.

"You rang?" The raspy voice of a life-long smoker crackled from the device.

"I'm here with Cat Holmes. Says she's been assigned to work with us for a semester as part of her chemistry BS program. You satisfied with her paperwork?"

"I am. You satisfied with her knowledge of chemistry?" A phlegmy cough punctuated the question.

"I'll know by the end of the day." Paul cut off the call and turned back to Bree. "You know what a Michael Addition Reaction is?"

Bree scanned her memories of organic chemistry reactions and came up blank. "Not specifically. But it's a standard organic reaction. I know exactly where to look up the details."

Paul stared at her for a minute then cackled with laughter. "You'll do, Holmes. Not afraid to admit there's something you don't know, smart enough to know how to find the answer, and plucky enough to give it to me straight. I like that."

He punched in an extension on the phone and picked up the receiver. "Tonya, we've got a new employee. A student intern from UIC." He listened for a moment. "Of course, I mean University of Illinois at Chicago. Is there another UIC? I'd like you to show her the ropes. . . . Yeah . . . in my office."

He hung up and grinned. "Tonya's all but taken over my place in the lab." He listed some of her accomplishments. "She's brilliant. PhD in chemistry and physics from MIT. I think it goes to her head." He raised his voice at the last words, making sure Tonya heard him as she stepped into the office.

"All this time, I thought you kept me around for my looks." A ripple of laughter followed the comment and Bree angled herself to study the trim young woman in a pristine lab coat. Her stylish haircut, warm mocha skin tones, and dazzling smile could have made a Hollywood talent scout do a double take.

Bree swallowed, more intimidated by Tonya's unconscious grace and easy femininity than by her MIT degrees.

"Only a fool judges a woman by her looks, Tonya. Not that I don't appreciate a beautiful woman. But it's your mind that appeals to me. That's why you'll be running this company after I retire."

"If there's anything left." Tonya's teasing disappeared behind the grim set of her mouth.

"You worry about the research. Leave the rest to me." Paul pulled a stack of papers to the center of his desk. "Get Cat settled while I review these patents. Someone's got to protect our inventions." With that, he shooed them out the door.

"Is something bad happening to the company?" Bree asked once they were in the hallway.

Tonya waved the questions aside. "It's nothing." Tonya led her out of the main building and across a parking lot to a cement block bungalow. "Our labs and offices are housed in here. Once *Naturalistics* vacates the premises, Paul and Lydia—that's his wife and business partner—will donate these labs to the college."

Bree caught the second reference to trouble in the company. She plastered a smile on her face and tried to pretend she was awed by the space Tonya led her into.

"This is our communal kitchen." Tonya gestured toward a smattering of small appliances. "There's always coffee. Food left on the table is considered fair game for anyone. If you're not sure about something, ask. We're a friendly and informal bunch."

Tonya led her around the corridor formed in a large rectangle, pointing out washrooms, conference rooms, and the small lab stockroom. "Labs are along three of the outer walls. Offices are on the interior. Unfortunately, that means no windows." Tonya stopped by an empty office. "You'll be sharing this space with our other visitor."

Bree scanned the room, pleased to note the office wasn't near anyone else's. The large desk dominating the space appeared occupied, so Bree dropped her purse into the bottom drawer of a much smaller desk, which was shoved into a corner between a bookshelf and a filing cabinet. If her office mate stayed AWOL, she would have privacy for her investigations. If not... she hoped her cover as a student intern would put her below everyone's radar.

"I'm eager to get started," she said, turning to Tonya. The young woman nodded and soon Bree was outfitted in a lab coat and escorted to the lab across from Tonya's office.

"Let's introduce you to the team. At present, there are only four of us: me, Jackie, Ricco, and Emily." Tonya pushed open the lab door. "Hey, Em," she called, "I have a new temp for you to meet. This is Cat Holmes. Looks like you're no longer the token white woman in the labs."

A tall blonde in torn jeans and a tee shirt emblazoned with the molecular structure of caffeine flashed a cocky grin and introduced herself as Emily Appleton. "If Paul's filling quotas, I'll have to give up my special privileges. Damn diversity initiative."

"You can laugh now," a woman across the lab chided, her Hispanic accent sharp with indignation. "In my day, people of color weren't running labs and making light of civil rights. Especially women. My generation fought and sacrificed to make your lives easier."

"Jackie marched in the civil rights protests in the 1960s." Tonya led Bree across the room to Jackie's bench top. "She's our conscience. And a damn good scientist."

The short, stocky woman slipped off a lab stool and tucked a strand of wavy hair—still more brown than gray—behind one ear. "I'm Jackie Torres," she said, pumping Bree's hand. "I've worked for Paul and Lydia Bender almost from the day they founded this company. Good people, the Benders."

She released Bree's hand, but kept her eyes trained on the newcomer. "I was a nurse's aide who expected to spend my life scrubbing soiled linens. Paul had other ideas. He and Lydia trained me for a chemist's job making twice what the nursing home offered. They made sure my son got an education, too, even if it meant kicking his lazy butt now and then. He's Dr. Torres, now." Pride shone in her eyes.

"Speaking of Ricco, where is he today?" asked Tonya.

"He's over at the new lab building installing the equipment you two designed. Should be back before the end of the day. Didn't he tell you?"

"Why would he?"

Jackie snorted. "I've got eyes in my head. I know you're sleeping together."

Dark cherry-red stained Tonya's cheeks. "My personal life is separate from my professional life."

"Ah, cariña, who says you have to choose? You can have both. Just don't hurt my boy."

Tonya mumbled something, then dragged Bree away for a tour of the rest of the labs. After spending an hour teaching Bree about safety and documentation, Tonya instructed her to create an inventory of the laboratory chemicals.

Bree drew a sigh of relief when she was finally alone in one of the lesser used labs. Tonya's detailed instructions had been perfect for a temporary technician who had yet to complete her BS degree in chemistry.

For Bree, it had been sheer torture as she struggled to remember she wasn't supposed to understand the hazard rating systems, the safety data sheets (SDS), or any of a dozen other things that were second nature to her.

At least no one expected a temp to be fast when creating the inventory—which gave her time to investigate. Bree worked quickly, making one set of data to give to Tonya and another to analyze for herself.

Tugood's instructions echoed in her memory.

The DEA needs this intel. Your mission is to determine if the lab is making meth or other drugs. If you believe they are, isolate the ring leaders and report back to me.

Bree moved from the organic chemicals to the acid storage area, pausing to strip off her old gloves and don new ones. The relationships at *Naturalistics* intertwined and wrapped around one another like a knotted ball of yarn. Or better yet, like a coiled polymer strand—every twist and turn creating a structure that influenced the whole in subtle—and not so subtle—ways.

"I'm here to observe, not to make friends," she muttered as she wiped the bottles clean. Even so, Bree found herself liking the people in the small, quirky lab. The thought of spying on them knotted in her stomach, nestling like toxic lead.

Yet, she couldn't abandon her mission, either.

Her snooping had already turned up evidence. Neat rows of chemicals and specialized equipment suitable for manufacturing narcotics filled the marble lab bench. Bree slowly placed the containers back into their scattered storage areas. *Just because they* could *manufacture narcotics didn't mean they* were *manufacturing narcotics.*

But someone at the DEA—Tugood's client—thought they were.

To learn more, she needed to get close to the team and earn their trust. She swallowed past a tightness in her throat as she folded one set of her inventory data into a small square and slipped it into the pocket of her slacks. Like it or not, someone at *Naturalistics* was probably involved in drug manufacture and possibly had ties to narcotics trafficking, distribution, and corruption.

One of the nice people she'd met today was a criminal.

Chapter 4

After a long day of sorting through dust and grime, Bree savored the cool brush of air against her bare hands when she stripped off her sweaty latex gloves. She shed her lab coat, placing it on a hook near the door, and pushed her safety glasses to the top of her head as she stepped into the hallway.

A murmur of voices from the opposite side of the building told her the researchers were gathered in one of their offices. Bree hesitated, debating whether to go into the occupied office or not. Getting close to the team was critical to her mission.

She ran her hand through the tangle of hair at her nape and made her decision. First, she would comb out the knots and pop a breath mint. Then she'd join her lab mates.

Bree headed away from the voices, toward her temporary office. At the sound of an unfamiliar voice inside the small room, she paused, hugging the wall. Quietly, she knelt, pretending to tie her shoe. With one ear alert to any sounds behind her, she focused the rest of her attention on the conversation in the office.

"Of course, my goal is complete integration," said a woman. Her low-pitched voice carried deference and a hint of defensiveness. "Give me a few more days to convince the staff. We can promise better benefits than the current owner. I'll have the rest of the IP *and* the inventors, just like I promised."

IP referred to Intellectual Property—in other words, patents. Bits of data lined up in Bree's mind, forming an incomplete, but intriguing, picture.

Paul Bender was worried about the corporate IP and determined to focus on it. Tonya had referred to the corporation being disrupted—perhaps sold or liquidated?—at least twice. Now, the unknown woman in her office was trying to get control of both the patents and the inventors.

Was *Naturalistics* being sold? Why? How did the sale effect the alleged production of illegal drugs?

Bree stood and backed down the hallway then retraced her steps to the office, whistling as she approached. "I know what's at stake," the woman inside said as Bree entered and headed for her desk.

"Who are you?"

Bree froze at the sharp demand. She turned slowly, ready to spin her cover story. "Hi, I'm Cat Holmes. I'm a—"

"Well, Cat Holmes, has no one ever told you it's rude to sneak up on a person?"

"I didn't sneak up on you," Bree lied.

The woman—who looked forty going on twenty-five—waved her comment aside with a slash of her hand. She flicked a hank of perfectly styled, inky-black hair over one shoulder. "What are you doing in my office?"

"I'm a new temp," Bree replied in a rush, gesturing toward the back of the room. "Tonya said I could use the spare desk. I didn't know anyone else was here."

She offered the woman a smile, which wasn't returned. Bree ducked her head and deliberately drew her lip between her teeth, trying to look young and uncertain. "I'll just ... just grab my purse and get out of your way." She dropped the inventory list on the desk and pulled her bag from the bottom drawer, unsure of her next moves.

"Hi, Cat." Tonya's voice interrupted her internal debate. Bree looked toward the door where Tonya stood flanked by Emily and a tall, handsome man who Bree guessed must be Ricco Torres. Jackie hovered in the background. "I see you've met Hannah."

Hannah thawed immediately and gave Tonya a warm smile. "Actually, Cat and I got off on the wrong foot. I hadn't realized you needed to hire temps."

"She's part of a university work-study program."

"I see." Hannah turned to Bree and offered her hand. "I'm Hannah Rogers, HR representative of *Elemental Fractions*. We recently acquired *Naturalistics*."

She pivoted back to Tonya. "I'm excited to have all of you as part of our company. The new venture will be a wonderful blending of talents. With the resources *Elemental Fractions* has at its disposal, you'll have a staff of technicians. You won't need to spend your time training undergraduates to help with the work. We pride ourselves on having the finest PhD researchers in the business."

From her spot to the side of the main conversation, Bree noticed Hannah addressed her comments only to Tonya and Ricco, ignoring Jackie and Emily. Beside Tonya, Emily stiffened.

Bree understood Emily's unspoken sentiment. Hannah probably didn't realize the young woman was "ABD" or all but degree. Emily had explained to Bree that her PhD thesis depended on her work at *Naturalistics*. Bree suspected Emily's confidence would be fragile until she passed her final examinations and thesis defense. No doubt Hannah's dismissive attitude toward her stung.

Heaven knew it made Bree want to blow her cover and put Hannah in her place. She clenched her fists against the temptation.

Ricco stepped into the office, oozing Latin charm. Ignoring Hannah, he introduced himself and offered his hand to Bree. His accent—thicker and somehow smoother than his mother's—was clearly a deliberate affectation, practiced and intended to seduce. Or something.

Whatever it was, it tingled along Bree's nerve endings— whether in pleasure or warning, she couldn't say. "Sorry we didn't meet earlier. I would like to invite you for a drink after work. My treat." He flicked a glance at Hannah. "You can come, too, if you like."

"We all wanted you to join us." Tonya moved to stand by Ricco. "Drinks at *All Mixed Up* are a tradition. A perfect way to welcome you to the team."

Next thing Bree knew, she was hustled from the labs and chauffeured to a local wine and martini bar, surrounded by her new friends.

Ricco made a show of opening the car doors for her and taking her arm as they walked across the gravel lot at the edge of town.

Tonya and Emily teased her about competing for the lone male scientist's attention. Jackie playfully pushed all the women aside and claimed Ricco's first love was his mother.

Hannah stood to the side and watched, a look of longing on her face until she stormed her way to the head of the group and herded them through the door.

Bree resisted the temptation to relax even as she pretended to join in the playful banter. Instead, she swallowed a bitter taste in her mouth, knowing she was working her

way into the confidences of a group of people she must ulti-
mately betray.

Tugood would have been proud.

"I'll buy the first round." Hannah's voice rose above the
din in the bar. Bree shuddered at the strident tone. Since
her gaffe in the office, Hannah had tried to be friendly—
without success. Her perky banter and backhanded compli-
ments grated on Bree's patience like a zester on a lemon,
peeling it away in painful, thin strips.

"I'm so impressed that you have group traditions for
your lab. Although you have to be careful. Alcoholism in
the workplace is a big concern."

One strip. And another.

The group found a table and Hannah waved a server to
them. "Bonding with fellow workers is important for high
functioning teams. I once led a phenomenal integration
team. Even though the end of the project signaled the end
of everyone's employment, they finished the task in record
time. With smiles on their faces."

More curled tendrils of shredded patience joined the
growing pile. Did Hannah not notice how Tonya rolled her
eyes at the absurd statement? How Jackie's fingers curled
into fists? Or how Ricco sat, arms crossed in a classic, closed-
off pose?

Bree made mental notes about her colleagues, cataloging their body language and interactions, observing the
inner workings of the team.

Other than their mutual dislike for Hannah—who
didn't stop her monologue until a waitress arrived to take

drink orders—Bree didn't know how she was going to bond with the staff.

Hannah picked up her topic again. "Gallup calls it the 'Best Friend' principle." Bree imagined Hannah in a cheerleader's uniform instead of a pantsuit while the words washed over her. What colors would a corporate cheerleader wear? Just-bruised-black-and-blue seemed to encompass Hannah's integration style. Performance-review-red was probably another popular choice.

"I've known my best friend since childhood," Tonya offered. "We used to do everything together before I went to grad school."

"That's not what we mean by best friend," Hannah corrected, her voice as prim and stiff. "A best friend is someone at work who you know has your back."

"Like Julio did when we got into a knife fight in sixth grade?" Ricco asked, an evil glint in his eye. Bree wondered if he was telling the truth or baiting Hannah. She'd have to ask Tugood if Ricco's background check had turned up anything of concern.

"Definitely not. Best friend means something entirely different in the context of work." Hannah flushed as she continued her explanation, but Bree lost interest.

She wasn't going to learn anything from the *Naturalistics* team while Hannah was around. Her head pounded. The topic of best friends reminded Bree she hadn't spoken to Kiki since Monday morning's department meeting. Right before Tugood had given Bree her latest assignment.

She excused herself and wound through the tables toward the ladies' room, guided by the light from the candy-colored neon martini glass lights on the walls. A banner on the back wall invited the patrons to attend the first "Mix Your Own Cocktail" party on Friday night.

Once in the safety of the empty ladies' room, Bree swallowed a couple aspirin and leaned against the cool tiles, savoring the silence.

I need just five minutes of normal. Not as undercover Cat Holmes. Not as Bree the spy. Just five minutes as myself. She located her phone and called Kiki. "What's your weekend look like?" She crossed her fingers and hoped Kiki didn't have plans. "I was thinking we should spring for a mani/pedi at the new spa by my condo. I could use some down time."

"So, work at the client's company has you drained?" Kiki asked.

Bree mumbled something about the fake company where her colleagues thought she worked, hating the secrets she couldn't share with her friend.

"Count your blessings." A stressful edge crept into Kiki's voice. "I don't know who thought Troy would make a good manager, but that person needs a sharp rap on the knuckles. Or worse. You're lucky you work offsite so much these days."

Kiki ranted about Troy's new policies while Bree cringed, hating the part she'd played on inflicting Troy on the team at Sci-PHi. "I guess, I'm just cranky lately," Kiki said. "I miss meeting you for lunch or coffee."

"Me, too." Bree laughed. "I even miss you forcing me to work out at the corporate gym."

"Workouts aren't the same. I almost never see you-know-who down there."

Oops. That was a can of worms she shouldn't have opened. Was it really only a few months ago when she and Kiki had gone to the corporate gym to ogle Matthew Tugood as he worked out? She hadn't known his true identity as an undercover agent then. Briefly, she'd even wondered if he was a contract killer.

"Hello? Bree? Are you still there?"

"Oh, yeah." Bree pulled her thoughts back to the present.

"I'm sorry. I guess things are a little strange with you and Matthew Tugood these days. I mean, now that he's your boss."

"It isn't like that."

"Sure, it is. Most of your work is run through his Special Projects Division. Personally, I think it's great because Troy can't stand having you report to someone besides him."

"And anything that annoys Troy amuses you."

Kiki's laughter burst through the speaker. "Guilty as charged. But as for Matthew, don't let an organizational chart stand in your way if you want to get up close and personal with him. I hear he's available again."

"First Troy. Now you. Why does everyone think his interest in me goes beyond professional?"

"Because I've seen the way he looks at you. And I've seen you look back at him the same way more than once."

"It isn't what you think," Bree insisted. Not even close, but she couldn't admit to Kiki that she and Matthew were … What exactly were they? Whatever it was, it didn't fit neatly into an organizational chart. Or anything else.

"Listen," Bree said, "I've got some work to finish up. So, are we on for the weekend?"

After confirming her plans with Kiki, Bree cut off the call and stashed the phone. Her five minutes of normal were up. Thoughts of Matthew, her cover identity, and her mission crowded out any pleasure from her weekend plans.

On the other side of the bathroom door a table filled with her co-workers contained possible drug dealers. It was up to her to figure out who was innocent. And who was guilty.

Chapter 5

B ree grabbed a tiny plastic cup from an oversized martini glass decorating the bathroom counter and filled it with a pale green liquid from a vodka inspired container. A sniff assured her it was mouthwash, not actual vodka.

She swished the mouthwash and refreshed her pink lip gloss. As she ran a comb through her shoulder length hair Tugood's words sounded in her mind.

You can disappear into a role. People won't remember if you're blonde or brunette. They won't remember your face. It's a rare and valuable quality in an undercover agent.

Tugood's idea of praise—pointing out her unremarkable features—didn't make her feel either rare or valuable.

Bree wished she could be memorable, at least, to someone. But she hadn't inherited her mother's red hair, green eyes, or vibrant personality. She'd taken after her dad.

She threw the comb in her bag and glared at herself in the mirror. Her silver peace sign earrings and peasant blouse covered with purple flowers made her look a dozen years younger.

Perfect for the role of Cat Holmes.

Thank heavens her mother had forced her to join the high-school drama club instead of the physics club. Mom had been right. Bree had needed to develop better people skills.

People skills her new job demanded she use in uncovering a narcotics manufacturing ring.

Bree grabbed a flyer describing the "Mix Your Own Cocktail" party as she made her way back to the table. She perched on a stool between Emily and Hannah.

Emily leaned close. "Don't desert me again. I've had about as much as I can take of Hannah's needling. She treats me like I'm stupid. I don't know how Jackie manages to sit near her without snapping her scrawny, dried-up little neck."

Jackie sat on the other side of Hannah, quietly watching while Hannah directed her comments toward Ricco and Tonya. Once, Hannah paused to scrutinize the flyer before pushing it away and continuing to court the PhD scientists.

"Just think of the fun you'll have when you finish your degree and can rub it in her face." Bree watched Emily's reaction to her words. "That is why you didn't tell her you were close to defending your thesis, isn't it?"

Emily blushed, confirming Bree's suspicions. "You guessed it. What about you? Did you ever think of going on for an advanced degree or are you going to stop with a BS?"

"I'll see how this job turns out first," Bree hedged, accenting her words with a shrug.

"Oh, good, the drinks are here." Hannah's voice demanded attention. "Miranda," she said, waving to the server, "and her father make the best margaritas in the business."

"Especially when you insist on a private, $500 per bottle tequila," the server muttered as she put a chocolate martini in front of Bree and a beer next to Emily.

"Oh, you found the flyer for our "Mix Your Own Cocktail" event," continued the server, changing the subject. "We're having a lecture on cocktail mixing, then a chance to try your hand at bartending. Your first drinks are included in the cost of the event. Plus, there's a contest. Bring in your own cocktail-inspired food or bar snacks to enter. If you win, your entry will be featured on our menu."

"That's ambitious," said Hannah, earning her a dark look from the server. "Is it your dad's idea, or yours?"

"My mother came up with the idea." Her tone, brittle as crystal and cold enough to freeze a straight margarita, caused Hannah's jaw to drop. "If you'll excuse me, I need to get back to the bar."

"Be sure to tell your dad I was in," Hannah called after her. The forced cheer in her voice didn't fool anyone. Bree—and everyone else—turned to their drinks as tension thickened the air around the table.

"So, Hannah, do you come to *All Mixed Up* frequently?" Jackie's direct question broke the awkward silence and forced Hannah to face her.

"I'm a regular patron."

"We come here every week, but I don't remember seeing you."

"I rarely leave the office before seven. I'm passionate about my work. Plus, I don't think it's fair to my employer for me to cut out early." She turned to Tonya, shutting out Jackie. "By the way, did I tell you about our Young Professional Program? It's for management trainees. I'd like to nominate you for the team."

Tonya swirled the olive in her martini glass, concentrating on the swizzle stick more than on Hannah. "I've managed the *Naturalistics* labs for years. As I understand it, your program is targeting entry-level candidates. Like Emily."

Tonya paused and turned to Emily, who blushed. "Emily is an accomplished organic synthetic chemist. She's come up with some techniques to—"

"—to clean up chemical mixtures," Ricco interrupted. He squeezed Tonya's hand and she turned her attention back to her drink. "Emily has a lot of untapped potential. As Tonya said, she's a good organic chemist. I'm sure she would be interested in your program."

Emily sent Ricco a look that Bree interpreted as gratitude, before she lowered her gaze to resume studying her beer bottle. She picked at the label with her thumbnail. The tension in the air closed around the table, muffling it in silence.

Bree's gut told her Emily, Ricco, and Tonya were hiding something. Drugs? Or something else?

"Of course, Emily would be welcome to apply as well." Hannah broke the silence, her eyes still trained on Tonya. "But we're concentrating on people with demonstrated potential."

"What makes you think I'd be a good candidate?" Something in Tonya's voice caused warning bells to ring in Bree's head.

Hannah either didn't catch the warning or ignored it in her rush to answer. "I have a good eye for talent. Trust me when I say you are exactly the type of candidate we're looking for."

Tonya nodded. "*Elemental Fractions* has a new diversity initiative, don't they?"

"They do. I'm proud of our commitments and accomplishments." Hannah took a swallow of her margarita and continued, her voice warming to the topic. "Last year, we increased the number of women, LGBT, and minorities in management positions by 5 percent. Our target is to get to at least 20 percent diversity in our upper management."

"So, you want me as part of your young professional program because I'm black? Or because I'm a woman? Or perhaps both?"

"Of course not. I'm recommending you because of your accomplishments."

"Name one."

Hannah took another drink, sipping slowly, as if giving herself time to think. "I admire the work you did with improving citrus extraction rates in your processes. The method is part of the reason we wanted to acquire *Naturalistics*."

Tonya nodded, satisfied.

Behind her, an older man with sandy-blond hair streaked with white approached the table. "Did I hear someone say citrus extract?" He kissed Tonya on the cheek. "I thought you came here to relax after work. Do you ever stop discussing scent and flavor extracts?"

"Not until after my second dirty martini."

He nodded then directed his attention to Hannah. "Miranda told me you were here. It's always good to see you, my dear. Are you enjoying your drinks?"

Hannah saluted him with her glass. "I am. You make a good margarita."

"My drinks are about to get better." He flagged down a tall, slender woman dressed in a tight black tee shirt, short leather skirt, and leggings. Even in ballet flats the woman stood nearly six feet tall. "Everyone, I'd like you to meet Jen Stands. She's my new mixologist. Jen is giving our drink menu a facelift. These folks were just mentioning citrus extracts. How about sending over a pitcher of your new concoction?" He looked to Hannah. "On the house."

"Sure." Jen gave them a smile and a wave, causing her collection of charm bracelets to rattle. "It's a twist on a classic Lemon Drop Martini that I call Tangerine Tango."

Jen chatted for a bit then headed off. Bree swiveled in her seat, craning her neck to get a look at the bar. It was too far away and the light too dim to get a good view. She turned back to the table and focused on learning about her colleagues. Finding out how a "mixologist" differed from a bartender would have to wait.

A few minutes later, Jen reappeared, carrying a glass pitcher filled with a bright, slightly fizzing orange liquid. Miranda, their server, followed with a tray of martini glasses and a bowl filled with fruit garnishes. Jen filled the glasses, plopped a skewer of fruit in each, and passed them around.

Bree took a sip. The orange flavor sparkled on her tongue. No harsh alcohol taste burned her mouth or lingered after she swallowed. She took a second sip. "It reminds me of a Mimosa," she commented.

"A Mimosa is straight champagne and orange juice," Jen replied.

"Jen's Tango is a bit more potent," said Miranda, giving Jen a wink. "Don't be fooled by the smooth taste. And don't drink too many unless you have a designated driver."

Miranda collected the empty glasses at the table while Jen stayed to chat. When the conversation drifted into flavor chemistry, she didn't bat an eye. Instead, she followed the discussion, eyes alight with interest.

"How did you get into your career?" Bree asked.

Jen gave her a hint of a smile. "I didn't start out dreaming of being a glorified bartender. I started college at Northwestern studying liberal arts. That's a fancy way of saying I didn't know what I wanted to do.

"Anyway, in my freshman year I took a course in their Science in Human Culture Department. *The Physics of Amusement Parks.* I learned a little bit about circular momentum and a lot about how fun applied science could be."

Hannah pushed her drink aside and sat straighter. "I remember that course. I was a business major, trying to get my science credits out of the way before graduation."

Jen's smile widened. "What a small world. It was a great program, wasn't it?"

"I could handle the tests, but the fieldtrip almost killed me." Hannah turned to the group, for once including all of them in her remarks. "We went to Six Flags Amusement park for a special tour. The lecturer would discuss the physics of a particular ride, then we'd try it out and have a sort of science debriefing after."

"That sounds like fun," Bree said.

"It was, until I threw up on my lab partner's shoes after the rollercoaster from hell. She spent the day smelling like puke. I spent it in the infirmary."

"Studying the physics of projectile vomiting?" Jen teased.

Hannah let out a bitter little laugh. "You could say so. I probably shouldn't have partied before the fieldtrip. In any case, I learned not to attend fraternity-hosted keg parties. And the value of drinking only high quality alcohol."

She fell silent for a minute. "Looking back, I feel sorry for my lab partner. When she joined my sorority house, the sisters dubbed her the *Puke Princess* and a host of other nasty names. I tried to stop them, but I got my share of ribbing, too." She shrugged. "It was a long time ago."

"Aside from being sick, it sounds like a great class to me," Bree said. "I love when science is applied to real life."

"Me, too." Jen focused on Bree. "To finish answering your question, the other applied science class I took was *Alcohol and Culture*. Basically, it combined the sociology of bonding over drinks and the chemistry of alcoholic beverages. The fieldtrip for that was a pub crawl, if I remember correctly."

"I'd love to learn more about the science of drinks."

Jen hefted the tray to her hip. "I spent years experiment-ing with drink mixing. Eventually, I took a bartending class, and here I am, a Master Mixologist. Having fun in a job I love. I'd be happy to share some drink making tips with you one day when we're not busy. But for now, let me send over another sample for you to try."

After Jen left, the group shared stories from their own college courses. Bree sat quietly, observing rather than par-ticipating. Hannah flirted with Ricco, flattered Tonya, and generally ignored the rest of them.

The next round of drinks came and Hannah waved off the offering, instead, asking for a second margarita. "You've got an admirer," the server said as she put the drink Hannah ordered and a second glass in front of her. "This is compli-ments of the gentleman over there."

They all looked at the man occupying a booth with his much younger date. Hannah took a sip, licked the salt from her lips and saluted him with her glass. He smiled in return.

"Is he a friend of yours?" asked Bree.

"No, but whoever he is, I'm grateful. Salt, lime and tequila is just what I need to clear my palate after that fizzy orangeade." She took a second sip and grimaced. "Miranda must have skimped on the ice. Plus, I can still taste that other nasty drink."

She rotated her glass so the salt encrusted rim faced her, then raised it and addressed the group. "Here's to a successful collaboration between *Naturalistics* and *Elemental Fractions*. May we continue to prosper together."

Quiet greeted her words. Bree wondered if the others would join in the toast or leave Hannah hanging. Slowly, first Jackie, then everyone else raised their glasses and echoed the sentiments of the toast. Bree drained the last of her drink and suggested they order snacks to cushion the effects of the alcohol.

Hannah grabbed a menu and stared at it for a minute before passing it to Bree. "I'm okay with anything you want to order." Soon chicken strips, loaded baked potato skins, and veggie tempura—for Emily, who didn't eat meat— arrived at the table and Bree switched from mixed drinks to Diet Coke.

Others opted for soda or coffee. Hannah stopped making everyone cringe with her comments and descended into an alcohol-induced silence, cradling her head in one hand. Her long, dark hair formed an impenetrable curtain between her and the rest of them.

Watching Hannah's bowed head, Bree forgot how annoying the woman could be and wondered if she was suffering the effects of overindulgence. Surely three drinks wouldn't do that to a woman, would they? Or had she had four? Bree had lost count.

Someone—Miranda? Jen?—brought Hannah a cup of coffee. She dumped cream and sugar into it and drank slowly. The bar owner offered to call a cab.

One by one, the team dispersed until Bree was left alone with Ricco. "I'm sorry you had to witness that," he said as he led her to his car.

"I'm not sure what you mean."

Ricco sighed. "Hannah's been in our labs off and on since Paul sold the *Naturalistics* patents to *Elemental Fractions*. She's trying to convince us to move to her company."

"I thought when companies merged, all of the employees merged, too."

"Maybe that's the way it works in other industries, but Paul Bender didn't sell the company outright. He sold the rights to our extraction patents. It's a different thing altogether." He opened the car door and waited until Bree fastened her seatbelt before moving to the driver's side.

"You'll eventually learn that chemistry is as much a business as it is a science. They don't teach you that in school." He flashed a smile, teeth white in the darkness of the car.

Bree noticed his accent has slipped. No longer thick and sensuous, he spoke with only a hint of Hispanic pronunciation. "Why the game?" she asked.

"What game?"

"Why do you put on the Latin Lover persona around Hannah?"

"So, you caught that, did you? Good observation skills. You must be a scientist." He was silent for a moment before adding, "Hannah's a cougar who sees what she wants to see."

"Did you deliberately try to scare her by talking about knife fights when you were a kid?"

Ricco laughed as if she'd told a joke. "Guilty as charged. Hannah looks at me like I'm some sort of exotic diversion. Giving her what she wants keeps her out of my business."

"What business is that?"

"Mine." Again, Ricco's smile flashed, white in the darkness.

Before Bree could ask more questions, he pulled into the company parking lot next to her car. "Are you okay to drive?"

Bree nodded and thanked him for the ride. While she started her car, he waited in the silent lot. A familiar chill made Bree shiver. Ricco hadn't corrected her when she'd accused him of playing games. Nor had he offered a reasonable explanation for his behavior.

Had she tipped her hand when she asked him about his accent? She didn't want him to be assessing her observational skills too closely if he was the brain behind the illegal drug manufacturing.

With shaking hands, Bree started her car. A friend would wait to make sure the car started. An enemy might wait for different reasons.

She pulled away and began the long ride home keeping one eye in the rearview mirror as she pondered a single question.

Which was Ricco? Friend? Or enemy?

CHAPTER 6

The next morning, Bree dragged herself to the *Naturalistics* site, feeling cranky and disoriented. No wonder the mixologist had warned her about the Tangerine Tango martinis. They packed a punch. Or maybe it had been worry over her conversation with Ricco.

She'd filed her report with Tugood and fallen asleep on the couch while watching the news. She would have slept for another hour at least, if Sherlock—her oversized orange cat—hadn't awakened her by yowling for his breakfast.

Now, instead of heading into the labs she cradled a cup of coffee and slumped on her corner desk. Hannah's desk was empty. Bree thanked her luck for small favors.

"You look a little worse for wear today."

Bree sat up as Tonya stepped into the office. "I didn't sleep well last night," she explained.

"Listen, real world chemistry isn't like doing a lab experiment in school. Being a straight A student isn't the same as wrestling with real world problems."

Bree remembered Ricco had said much the same thing the night before. What real world problems were Ricco and Tonya wrestling with?

Tonya perched on her desk and nodded toward the empty chair across the room. "Not everyone understands, or appreciates, your skills. *Naturalistics* values all its employees,

PhD, BS, and student interns. Don't let Hannah get you down."

"But *Naturalistics* doesn't exist anymore, does it? I mean, didn't *Elemental Fractions* buy your company?"

"They bought some of our technology. They didn't buy us."

Bree noted that Tonya's answer to the question, much like her observation a moment ago, correlated with what Ricco had told her last night. Clearly the *Naturalistics* employees weren't jumping at the chance to join Hannah's company. Because illegal drug manufacturing was more lucrative? Or were there other reasons?

"I guess it doesn't matter to me, anyway," Bree said, dismissing the comments. She finished her coffee and stood. "I'm only here for an internship. Whatever happens won't affect me."

"Maybe. Maybe not. If Paul Bender likes your work, he might offer you a permanent position. You seem to be comfortable in the lab. Would you like to try your hand at a couple of reactions today?"

Bree jumped at the chance. The closer she got to the actual reactions, the closer she got to uncovering who was responsible for drug creation.

As Bree was buttoning her lab coat, Hannah entered the office. Actually, lurched more accurately described her movements. Her skin had an odd tinge and the oversized sunglasses covering her eyes hinted at other issues.

"I should know better than to mix margaritas with martinis," Hannah declared as she sat and groaned. "My head feels like the university marching band is stomping through it. I need coffee."

"I'll get it." Tonya scooted out the door before Bree could open her mouth.

Hannah booted up her computer and tossed her sunglasses aside as she squinted at the screen. She rubbed her eyes and looked again. "Where are my reading glasses?"

Bree watched as Hannah rummaged through her designer bag. When she stopped and put a hand to her mouth, Bree gave up trying to be aloof.

"Hannah," Bree knelt to look into Hannah's bloodshot eyes, "do you need me to help you make it to the bathroom?"

Hannah swallowed and shook her head. "It's passed now. I swear, I never get sick unless I drink cheap alcohol. Everyone at *All Mixed Up* knows that. Did the orange drinks bother you?"

Bree shook her head, trying to ignore Hannah's alcohol scented breath. "Let me try to find you something to settle your stomach." She left the office to join the others in the kitchen.

Tonya stood by the coffee pot, tapping her foot while waiting for it to brew. Emily sat at the table, sorting through her purse. "I've got some aspirin in here," she said. "Maybe that will help." She pulled out a couple of capsules.

"She needs food." Jackie slapped a plate of buttered toast onto the table.

"What's on it?" Bree asked, looking at something dissolving in the butter.

"Cinnamon and sugar. Helps to calm the stomach and metabolize the alcohol, according to my mother and her mother before her." Jackie shrugged. "It can't hurt."

Tonya took the plate, aspirin, and coffee and headed back to Hannah's office. Bree followed with a glass of water. Once they had Hannah settled, they made their way to the labs.

At the bench, Tonya showed Bree how to purify a muddy green mixture she called clover extract. "This," Tonya said, holding out a cone shaped piece of glassware fitted with a valve at the small end, "is called a separatory funnel. Use it to shake oil-based solvents with the water-based plant slurry—like mixing salad oil and vinegar. Then let the components settle and drain off the bottom fraction."

Bree nodded, hoping she didn't look bored. "What are we mixing?"

"We're extracting clover sent. It's used to add freshness to outdoor inspired candles, fragrance sprays, and personal care products."

The lab didn't smell fresh to Bree. The sting of acetone and the sweet, sickly scent of toluene and other solvents assaulted Bree's nose, despite the ventilated fume hood. She eyed the mixture. Was it really clover? Or something else? Something illegal?

"So, Cat, do you like to cook?" Tonya chatted as she worked.

"Cook what?" Bree asked cautiously. Was Tonya using the slang term to ask if she liked to synthesize—cook—meth? Had she cracked the drug ring that easily?

"Cook anything. Most chemists like to play around with recipes. Molecular gastronomy—the merger of science and cooking—fascinates me."

"I enjoy puttering in the kitchen."

"You might like synthetic organic chemistry if you enjoy cooking. Speaking of that, Emily and I are thinking about whipping something up for the "Mix Your Own Cocktail" party at the bar on Friday. Do you want to join us?"

"That would be great." *Cocktail inspired foods.* Bree had put some chicken breasts in a pineapple-soy marinade this morning, intending to grill them for dinner. Maybe she could tweak the recipe to create a Pina Colada chicken strip with tropical chutney. Mentally, she composed a shopping list. Onion. Sweet bell peppers. Coconut. Pecans—or maybe almonds—to crush for the coating.

"You're smiling," Tonya teased. "You already have a recipe in mind, don't you? What is it?"

"If it works, I'll tell you." Bree secured the funnel on a lab stand and let the layers separate. "Until then it's a trade secret."

"No fair keeping secrets from colleagues." Tonya checked Bree's work. "That looks good," she said, referring to the experiment. She outlined the next steps in the separation process while Bree took notes.

"I hear the word secrets and then find you two conferring in private." Both women looked up at the sound of Ricco's voice. "What brilliant idea do you have now, Tonya? And should I be worried that you're sharing it with Cat instead of me?"

"It's not my idea, it's Cat's. And yes, you should be worried."

The grin on her face belied the warning in her words, but Ricco's brows snapped together and he flashed them a look of annoyance. "Ideas developed in these labs are the property of *Naturalistics*. Don't forget that. Be careful who you talk to."

"It's not chemistry," Bree interjected. "It's a recipe. For the contest at *All Mixed Up*."

"My misunderstanding." Ricco colored as he gave them a curt nod. "I'll just go check on my reactions in the other lab." He ambled away, muttering something under his breath in Spanish.

An hour later, Bree slipped out of the lab while she waited for another mixture to separate into layers. She took the long way to her office, going first to the kitchen for a second cup of coffee before heading to the space she shared with Hannah.

As she approached the door, she spied Hannah, slumped at her desk, a half-eaten piece of toast nearby and a coffee mug at her elbow.

Bree stepped to the desk, intending to shake Hannah awake and send her home. The minute she touched Hannah, Bree's senses went on alert. The fine hairs at the back of her neck stood.

Hannah was stiff.

Hannah was cold.

Hannah was dead.

CHAPTER 7

A cting on instinct, Bree called 911 from the lab phone. Ignoring the operator's insistence that she stay on the line, Bree placed the receiver on the desk, grabbed her purse, and left the office, pulling the door closed behind her.

Leaving the 911 operator hanging assured the police would arrive soon. Bree's gut told her the office was a crime scene, not simply the scene of a death.

In the day she'd known Hannah, the woman had irritated everyone at the lab. Herself included, Bree reluctantly admitted. Given that, Bree could imagine—no, make that logically construct—a case for anyone wanting Hannah out of the picture.

Bree sent a quick text to Matthew then pulled a notebook out of her purse. She'd planned to use it for notes on her narcotics investigation. Now, it became her murder notebook.

She leaned against the hard door and closed her eyes as an eerie sense of familiarity settled over her. The day her former boss was found dead, she'd fought off panic by meticulously recording her observations, retreating into a realm of pure science, where fact, not emotion, ruled.

Then, she'd been a prime suspect in the murder investigation. Today, she was … She slid down the door and huddled against the cool tiles, knees drawn up to her chest, head in her hands.

What, exactly, was she? Besides in over her head.

A dead body changed everything.

She clutched the notebook, its edges biting into her hands, fighting the desire to curl up in a tight ball and forget her assignment. Or run home and pull the covers over her head while her cat snuggled at her feet. She was just a scientist. Had she really thought she could be a spy? Or a detective?

Her phone vibrated. A cryptic text from Tugood—keep your cover—did little to calm her nerves.

Bree focused instead on the facts. Her scientific skills were the means to finish her undercover mission *and* determine who killed Hannah. She shook off its stupor and assessed the situation, planning her next moves, just as she'd planned thousands of experiments.

Her vantage point on the floor outside the office meant she could keep the crime scene untouched. If anyone questioned her, she could claim to feel distraught and unfocused.

So far, so good.

Bree frantically scribbled notes, detailing what she remembered about the area around Hannah's body. Next she closed her eyes and mentally reconstructed the events of the morning.

Hannah had entered the office at about 8:40 with a hangover. She'd complained of a headache and begged for coffee.

Coffee Tonya rushed to get. From everything Bree had seen, Tonya disliked and distrusted Hannah. So why fetch her coffee? Bree jotted the questions in her notebook.

Who else had been present?

Emily was in the kitchen and quick to offer aspirin. She'd pulled the medicine from her purse. *Capsules.* Not tablets.

Jackie has also been in the kitchen. She'd fixed food for Hannah. Three people with easy access to chemicals had offered ingestible substances to a woman who was inexplicably dead a few hours later.

The plot line from *Murder on the Orient Express* flashed through Bree's mind. No one in the labs liked Hannah, but did they conspire to kill her? Bree could easily see the group banding together against her. But murder? She shook her head to clear it and focused on the facts.

Coffee. Aspirin. Toast. Any of which could have been laced with poison.

Or could it have been something else? Bree forced her thoughts back to the morning, focusing on what she observed, not on the how or why of the situation. First, remember the what.

After Tonya left to fetch coffee, Hannah had removed her sunglasses, revealing bloodshot eyes. She'd searched for reading glasses until nausea threatened. Bree's nose stung at the memory of Hannah's alcohol-laden breath.

Once she left the office, Hannah had been alone. Jackie, Tonya and Emily all clustered in the kitchen. Ricco had been... She didn't know where Ricco had been.

Bree flipped to a page near the back of the journal and started a table to keep track of everyone. She added columns for their whereabouts, possible motives, and alibis. What else did she need to record?

When the body language doesn't match the words, you're close to uncovering a secret. Bree's mother—a PhD psychologist— had offered those words of wisdom when Bree was trying to solve another murder. The trick had worked. Bree added a column for "body language" and filled in her observations.

She flipped back to the page detailing the events of the morning. She'd left the office and spent the morning with Tonya in the extraction lab. Emily and Jackie had been...elsewhere.

Midmorning, Ricco had come in, then left quickly, followed by Tonya. It had been at least another hour before Bree discovered Hannah.

Bree hadn't seen any of them—in the lab or near her office—when she'd found Hannah. She tilted her head, listening. Hushed sounds snaked through the corridor, but before she could identify who the voices belonged to or where they originated, the wail of a siren drowned out everything else.

Bree shoved her notebook in her bag and buried her face in her hands as emergency responders—followed by the lab staff—raced into the hallway. In the resulting chaos, a paramedic walked her to the kitchen and examined her for shock.

But she wasn't in shock. She was on full alert.

In the middle of an investigation.

Undercover.

Bree slumped at the kitchen table, head in her hands, pretending to be distraught as she watched the paramedics wheel Hannah from the building. Ricco appeared, dragging Paul Bender behind him. The tattoo on Paul's neck stood out, its faded colors suddenly vibrant against the unearthly pale of his face when the gurney passed him.

A medic rushed to Paul while Ricco huddled together with Emily, Jackie, and Tonya. The flash of red and blue lights pulsed through the kitchen windows. Medical personnel, uniformed police officers—from the campus and the city—and others, crowded into the small laboratory complex.

In truth, Bree wasn't as calm as she pretended. But at least, it wasn't the first body she'd found. The others appeared more shaken than she was. Even the murderer, if he or she was one of Bree's lab mates.

A blare of music—*Wild Thing*—broke through the soft sounds of friends comforting one another. Tonya looked up, eyes wide, with a dull sheen to them. Emily pulled her phone from her pocket and shook her head. The song faded into silence then started up again within seconds. Finally, Jackie broke from the group and laid a hand on Bree's shoulder. "It's your phone."

Bree gaped at her before digging the phone out of her purse as the music reverberated through the kitchen. *Who changed my ring tone?* Caller ID flashed on the screen. "Your Boyfriend."

"Hello?" Bree's hand shook as she answered the phone.

"Did you see my ID?" Matthew Tugood's voice poured over the line, cheerful but with a hint of strain.

"When did you program my phone?" she asked.

"I did it the last time we were together. I couldn't have your new friends thinking I was just some random guy, could I?"

"Staking a claim?" Bree asked dryly.

"Well, can you blame me after the incident with Troy the other day?"

Out of the corner of her eye, Bree noticed the others pretending not to be interested in her call. Something clicked in her mind. Without her Bluetooth headset, his call could be overheard by someone standing close enough. So he'd chosen to live the lie Troy had insinuated of them: that they were dating. Or lovers. Or something. When she saw Tugood next, she'd have to clarify just what their fictional relationship consisted of.

Meanwhile, two could play his game. "Oh, honey bear," she said in the most saccharine tone she could muster, "You're so sweet. And romantic. I'm really glad you called."

"Don't call me that." Bree imagined Matthew forcing the words through clenched teeth.

"But, honey bear, I love you."

Bree watched her coworkers while Tugood grumbled at her over the phone. Ricco grabbed Tonya's hand and whispered something to her before moving out of earshot. Emily's cheeks turned red. She shuffled over to Paul and sagged on the wall next to him. Jackie rolled her eyes and joined Paul as well.

In addition to annoying Tugood, Bree's love talk had driven them further away, reducing the chance they'd eavesdrop on the conversation. Now, she needed to convey critical information to him without drawing the wrong sort of attention to herself.

A uniformed medic pushed a gurney into the hall. Bree stared at Hannah's lifeless, sheet covered body.

"Can I see you tonight? Please?" She injected a hint of panic into the syrupy love talk, hoping Tugood would catch on. "I'm afraid I'll have nightmares. One of the girls in the lab died and now the police are here."

"Anyone we know?" Tugood's voice dropped to a near whisper.

"Yes."

"O'Neil?"

"I think so."

"Shit. He knows you. He'll see right through your cover."

"What do you want me to do?" Bree had helped James O'Neil when he investigated the murder of her boss a short time ago. They'd met for coffee several times since and become friends. At least, that's what she thought they were. For now...

"Get him alone if you can," Tugood instructed, breaking her train of thought. "Don't let him blow your cover in public. We can meet later and brief him on your mission."

Detective O'Neil started to approach the group. Bree raised her voice. "What do you mean you can't come over tonight? No," she wailed into the phone. She put every ounce of her acting experience to work in this little bit of improv while Tugood sputtered in annoyance on the other end of the line. "I need you. Can't you play basketball at the gym tomorrow?"

Bree dissolved into tears, letting her hair fall into her face before she buried her head in the crook of her elbow and collapsed on the table. Her shoulders shook with mock grief. With luck, O'Neil would see a distraught twenty-something in the throes of a break up, not the woman who'd shared a mocha whipped latte with him last week.

Between fake sobs, Bree listened to the muted sounds around her. James O'Neil, his voice calm and sure, questioned her lab mates.

"She's Cat Holmes, our new temp."

"We found her in the hallway outside of her office."

"She must have been the one to call 911."

"She shared an office with Hannah. The one who…"

Bree didn't bother to try to sort through the cacophony as Paul, Tonya, Emily, Jackie, and Ricco all talked over one another trying to answer O'Neil's questions. Soon the voices drifted into silence.

Bree felt someone put a hand on her back, then squat down beside her. Warm breath touched her chilled arms. "Miss Holmes? I'm Detective James O'Neil. I know you've been through a terrible shock, but I need to talk to you. Okay?"

Bree mumbled a reply, keeping her head buried.

"You can use the conference room," Paul offered. "Tonya, get Cat some water."

O'Neil patted her on the shoulder. "This won't take long, I promise." Bree felt him move away and heaved a sigh of relief. Once he was set up in the conference room, she could talk to him in private.

Minutes later, head still bowed, Bree let Tonya lead her to the conference room. Keeping her face hidden, she turned to O'Neil's partner as soon as Tonya left. "Could I have some more water, please?" she asked in a timid voice.

As soon as the woman left, Bree flipped her hair out of her face and turned to O'Neil. Recognition—and confusion—fought for control of his handsome features.

Bree's stomach knotted as she looked him in the eye.

"Please, don't blow my cover."

CHAPTER 8

"**W**hat the hell has that idiot Tugood gotten you involved in now?" James O'Neil paced the small conference room like a caged wildcat, fury reverberating in his low-pitched voice and agitated steps.

Bree glanced at the closed door, behind which O'Neil had asked his partner to stand guard. "It's complicated," she hedged. "Something we shouldn't be discussing here."

"Give me the short version."

"One of Matthew's contacts at the DEA suspects—and I've found evidence for—illegal drugs being produced at this site." She told him about her inventory.

"First," he interrupted, his green eyes snapping, "I've done time in the narcotics division. Some of it undercover. The DEA doesn't use retired spooks, and God forbid, civilians to do legitimate undercover work. Second, even if you were qualified, no one sends a rookie in to do a job like this. It's dangerous."

"How many of your undercover cops could pose as a chemist?" she shot back.

"We have a few."

"In Plainville County?"

James ran a hand through his hair, mussing the precisely cut blond strands. "I'll concede your chemistry knowledge makes you well suited for the task. But you're not trained in undercover work, or self-defense, or any of a hundred other skills you'd need to stay safe. He had *no business* putting you in harm's way."

James flattened his hands on the conference table and leaned toward her. "I wouldn't have done it." His voice took on a softer edge. "No one who cares about you would have done it."

Bree touched his cheek, savoring the slight feel of hours-old stubble beneath her fingertips. The concern reflected in his eyes drew her in. Her gaze drifted to his lips, so close to her own. If they weren't in the middle of an investigation ... But they were. She shoved temptation aside and settled for the truth. "I know. And I appreciate your concern."

The last of the anger faded from his eyes. "I'll keep your secrets. For now. But after I finish questioning the lab personnel, you and I are due for a long talk. At the police station where we won't have to worry about prying eyes and ears."

"Thank you." Bree took a seat at the table and composed herself.

"For what it's worth, I'm glad to have a set of eyes I can trust on the scene. I gathered from your lab mates that they found you outside the office door when the emergency personnel arrived."

"I was trying to keep the scene clean. In case it..."

"In case it's a murder?"

Bree nodded. "I have notes. Just like last time."

"Good job," O'Neil said. "But save them. We'll talk about it later. When you're not masquerading as Cat Holmes." He gave her a tight smile that didn't reach his eyes then crossed the room. "Ready?"

When she nodded, he opened the door and ushered his partner inside. "She seems calmer now," he said.

The female officer's eyes skittered toward Bree and back to O'Neil. "Good. But next time, maybe you should guard the door and let me handle the hysterics."

O'Neil nodded and took a seat. He turned to Bree. "Now, for the record, would you tell me your name?"

"My name is Catherine Holmes. I'm a student chemist..."

For the next hour, Bree's fictional world and the real world wove together in knotted, murky patterns as O'Neil took notes and asked questions regarding the suspicious death of Hannah Rogers.

Except that he didn't really want to know what she'd discovered. He wanted only what Cat Holmes might have noticed. He frowned, glowered, and acted generally obnoxious every time she gave him an answer. Even his partner— whose name Bree had never managed to catch—stared at him with a furrowed brow and disapproving frown.

When O'Neil finally dismissed her with the standard warning to stay available for further questioning, Bree made an excuse to Tonya and left the labs.

Despite being weary to the bone, she knew the day was far from over.

Tension knotted Bree's neck and shoulders as she drove into her condo garage. The brief respite she'd felt while picking up supplies at the grocery store evaporated the minute she opened her purse to pay and spied her "murder notebook." Soon, she'd have to relive the ordeal for James O'Neil in the privacy of the Plainville Police Department. For real, this time.

Inside the condo, she spied her large orange cat, Sherlock, curled on the sofa. He opened his eyes, sniffed, then buried his nose in his paws. Food was generally high on his list of interests, but apparently, the ingredients for her new chicken recipe didn't qualify. "Guess you were hoping for a juicy piece of salmon, huh, boy?" Bree rubbed his ears. "Sorry. Not this time."

She unpacked her supplies and grabbed a notebook filled with her recipes and other kitchen experiments. She started a page labeled "Pina Colada Chicken Strips" and set to work. The recipe would give her an excuse to mingle with the bar staff and regulars at cocktail party, aiding her investigation. As Bree made notes about the recipe, she allowed her subconscious to mull over events at the lab.

Marinade with pineapple juice. Soy sauce. Brown sugar. Vegetable oil.

She wasn't thinking about Hannah's death. Really.

Crunchy chicken coating with crushed corn flakes. Sweetened, flaked coconut. Finely ground pecans. Lime zest, red pepper, salt.

Was Hannah's death related to the narcotics investigation?

Bree set up a dredging station, adding lime, sugar, and rum extract to a frothy egg-white mixture. The fresh scent of citrus reminded her of Hannah's preference for margaritas.

At the bar, Hannah's chatter had everyone at the table gritting their teeth so hard, it was a wonder they could eat the appetizers Bree had ordered.

Bree grabbed a piece of chicken and recoiled at the cold, clammy feel. Like Hannah's lifeless hand. She dumped it in the dredging mixture and forced her thoughts back to last night's bar snacks. Hannah hadn't ordered a single item from the menu. After taking charge of everything from the conversation to the drinks orders, she'd suddenly passed the food choice off to Bree.

That was odd. Bree slid the chicken into the oven before grabbing her crime notebook. *Review Hannah's behavior at the bar,* she wrote.

Satisfied that she wouldn't forget, Bree showered and changed into jeans and a polo shirt. Her tension eased as she wadded up the Cat Holmes costume and tossed the clothes into the hamper along with her worries.

When she padded back into the kitchen, Sherlock followed, batting at her bare feet and mewing for his dinner. Bree fed him and then took the chicken from the oven. The strips were crispy and golden, just the way she wanted.

While Sherlock was busy with his dinner, Bree created a sweet and savory dipping sauce, then packed her supplies away. She snagged a left-over chicken strip and swiped it across the pan. Sticky dipping sauce dripped from the chicken and smeared her lips as she took a bite. Yummy. Exactly the right crunch. The touch of peppery heat complimented the sweetness of the coconut and fruit as she'd hoped.

Bree had just finished putting more chicken into a fresh batch of marinade when the phone rang. She glanced at the caller ID. Plainville County Police Department.

She took a deep breath, ignoring her growling stomach and the combination of guilt, fear, and adrenaline that flooded her body at each ring.

Playtime was over.

Duty called.

❧   ❧   ❧

Twenty minutes later, Bree sat across from James in his quiet corner of the police department. Most of the day shift had left. Members of the small evening shift trickled in and clustered around the coffee machine, ignoring James and Bree.

"Thank you for coming." The quiet flatness of his voice unnerved Bree. Where was the hint of intimacy and friendship they'd shared earlier?

"Of course, I came. I promised you I would. Especially after you kept my secret."

O'Neil's face darkened at the reference to her cover identity and their earlier discussions at the *Naturalistics* laboratories. "Do me a favor and don't bring that up."

He leaned back in his chair, crossed his arms, and stared at the ceiling, a frown puckering his brow. After a couple of minutes, during which Bree pulled out her murder notebook and studied her entries in silence, James sat up abruptly.

"The thing is," he said putting his hands on the desk and leaning close to her, "the captain is especially interested in this case. The college president called him—personally— and asked about the status of the investigation. Shortly after that, the Plainville mayor also called. Everyone wants this case solved, and solved fast."

"I take it President Jenkins and Mayor Greenwood are old golf buddies?"

"Something like that. At the very least, they belong to the same country club. Both come from old money."

"Money talks?"

A ghost of a smile lightened O'Neil's face. "In this case money shouts. And whines a bit, too. When parents spend the equivalent of a couple luxury cars on a kid's education, they tend to get pissy if the kid calls home claiming a murder occurred in the chemistry labs."

"The labs don't belong to the university, yet. Paul Bender planned to donate them in the future, but no one takes classes in the *Naturalistics* labs. Besides, we don't even know if it really was a murder. Hannah could have died of natural causes."

"The parents don't want to hear that. They want to hear the campus is safe for their little darlings and the evil villains are under lock and key. Which brings me to the second reason we need to solve this case."

O'Neil opened a desk drawer, pulled out a thin file, and pushed it across the desk to Bree. "The campus cops are in over their heads. This is the sum total of their experience. Ninety percent of it involves breaking up drunken frat parties."

Bree scanned the file. "Looks like they are recent graduates of the police academy."

"This is a first assignment for both of them. They're essentially highly paid private security guards with good uniforms but no investigative experience."

"So, the Plainville PD is taking the lead on the investigation?"

"Not exactly." O'Neil's eyes shifted left, then right. Bree followed his gaze. The officers by the coffee pot had drifted away, leaving Bree and O'Neil alone. "I've also been told to keep the investigation as quiet as possible. No uniforms on site. As little visible police presence as possible. Basically, they've told me to catch a killer while handcuffed to my desk."

"That sounds impossible."

A calculating gleam came into O'Neil's eyes. One Bree didn't trust. "The good news is, I've been given access to some discretionary funds. The captain approved hiring private consultants. And since you are already on site—"

"You hired Matthew's company to investigate—"

"No." O'Neil cut her off with a grimace of distaste. "I didn't hire Tugood's company. I hired you. To be my eyes and ears." He shoved another file at her. "It's a standard contract. Read it over tonight and give me your answer in the morning."

Bree put the folder in her purse, unsure what to do next. Before she could get to her feet, James sighed and dragged a legal pad out of a drawer. "For now, I still need to get an official statement from you about the events leading up to Hannah's death. The statement of Cat Holmes won't do."

"Has it been decided that we're definitely looking at a murder?"

"No." He fiddled with his pen, tapping it in staccato bursts against the legal pad before finally looking her in the eye. "The parents, students, and college president are unofficially calling it a murder. The captain isn't saying anything. Despite everyone's clear opinions, the investigation still hasn't determined if we're looking at an accidental death, a natural death, or a murder."

"The investigation? Or you?"

"At this point, it's one and the same." He glanced at the paper pad. "What's your theory?"

"James, you know me. I don't have theories. I'm a scientist." She tapped her crime notebook significantly. "I make observations."

"Right." He flashed her a hint of a smile. "Before you begin your lecture, Dr. Mayfield-Watson, let me review this lesson. Scientists make observations. Based on the observations, they form hypotheses. That's science-speak for an educated guess. How am I doing so far?"

"And a theory is based on a set of hypotheses that have stood the test and not been disproven." She opened the notebook. "There's hope for you yet, O'Neil."

"Tell me, what did you observe regarding Hannah and the others at the labs?"

"For one thing, even though I'd known her for less than twenty-four hours, I could see she was the type of person anyone would fantasize about killing. She collected enemies like teenage boys collect comic books."

"Did you fantasize about killing her?"

The question shocked Bree, but not as much as the stoic look on O'Neil's face when he asked it. "No, Detective," she said in as cold and expressionless a voice as she could muster. "I didn't. I wasn't her enemy."

He nodded. "I had to ask. For the record." He shifted uncomfortably in his seat. Bree caught a hint of embarrassment as his impassive mask slipped a bit. "What else did you observe?" he asked.

Bree consulted her notes and started at the beginning—two days ago when she'd first entered the *Naturalistics* labs and met first the staff, then Hannah.

James listened, scribbling notes on his legal pad and asking questions to clarify points. Once, he interrupted her to request a photocopy of her notes. Gradually, the tension between them eased as they focused on motive, opportunity, and alibis for each person in the lab.

After nearly an hour, a uniformed officer stuck her head into the bullpen from the department's reception area.

"O'Neil, you've got a delivery," she called.

"Put it in the interrogation room. Don't mess with any of it. I'll know if you do."

"You're the boss." She disappeared.

O'Neil grabbed his legal pad, rose from his desk, and motioned for Bree to follow him.

CHAPTER 9

"What's going on in the interrogation room?" Bree asked as she hesitantly followed James O'Neil through the police department corridor.

He turned to her, a hint of mischief sparkling in his green eyes. "You. Me. A massive order from Chong's Chinese Delivery. I figured after dragging you down here at dinner time, the least I could do was feed you." He flashed her a grin, the friendly, boy-next-door kind she expected from him rather than the moody looks he'd been giving her.

"We can talk privately in interrogation and keep the rest of the department from stealing our food. If you don't mind, that is."

"Privacy? In an interrogation room with a one-way mirror and a viewing area attached?"

James chuckled. "Don't worry. We'll dim the lights on our side."

"So now you're suggesting adding romantic ambiance to cover our activities?"

"Romantic ambiance might be nice," he mused. "But no; one-way glass works because the interrogation room is brightly lit, making the glass reflect images while the viewing area is dim, making the glass transparent. If we switch the lighting, we get privacy."

"Privacy and a view of anyone trying to spy on our dinner?"

"Exactly." James opened the door to the interrogation room and ushered her inside. He dimmed the lights. "If it's okay with you, I'll grab some drinks and turn on the lights in the other room."

A surge of panic hit Bree the minute the door clicked shut, locking her in a room designed to intimidate. Before it could take hold, James stuck his head back inside. "The door won't be locked," he said, giving her a reassuring smile.

"Thanks." Tension still coiled in Bree's stomach. After James left, she counted to ten, then walked over and twisted the knob. To her relief, the door opened. Nevertheless, unease continued to prickle between her shoulder blades despite the tempting smell of Kung-Pao Beef wafting through the room.

To distract herself from her surroundings, Bree opened the plastic bags of food and lined the cardboard takeout containers on the table. The Kung-Pao Beef, General Tso's Chicken, Szechwan Pork, Egg Rolls, crispy Crab Rangoons, vats of Hot-N-Sour *and* Egg Drop soup, and other delicacies crowded the space.

James had ordered enough to feed the entire depart-ment with ample left over. Bree smiled, knowing the wide selection was his way of being sure to get something she liked.

The atmosphere of the room lightened. Bree folded up a hard metal chair and placed it against the wall, giving her space to arrange the two office chairs in more comfortable positions. When James returned loaded down with plates, bowls, cups, cutlery and drinks, she'd almost forgotten where they were.

"How many egg rolls are there?" he asked.

Bree took a quick count. "Six."

"Looks like the desk sergeant managed to snag a couple." He grinned. "There should be eight of them. I always tell her to keep her hands off and she ignores me and steals two. Every time."

"I think we can make do with six," Bree said, returning his smile. "After we're done, we can feed the homeless shelter for a week."

"I guess I overdid it."

Bree gestured dismissively at her figure. "Do I look like the kind of woman who can be bribed with food?"

"If you're fishing for compliments, you should know that as tempting as I find the wrapping," he let his gaze slide down her body in a slow visual caress, "I'm even more intrigued by what's inside."

Bree's face grew warm. A reply froze on her lips. The silence shimmered between them, full of promise—and risk. This could be more than an innocent coffee date. Much more, depending on how she responded. Bree jerked her gaze from his and grabbed a plate. Pretending a nonchalance she didn't feel, she spooned out beef, chicken, and rice before grabbing a pair of chopsticks. She captured a slice of beef. "As long as we're clear about what part of me you're trying to bribe."

James glanced into the observation room, then dragged his chair around the table to position it on the same side as Bree's. He leaned forward, elbows on his knees, hands relaxed. "And that would be?"

Bree snorted. "My mind, of course."

"Would you be open to bribery on other fronts?"

The expectant silence descended again. The chopsticks dangled loosely from her fingers.

James moved a fraction of an inch closer and she forgot about food.

He lifted his eyes to her face, and she forgot about everything.

She licked her lips. His eyes followed the movement. "I," she swallowed, "I'm not sure what you mean."

"Aren't you?" He touched her knee with his fingertips.

Bree struggled to collect her scattered thoughts. How did she feel about James? He was kind, she thought, cataloging all the attributes she liked about him. Steady. Dependable. His clean-cut good looks, along with a killer smile and twinkling green eyes, were straight out of a feel-good novel or a made-for-TV movie. She felt safe with James. Protected.

The erratic thump of her heart accused her of lying to herself. Protected, maybe. But safe? Not at the moment.

That was a definite shift in the state of affairs.

They'd been enjoying casual coffee dates for weeks. Yet he'd never tried to deepen the relationship. Until today. He'd admitted he cared for her. Was this dinner a way of saying he wanted more?

Before she could respond, James withdrew his hand and slid his chair away with a mumbled sound of disgust. "I'm sorry. It's the room." He stood and paced across the small space. "Sometimes when we want information, we invade a suspect's personal space. Try to overwhelm them. It's almost a reflex."

He ran a hand through his hair and turned to Bree.

"James. It's okay." She gave him a tentative smile. "For what it's worth, I didn't really mind. But let's take things one bribe at a time."

"Fair enough." He dragged his chair back to its place across the table from her. "I guess I'll have to settle for picking your brain. Suppose I tell you I have a theory—sorry, make that a hypothesis—that Paul Bender killed Hannah. What would you say?"

"Well, if I wanted to use the scientific process, I'd try to test the hypothesis. See if I could disprove it. If I couldn't..." She shrugged. "It wouldn't mean you were right. But we couldn't dismiss it as wrong, either."

"So, test it." James filled a plate and focused his attention on her as he nibbled an eggroll. "Poke holes in my... hypothesis."

One by one, they cast each lab member as the main suspect in a murder. And one by one, Bree and James built a case both for—and against—the supposition.

By the time they'd polished off the savory dishes and cracked open fortune cookies, they'd included the college president, the groundskeeper, and everyone in between on their list of suspects.

Bree dissolved into laughter when James suggested the college mascot—a dancing purple gopher—might be the real killer.

"I can see it now," she said as she pushed her uneaten fortune cookie away. "It was Gleason Gopher in the science lab with a syringe."

"And that, folks, is how we play the game of *Clue*." James leaned back in his chair and chuckled. "This ranks as one of the most unusual dates I've ever had."

Date? Hadn't they dismissed that idea earlier? Bree felt her smile slip as the sensual pull snaked between them, disrupting the earlier, easy camaraderie.

The door banged open, cutting off her musings.

"Isn't this a cozy little evening?" Matthew Tugood's voice dripped with sarcasm as he shouldered his way past his escort into the interrogation room.

"Matthew, what are you doing here?" Bree clutched the metal arms of her chair, determined to remain calm in the face of his prodding. A frown etched his features as he swiveled toward her. Bree fought her instincts. She refused to cower under his anger. But she also knew the futility of fighting him. She settled for matching his steely gaze in silence.

"My operative witnessed a murder, then disappears into police custody without so much as contacting me. Why wouldn't I be here?" His gaze softened a bit, although his voice still carried a razor-sharp edge. "I was worried about you, Bree."

O'Neil snorted. "That's rich, Tugood. You didn't worry when you left her on her own in a suspected meth lab. I'm not buying it. You're jealous because she's here with me."

"This is none of your business, Detective."

"The hell it isn't." O'Neil shoved his chair back and leaned across the table, bringing his face close to Tugood's. "The campus is in Plainville County, which puts it squarely in my jurisdiction. A suspected murder makes it my business."

"My investigation supersedes that."

"Really?" O'Neil's voice was cool. He crossed his arms and sauntered around the desk. "Is that because you're part of a federal investigation? Wait. That can't be it. You're not with the FBI. Or the CIA. Or any government sanctioned agency. Are you, Tugood?"

CHAPTER 10

"Stupid, posturing baboons." Bree checked her pacing long enough to give Sherlock a pointed stare. His tail twitched and he gave her a sleepy blink.

"They did everything except pound their chests." Bree focused on the cat. "I doubt they even noticed when I left."

She stomped into the kitchen and collected the ingredients she needed to reproduce her Piña Colada chicken strips at tomorrow's party. By the time she was finished, images of James and Matthew standing toe-to-toe trading insults faded, replaced by memories of Hannah's dead body.

Tomorrow she'd sign O'Neil's contract and resume her cover as a wide-eyed undergrad to see what secrets she could pry out of her lab mates. For both of her investigations.

After work, she'd head with them to the bar and the "Mix Your Own Cocktail" party. Since Hannah had been a regular at the bar, Bree's list of suspects had to include bar staff and patrons.

The bar owner and his family had clearly been acquainted with Hannah. Had the other patrons known her as well? Hannah had frequented the bar at times when the *Naturalistics* staff didn't, so Bree would need to do so as well if she wanted to talk to everyone who knew Hannah.

After scrawling a few notes, Bree stashed the crime book in her purse. Still restless, she paced from the living room to the fridge under the watchful eyes of Sherlock. She scanned the pristine kitchen counters, idly thinking about Piña Colada cupcakes. Baking took the edge off when she was restless.

Sherlock's meow drew her attention from the kitchen to the spot on the couch where he was curled up. Too bad she couldn't talk to him and get an intelligent response in return. Meth labs and murder swirled in her head, battling for her attention in the way O'Neil and Tugood had battled for dominance in the police interrogation room.

"I've got to get out of here," she muttered as she passed the drowsy cat on her final lap around the room. She grabbed her purse, and the chicken from her early cooking frenzy. A walk would help calm her frazzled nerves, she thought as she set out to visit Horace and Wendy at *The Barkery*.

An evening breeze ruffled her hair, bringing with it scents of roasted coffee, fresh baked goods, and more as Bree strolled along the pedestrian walkway. The quaint ambiance of Plainville, Illinois calmed her nerves. She passed the kitchen store, where a culinary class was in session, and continued down the block to the storefront that housed *The Barkery*. As she approached, Bree wondered—not for the first time—if her friends lived in rooms at the back of the store. She shrugged off the thought. Best not to look too closely at any blurry lines the Clarks crossed.

When she arrived, the sign on the door indicated they were closed. Bree peeked in the shop window and spied the couple near the back of the store. Horace's lean, weathered frame towered over his petite wife, Wendy, as they focused on something out of Bree's line of sight.

Since they were in the store, Bree tried the door. It opened and the chimes above it tinkled.

"Hey, Doc Bree," Horace's face split into a grin and he motioned her into the shop. "Don't pay no mind to the sign. Friends are always welcome."

Wendy hurried over and enveloped Bree in a warm hug. Bree closed her eyes and breathed in the scent of fresh bread that clung to the older woman. Like a true earth mother—or maybe a pioneer—Wendy avoided preservative-laden supermarket fare and did most of her cooking from scratch.

"What brings you to the shop tonight?" she asked.

Bree waved the plastic containers at her. "I tried a new recipe and wanted your opinion."

"And by that, she means my opinion." Horace brushed past Wendy and grabbed the food.

"Horace Clark, you know very well that I'm the expert when it comes to cooking." Wendy thrust her hands on her hips and frowned at her husband as he pried open the container.

"You may be the expert on cooking, but I'm the expert on eating." The skin around his faded blue eyes crinkled into smile lines. "Besides, I'll share."

He snagged a chicken finger, and at Bree's instruction, dipped it into the sauce. A moment later his Adam's apple bobbed as he swallowed and he gave Bree a quick thumbs up before devouring another stip. Bree doubted he'd even tasted it.

Wendy slapped his hand away and stepped between Horace and the food as he reached for a third piece. "Give me a chance to taste it." She dipped one end of a chicken strip in the sauce and took a small bite. Her brow tightened in concentration. Next she took a bite from the end of the strip without sauce. After a minute, she shifted to give Horace access to the food.

"Great job, Bree. I really like the crunch. What did you use?"

Bree filled Wendy in on the recipe and compared notes with her while Horace finished the rest of the chicken.

"Mighty good, Doc Bree," he said after he'd licked his fingers. "Now it's my turn to show you something. Wendy and I have a new family member."

He issued a terse command and Bree heard the click of tiny claws on the hard floor. A small beagle with floppy ears toddled around the counter and headed to Bree, tail wagging. Horace issued another command, then told Bree she could pet the dog.

"He's adorable," she cooed, rubbing his ears and getting a puppyish howl in response. "Is this the newest *Dog on Guard*—I mean *D.O.G.*—team member?"

Between *The Barkery*, *D.O.G.*, and Wendy's pet parties (doggie birthdays, baptisms, and bar—or rather bark—mitzvahs), the couple's crazy businesses took up every minute of their time. Wendy's ideas were quirky, but Horace's were downright...

"Nonsense. Rookie, here, ain't cut out to be chasing critters like Krupke and the boys," he said referring to his other dogs. "Rookie's a genuine police dog. All the way from California."

Bree stared at Rookie, who rolled over for a belly rub. What did he do as a police dog? Distract the suspects with cuteness while the cops snuck up on them?

"Actually," Wendy said, "Rookie is a former police dog. We got him from a rescue society."

"I'm gonna rehabilitate him." Horace squatted next to Bree and scratched the dog. "He's a dropout from drug dog school. But we're gonna find him a new purpose in life. Aren't we, Rookie?"

"At the very least, he'll have a good home here with you and the other dogs," Bree said.

"Yup." Horace stood. "It's been quiet here since we found homes for the last rescue litter."

"What about the contracts you have for *D.O.G.* services?"

"My sons are taking over D.O.G. Them boys have got so many new customers, we're busier than a long-tailed cat in a room full of rocking chairs. While they take care of business, Rookie and I have plans. He starts training in the morning."

"Training for what?"

"You'll see." Horace winked at Bree then snapped a leash on Rookie. "He's a special boy with a great nose. Rookie could learn to sniff out anything from diabetes to designer drugs. We're gonna see where that nose takes us." With that, he headed out for a walk.

"That man's full of crazy ideas." Wendy smiled as she talked about her husband. "The trouble is, you never know in advance which of his ideas are crazy-good and which are just plain crazy. Time will tell."

No amount of wheedling could get Wendy to give Bree more information, so, after a few minutes, Bree said goodnight and headed back to her condo.

She took the long way home, detouring through the blocks of retail merchants before returning to the pedestrian shopping mall that lined her street. Window-shopping in the balmy evening air restored a sense of balance she'd been missing lately.

For once, she didn't have to think about her cover ID, the lies she told her friends and family, her multi-layered relationship with the Plainville PD or her enigmatic handler. She could relax and just be...

Something moved in the shadow of a building. Bree snapped to full alert. Her hand curled around the pepper spray she carried in her pocket. Her feet planted themselves into a secure defensive stance.

With a screech, a cat flew across the street in front of her, chasing its invisible prey.

Bree relaxed her grip on the self-defense spray and eased out of the fighting stance. But for the rest of the walk home, her eyes sought the shadows and her mind raced.

Being a spy wasn't something she could leave on a hook by the door with her spring jacket.

Not with an illegal drug ring and a murderer on the loose.

A hungry cat is more effective than an industrial strength alarm clock, Bree thought as Sherlock tapped her on the cheek for the third time.

Merooww.

"Don't take that tone with me, Sherlock. I'm the one with opposable thumbs who knows how to use the can opener." She pried her eyes open and stared at him.

Satisfied that she was awake, the orange cat perched on Bree's stomach and purred while shifting his weight from paw to paw. The effect was like being awakened by a jackhammer. One with claws. Bree moved under the covers to dislodge the cat. "All right. I'll get your breakfast."

Thirty minutes and one well-fed cat later, she stepped from the shower, pulled out her cosmetic bag and eyed her reflection in the mirror. Time for Dr. Bree Mayfield-Watson to disappear into the persona of Cat Holmes, college senior.

She went to work, thankful for her years of practice with theater makeup, plus the tips the Sci-Spy makeup artist had taught her. Fine smile lines disappeared beneath a plumping agent and a concealer. Eyeliner to create a wide-eyed look.

A few minutes with the blow drier tamed her normal body and bounce into a straight, flat, lifeless mass of nondescript brown locks.

Bree stared in the mirror, hating the way Cat's center part drew attention to her nose. But wasn't that the point of a disguise? To create an image unlike your own?

She slathered pink berry stain and thick gloss on her lips and examined the result. A hollow ache gripped her stomach as the eerie image of Cat Holmes stared at her from her own mirror.

"I'm still me," she muttered as she moved from the mirror to her closet. But the ache in her stomach didn't abate.

"Still me." Bree pulled on tattered jeans, a baby-blue tank top, and a sleeveless stripped shrug with slit-open sides. The shrug hid the curve of her hips, but exposed her arms. Bree hoped her pudge and love handles passed for baby fat, not sedentary spread.

A once-over in the mirror on the closet door confirmed that she looked more like a chemistry student than a mature scientist. She turned from the disturbing image, grabbed her phone—which she'd silenced for the night—and checked for messages.

Three from Tugood. Two from O'Neil. And one from her grandmother. She ignored both her handler and the detective and keyed in her grandmother's number.

"Hey, sugar, it's about time you called." Her grandmother's thick southern drawl oozed across the line and wrapped around her like a hug.

"Hi, Gram. How are things in Chattanooga?"

"It's so hot down here, my peach tree smells like pie."

Bree giggled. Gram knew how to turn a phrase. "Maybe you should come up north to visit me. It's still pleasant in the Chicago area."

"You couldn't pay me to visit that cesspool. You should high-tail it down here. I've been worried sick about you ever since you found your boss dead last March. Why on earth would you want to work at a company where folks are killing one another?"

"The police caught the killer. He's in jail." Bree left out the part about the murderer having his hands on her throat when the detectives had kicked in her door.

Gram snorted. "Pick one flea off a dog and what've you got left? I'll tell you. A dog with fleas."

"It's not like that. Our new owners brought in state-of-the-art security. The building is as safe as a bunker." Literally, if you counted Tugood's office and the Tech-Ops center.

"So, now, you've got cameras watching your every move?" Another snort. "If I were in your shoes, I'd spend more time with that nice young detective and less time in the chemistry labs. I wager he'd keep you safe and make your life interesting."

"My life is interesting." Bree stuffed her crime notes into a denim tote. A crystal bedazzled *Hello Kitty* logo winked in a shaft of sunlight from the French doors overlooking her balcony. She sighed. Cat Holmes had tacky taste.

"Why the heavy sigh if your life is so interesting? Boyfriend trouble?" Gram's voice held a note of hope.

"No steady boyfriend, yet," Bree said as she rummaged in the fridge. "But I am going to a party with some friends from work." She shared her recipe with Gram as she packed the ingredients into a thermal bag.

"Sounds too fancy for me. I can give you a man-pleasing recipe or two if you want."

"What?" Bree held back a giggle.

"If you want to keep a man happy, you've got to feed him right. Every woman knows that—even your ma. Didn't she teach you anything? Or did she lose her little bit of God-given common sense when she married that Yankee?"

Bree stifled a defense of her dad. Her southern grand-mother never quite forgave her Michigan-born father for marrying Bree's mother.

"It don't matter anyway. You listen to your grandma, Gabrielle Catherine. Feed your man. My macaroni salad will turn a Wanderin' Willie into a Steady Eddie in no time. You'll see."

"Thanks, Gram. Can you e-mail the recipe to me?" Taking Gram's advice—or pretending to—was the fastest way to get her to let go of a topic.

"I'll mail it to you, but you know I don't go for that computer crap. Too easy for busybodies to get in your private affairs."

Oops. Gram had obviously never heard of mail fraud, but Bree resisted the temptation to drag her into the modern century. Instead, she told Gram she loved her and cut the call off.

Bree took a cleansing breath, closed her eyes, and ran through a meditation exercise she'd learned in drama class. With each exhale, she let go of herself. With each inhale, she took on the persona of her role.

Out with Bree.

In with Cat.

Out Bree. In Cat.

Out. In.

Once the cover was in place, she breezed out the door ready to take on her investigations, her handlers, and what-ever else the world decided to throw at her today.

CHAPTER 11

"Cat, how are you doing this morning?" Tonya greeted her in the kitchen of the lab complex and gave her a critical once-over. The shadows under Tonya's eyes indicated a lack of sleep but did little to detract from her perfect features.

"I didn't sleep well," Bree said, hoping to bond with Tonya over restless nights.

"Me, neither. Between the police and seeing Hannah like that, I—" She crossed her arms and hugged them to her chest. "Every time I closed my eyes, I saw her. I can't imagine what it was like when you found the body. I'm amazed you had the presence of mind to call 911."

"Just instinct, I guess." Bree deliberately pulled her bottom lip through her teeth and let her gaze skitter around the kitchen, wondering if the killer had left traces of poison or any other clues nearby.

"Want some coffee?" Tonya poured herself a cup and held the pot out to Bree. "It's fresh."

Bree hesitated, then hefted her commuter mug. "I still have almost a full cup." No way was she drinking from a coffee pot—or mugs—that might have been tainted.

Tonya put the pot back and sat at the table. "You expect to see your grandparents' generation die. And even your parents'. But Hannah was closer to my age. Her death makes me feel so vulnerable." She glanced at Bree. "At your age, I felt immortal. Not so much anymore. You'll understand when you're a few years older."

At least, Tonya was still buying her disguise. Bree took a seat. "Does anyone know how Hannah died?"

"Hidden coronary disease? Undiagnosed aneurysm? Diabetes? Who knows?" Tonya shrugged. "I didn't care much for her, but now that she's gone I keep wondering if I shouldn't have been nicer to her."

"She didn't look good when she came in yesterday."

"I assumed she had a hangover. I wouldn't have pegged her for a lightweight since she was a regular at the bar. Plus, she didn't drink that much—at least, not that I can remember. I wasn't keeping count."

"Maybe she had more drinks at home," Bree suggested. A thread of hope wove through her doubts. Hannah could have died from natural causes. Her breath had been foul with alcohol and something else that teased the edges of Bree's mind.

Didn't diabetics exhale a specific chemical mix when they were in a hypo or hyper-glycemic state? Tonya could be right about Hannah's death being from natural causes.

Bree dug in her purse for her crime notebook but changed her mind. Tonya might be suspicious if she saw the book.

Instead she grabbed her phone and pretended to text something while jotting her observations in the note-taking app. Just as she finished the phone vibrated, reminding her it was still muted. Tugood's number popped up under the alias "Your Boyfriend" that he'd programmed into her phone. She ignored it and turned to Tonya.

"Maybe we should get to work to distract ourselves from thinking about Hannah's death," she suggested.

"Spoken like a budding scientist. When under stress, bury yourself in the lab. I'll meet you there in ten minutes." Tonya gave her a weak smile and left.

Bree hurried to the privacy of her office. Thankfully, it wasn't cordoned off as a crime scene today. O'Neil and team had been efficient. She closed the door and dialed Tugood.

He picked up on the first ring. "Where the hell have you been and why aren't you answering your phone?"

"Good morning to you, too."

"Where are you?" he repeated.

"I'm at work. Doing a job you assigned me to, in case you don't remember."

"Part of that job is checking in with me. I shouldn't have to hunt you down like I did last night."

"You knew where I'd be. You told me to brief O'Neil on my mission after he left the labs."

"No, I told you *we* would brief him. Big difference."

"Fine." Bree huffed and tried to regain her focus. "So, I assume after the two of you stopped trading insults, you finished briefing one another on the investigations?"

"We agreed that you need backup. And that the three of us will work together to solve both cases. Not that a city cop like O'Neil could solve it on his own anyway."

"He probably has something similar to say about you."

"Not the issue, Bree. What I need now is your assessment of the situation and your action plan so I can support you."

"Matthew," Bree hesitated, "do we know for sure that Hannah didn't die of natural causes?"

"We won't know anything till the autopsy comes back. Maybe not even then. But O'Neil put a rush on it and his captain approved it—to keep the mayor and the college president happy. Until we know for sure, treat her death like a murder. Don't trust anyone in the labs. And don't miss another check in."

His voice softened. "Please. I wasn't kidding when I said I was worried about you. I don't have eyes or ears in the lab yet. When we meet tonight, I'm giving you a couple of bugs to plant to remedy the situation. Till then, be careful."

"I will. And I promise, I'll check in on schedule." She heard him sigh in relief. They agreed on a schedule then Bree stashed the phone in her pocket and headed to the lab.

The staff stood clustered around Paul Bender when Bree entered the lab. No one noticed her so she crept to a lab bench and pretended to sort through a stack of safety data sheets.

"The good news," said Paul, "is that *Elemental Fractions* isn't pulling out on the acquisition deal."

"Why would they want to pull out?" The accent indicated this came from Jackie.

"It was," Paul hesitated, "something that doesn't matter anymore. The bad news is that they want to close the deal soon." He named a date.

A collective groan followed this announcement. "This is terrible." Emily's voice rose to a painful, enraged pitch. "Hannah was already pushing for such a fast integration that I could barely keep up with my work. Why would *Elemental Fractions* speed things up now that she's gone? Don't they have to take time to go through her notes or something?" Her voice cracked at the end of the tirade.

"Em's right," said Ricco. "She can't possibly finish her work that soon. Neither Tonya nor I can supervise—actually, it's more like consult—on her work if we're still planning to move to the new labs when the acquisition finalizes. I'll need Tonya's help to get everything set up."

Bree noticed his accent was nearly absent today.

"Calm down, everyone." Paul's voice sounded closer. Bree looked up to see he'd stepped away from the group and turned toward her. "Cat, come join us."

She edged closer to her lab mates.

"We don't need to vacate the labs before the integration. I can negotiate as much time as we need from the university. *Naturalistics* doesn't hold the lease. I do."

One at a time, Paul pointed to the team members. "Ricco, you and Tonya concentrate on the new labs. Emily, practice your leadership skills by drafting your final series of experiments and teaching Jackie and Cat how to run them. Streamline the tests, if necessary. If everyone works together, we can accomplish everything we need to before the deadline."

The group dispersed. Paul left first, an overflowing stack of paper-crammed file folders under one arm. Ricco gave Emily a one-armed hug and a wink, then left the labs hand-in-hand with Tonya. At last, only she, Emily, and Jackie remained in the lab.

"What's the deal with the integration?" Bree asked Jackie, trying to sound young and unsure instead of keenly interested. "It seems to have everyone on edge."

Jackie's gaze remained glued to the door. "It's probably nothing. *Naturalistics* is Paul's baby."

"Why would he want to sell it?"

Jackie shrugged and turned her head toward Bree. "Money. Why else?"

"He didn't strike me as the type to sell out for money."

"Selling isn't selling out." Jackie spit the words through gritted teeth. "Paul is an honorable man. Something a busybody like Hannah didn't understand. If she thought she could twist him around her fingers, she was wrong."

A chill washed over Bree at the vehemence in Jackie's voice. She shivered and turned her attention to Emily. "So, boss, what are my orders?"

"I was planning to run some separation columns today. Jackie was helping me. But since Paul dropped that bombshell on us, I'd better hole up in my office and plan the rest of the experiments. Can you run one of the columns for me?"

"Sure." Bree smiled at Emily, trying to ease the young scientist's nervousness. "All you have to do is explain what a column is, why you want me to run it, and what exactly I have to do."

Emily led Bree to a bench. "This is a chromatography column," Emily explained, pointing to a long glass tube. "It's filled with a special—and very expensive—material. I'm working on a process to separate a mixture of chemically similar species. Have you studied chiral molecules?"

Bree struggled to keep her features blank while she answered Emily. "I studied chiral molecules. They are like a person's right and left hands. They look the same, but the right hand won't fit in the left-handed glove."

"Exactly. Good memory, Cat. Vitamin E is an example of a chiral molecule. The body can use one form but not the other. Lab synthesis of vitamin E produces both forms. Nature only produces the form the body uses. That's why natural vitamin E is twice as potent as the synthetic form."

Emily was both sharp and patient. She'd make a good teacher if she chose that path. Bree nodded to the column.

"What does vitamin E have to do with the column?"

"Good question. The media separates the two molecular forms. We could pour a mixture of synthetic vitamin E into the top and collect a single isomer from the bottom of the column."

"So, that's what your research is?"

"I couldn't get my PhD with something that simple, but yes, that's the idea behind most of my research. The solution we're separating isn't just a single molecule with right and left hand forms. It's a mixture of many chiral molecules. I'm trying to see if we can separate both the molecules and the isomers—sorry, I mean the right and left hand forms—in a single step instead of multiple steps."

"Wow, that sounds cool." Bree kept her eyes wide and her voice slightly awed. "What molecules are you separating?"

Emily turned away and grabbed a flask of liquid, not meeting Bree's eyes. "Like I said, it's a bunch of stuff. Nothing you need to worry about. It's not dangerous to handle."

She handed Bree a series of vials, a large flask of liquid, and explained how often to collect samples.

Bree asked a few more questions, then breathed a sigh of relief when Emily left the labs. The girl had been chatty until Bree prodded her about the contents of the reaction mixture. Bree eyed the flask and its contents with suspicion. If the reaction contained an unpurified version of meth—or some other street drug, it could explain the girl's reluctance to answer.

After a quick check to assure no one was watching, Bree filled several vials with the fluid and pocketed them. Later, she'd take them to her colleague Nate Rayburn for analysis.

Nate, who came from the same region of the South as Bree's grandmother, also worked on the Sci-Spy team. His slow drawl and good-old-boy aphorisms fooled most people, but not Bree. His analytical skills were as sharp as crocodile teeth and his grip on a problem just as fierce. Bree was sure he'd identify the mixture.

Over the next several hours, Bree pulled samples for Emily and pocketed duplicates for Nate, wondering which of the fractions interested Emily most. At the bar, Tonya and Ricco had mentioned a special separation process Emily was working on. So all three of them were likely involved in whatever the girl was doing.

"How's it going, Bree?"

She jumped at the sound of Jackie's voice near her ear.

"Sorry, *cariña*. You were lost in thought. Did you need some help? Or have any questions about the process?"

Did Bree imagine it or was Jackie looking at her bulging lab coat pockets? She forced herself to relax.

"I think I've got it," she said as she positioned another vial under the stream of liquid exiting the column. "What about you? Are you working with the same thing I am?"

"No." Jackie leaned on the lab bench. "My media is different. Emily's evaluating lots of reactions and media. That girl bit off a big chunk of research when she proposed her dissertation work. But she's got the guts to see it through. Our Emily looks fragile, but she's tough as an old rooster when she needs to be."

Tough enough to kill if someone got in the way of finishing her research? The question flitted through Bree's mind and refused to leave. At Paul's impromptu group meeting, everyone had been concerned about the speeded-up integration timetable. But only Emily had connected it to Hannah's death.

Don't they have to take time to go through her notes or something? She'd claimed Hannah's desire to integrate the companies quickly impacted her work. Emily had been desperate to gain more time for her research—or whatever it was she was doing. And she'd seemed surprised that Hannah's death hadn't slowed down the integration process.

The vials weighed heavily in her pocket as Bree pondered the question that refused to leave her mind.

Was Emily desperate enough to kill?

Chapter 12

After her check-in with Tugood, Bree stashed the chemical samples and updated her crime notebook with information she'd gleaned about the others in the lab. Tonya, Jackie, and Emily all had an opportunity to kill Hannah, but now Emily had a potential motive.

As for the other two... Tonya seemed genuinely upset that Hannah had died. Nothing in her manner had contradicted her words when she had talked with Bree, which made Bree want to dismiss her from the suspect list. She jotted her observations in the table under the body language column.

Jackie, on the other hand, didn't seem distressed about Hannah's death. She'd all but accused Hannah of—Bree stopped short. Jackie had only insinuated that Hannah tried to manipulate Paul. But her anger, and the insistence that Paul was a good man, left Bree with questions.

Was Paul aware of the lab's alleged illegal activities?

Did he condone them? Or had he tried to stop them?

Paul's actions were consistent with a man of principle. He hired—and empowered—women and minorities. No criminal record, except for a few citations for old Vietnam War era protests, all of which were peaceful. In short, he seemed to be above suspicion.

Was his reputation the truth? Or a carefully constructed lie?

Bree grabbed a peanut butter sandwich from her tote and headed to the kitchen where she'd left a Diet Coke in the fridge. Voices drifted to her from the eating area where Jackie and Ricco chatted while they ate.

"Hey, Cat, come join us." Ricco waved her over. "Mom made cheesy chicken and rice. As usual there's more than enough for two. Grab a plate. I guarantee it's better than that sad looking sandwich you're holding."

Bree eyed the covered dish and decided it was worth the risk. Both Jackie and Ricco were eating from it. Besides, she had to get control over her poison phobia. Unless someone had coated the dishware and cutlery with arsenic, she would be safe.

She grabbed a plate and spooned some of the casserole onto it. "Thanks, I'm starving."

"So Em's working you hard today?" Ricco grinned at her.

"It was a lot different than the kind of stuff we did in chem lab at school. Her research sounds interesting. Why does she have to finish it so fast?"

"No technical reason. Like I told you, chemistry is as much a business as it is a science. *Naturalistics* sponsored Emily's graduate research. Once the company dissolves, paperwork and funding issues could get sticky. Paul wants everything associated with *Naturalistics* wrapped up before he finalizes the transfer of IP to *Elemental Fractions, Inc.*"

"The company's dissolving?"

"Yes. Gone. Poof." He gestured like a magician. "As of the integration day, *Naturalistics* will be no more."

"What about your jobs?"

"Paul looks out for his people," Jackie replied. She patted Bree's hand. "Don't worry. If he likes you, he'll find a place for you."

"At the new labs?"

Silence greeted her comment. Ricco frowned, the action drawing his brows tight and giving him a foreboding, glowering look. After a minute, he relaxed and focused on her.

"Not all of our discoveries are owned by *Naturalistics*. And not all of the IP we developed was sold to *Elemental Fractions*. Paul's already started a new corporation to take some of our discoveries forward. That's what will take place in the new labs. Understand?"

Bree nodded.

"Ricco helped Emily with her research when she first came on board," Jackie added. "Her studies formed a bridge between the old company and the new one. She needs to wrap up her old work so she can focus on the new."

"Won't the university own the IP from her work?" Bree watched closely for their reactions to her comment.

"Cat's a sharp one, Mom. She's catching on to the business side as quickly as she's catching onto the chemistry side." He turned to Bree. "But to answer your question, yes, the university normally owns any IP generated by its graduate students. But Paul and his IP attorney were very specific with their agreements. We're protected."

"Like I told you, Cat," said Jackie, "Paul takes care of his own. He's a good man. He wouldn't let anyone take advantage of his team."

"Was Hannah trying to take advantage of him?"

Jackie uttered an obscenity, then crossed herself and muttered a prayer in Spanish before turning to Bree. "I knew that woman was trouble the minute she marched her skinny behind into Paul's office."

"What happened?" Bree asked in a breathless voice as she leaned toward Jackie in a move calculated to inspire confidences.

"Mom, stop gossiping."

"It isn't gossip. I saw—and heard—everything myself."
Jackie skewered Ricco with a look. He clamped his jaw shut.
"I was dropping off a supply order with Paul's admin, Alice,
when Miss Thing sashayed past us like we didn't exist. If she
thought flashing her boobies and strutting in her tight little
pantsuit would sway Paul, she was mistaken. He walked her
out in less than five minutes."

"What did she want?"

Jackie shrugged. "Whatever it was, Paul told her it wasn't
part of the deal. She said everything had a price. Next thing I
know, she'd moved into an office and set her sights on Ricco."

"Who's got sights on Ricco?" Tonya entered the kitchen
bringing with her the scent of fresh air and sunshine.

"Nothing you need to worry about, beautiful." Ricco
gave her a kiss on the cheek. "It's old news."

Tonya stiffened and turned from Ricco. Dark color
flooded her cheeks. "Hannah. That bitch couldn't keep her
hands off you, could she?"

"Trust me, the woman's better off dead." Jackie stood
and faced Tonya. "Nobody hurts my boy. And you," she
jabbed a finger in Ricco's direction, "you know better than
to mistreat your woman. I won't let you treat her like your
father treated me."

"Don't worry about me," Tonya said. "I can handle
myself. And take care of anyone who gets in my way." With
that, she turned and walked out of the room.

The hairs on the back of Bree's neck lifted.

Tonya was back on the list of murderer suspects.

Tensions in the lab eased a bit in the afternoon. Bree managed to sneak samples from the columns Jackie was running

but before she could get them to her office, Tonya entered the lab.

"Time to get ready for the cocktail party," she announced. Bree hugged her lab coat close, the vials weighing heavily in her pockets as Tonya steered her toward her office.

Tonya stayed nearby, chatting while Bree turned her back and shifted the vials from the lab coat to her bag. Next, she checked in with Tugood via text. Shortly after, she and the rest of the team were on their way to *All Mixed Up* for the mix your own cocktail party. Tonya hitched a ride with Bree.

"Still angry with Ricco?" Bree asked.

"Not really. But it doesn't pay to let him off the hook too easily."

"Do you honestly think he'd cheat on you?"

"He's a man." Tonya pulled out a tube of lipstick and applied a fresh coat. "If Hannah thrust the goods in his face, he'd be tempted."

"Somehow, I doubt that," Bree said. "He didn't seem to like her much."

"You don't have to like it to bang it." Tonya put the lipstick away. "But you're right, Ricco has integrity. He wouldn't have let her get to him. Still, I don't like him flirting with other women. That flirting is going to cost him."

"Wh- what do you mean?" Bree clutched the wheel to keep her hands from shaking. After Tonya's outburst at lunch, she no longer seemed incapable of violence.

"I mean the man's not getting away with a load of sweet talk and a couple of drinks. Jewelry or a romantic weekend and a lot of groveling could do the trick. But not a drink. Don't ever let a man think he has the upper hand. You're smart, attractive, and a good catch. Make sure he knows what a prize he's getting."

Tonya saw all that in Cat Holmes? What would she think if she knew the real Bree Mayfield-Watson? Smart, yes. Attractive? Maybe. A good catch? If so, why was she still single?

She shrugged the thoughts off and pulled into the parking lot at the bar. Tonya helped Bree gather her ingredients for the cooking contest and they met up with the others at the door.

"Cat, it looks like you're ready to do some kitchen chemistry." Emily gave her a smile. "Good for you. After yesterday, I didn't feel like coming up with a recipe."

"It's just chicken. And I still have to cook it. Do you think I can use the kitchen?" Bree hoped she could get some of the staff chatting about Hannah while she cooked.

"We'll ask. I'm sure we can work something out." Tonya led Bree through the crowd until they reached the owner. "Cat, this is Edward Tinsdale. Edward, Cat is our new intern. You met her the other night."

Edward held out his hand. "Welcome back. Any friend of Tonya's is a friend of mine."

Bree juggled the plastic food containers until she could shake his hand. No doubt her lack of coordination fit well with her cover disguise. "Hi. Um... I was wondering if I..."

"Cat needs to cook her entry for the contest. I told her you wouldn't mind."

The older man grinned. "Normally only staff is allowed in the kitchen, but in this case, I can make an exception. Follow me, Cat. What is it you're making for us?"

On the way to the kitchen, Mr. Tinsdale introduced her to his wife, Liz, and his daughter, Miranda. Bree recognized Miranda as the server who'd brought them drinks her last visit.

"Nice to see you again," said Miranda. "Let me help you with those containers. What do you need in the kitchen?"

While Miranda outfitted Bree with an apron and hair net, they chatted about the party. Eventually Bree steered the conversation in the direction she wanted.

"No one else from the lab brought anything," she said as she dredged the chicken in the egg mixture followed by the crunchy coating. "But when I'm nervous, I cook."

"Why are you nervous? The party's all about having fun. No pressure."

"Didn't you hear?" Bree widened her eyes and turned to Miranda. "Hannah Rogers died yesterday morning. I found her body in the office."

"Oh, my God." Miranda froze, a baking sheet in one hand and a blank look on her face. "What happened?"

"I don't know." Bree took the baking sheet and arranged her chicken strips on top. "But the police and the paramedics came and the lab was in chaos. It was creepy."

"That's fitting. Not to speak ill of the dead, but I never liked her."

"Did you know her well?"

"Know her? She's been a regular bar patron since day one. She used to work with my dad."

"What did they do together?" Bree watched as Miranda's face contorted in a grimace.

"What didn't they do? They went to conferences together. They spent late nights in the office together. They worked," Miranda used her fingers to add air quotes to the word "or so they said. I can read between those lines."

"No way." Bree hid her grimace at the juvenile expression by sliding the chicken strips into the oven. "You mean your dad and Hannah were hooking up?"

"Dad says they didn't, but my mom cried herself to sleep every night during some of those so-called conferences. When Dad finally quit the job to follow his dream, he welcomed Hannah to the bar with open arms." Miranda shrugged. "Open arms and a private bottle of expensive tequila."

"Yeah. What's the deal with that? I mean, how much different can one bottle of tequila be from another? Right?"

"It's an acquired taste. The more money you make, the more expensive you want your liquor to be. No matter who's paying for it. You'll see one day."

Bree spooned her dipping sauce into a container and put it in the microwave to take the chill off. "Do other customers have private bottles?"

"No." Miranda pointed to a corner shelf in the kitchen. "I guess it's time to retire Harpy Hannah's bottle forever. Sorry, I shouldn't have called her that, but if the shoe fits..."

Bree nodded in sympathy. "It must have been hard, seeing her here all the time. I mean, she was a regular, wasn't she?"

Another shrug. "Yeah. She hung out here with the late crowd. I tried to make sure Mom never had to deal with her. My mom didn't deserve any of that witch's snotty attitude."

Bree mentally added another two suspects and a chore to her list. Miranda and Liz Tinsdale both had reason to want Hannah out of the picture. Which meant Bree needed to get a sample of the private-label tequila to check it for poison.

CHAPTER 13

The back of the bar had been set up with long tables for the food contest and a center stage where Jen Stands emceed the events. Tonight, sparkling drop earrings and a colorful crystal necklace glinted against her black top when a spotlight hit her.

She stepped up to the microphone. Between her jangling charm bracelet and her staccato taps on the microphone the crowd soon quieted.

"Ladies and Gentlemen, welcome to *All Mixed Up*'s first ever 'Mix Your Own Cocktail' party." Jen introduced the staff and explained the evening's events.

Bree lined her chicken strips in with the other entries then turned to study the crowd. Button-down shirts and business casual attire indicated most were young professionals ready to start the weekend.

A scattering of older patrons sat in shadowed booths, ignoring the festive atmosphere. None of them looked like people she'd seen the last time she'd been at the bar. But then, she hadn't been interested in anyone except her lab mates last time she was here. Now any one of the others could have known Hannah, and wanted her dead.

Focus on what you can do, not on what you can't.

Bree waited until the tasting began, then edged away from the tables. She walked in the direction of the ladies'

97

room then ducked into the kitchen instead. A lone line cook manned the griddle, his back turned to her.

Bree grabbed her empty commuter mug from her tote, hands shaking as she unscrewed the cap. Quickly, she reached for the private bottle of tequila and poured a measure into the mug. Just as she replaced the bottle on the shelf, the line cook turned.

"Hey, what are you doing in here?"

Bree screwed the lid on her mug but the threads didn't line up. She plastered a weak smile on her face, battling internal panic. "I…um…" *Unscrew the cap and start again.* "That is I came in to get my food containers…" The threads caught and the cap screwed into place. "I left them here when I was cooking my chicken."

The cook glared at her, his eyes slipping to her mug. He jerked his chin toward her plastic ware. "Your stuff's over there. And guests belong in the bar, not the kitchen."

Bree hustled out, her heart pounding so hard, she was sure everyone could see it beating. The mug of tequila weighed down her tote. Or was it her conscious that felt weighed down? If anyone got close enough, they might smell tequila on the bag.

She edged up to the makeshift bar where Miranda and several others were helping party-goers mix their own cocktails while Jen made suggestions. A tray with half-finished drinks and discarded concoctions sat nearby. She bumped in to it, sending a slosh of mixed liquor onto her bag. So much for the smell.

"Oh no!" Her fake outrage turned a few heads and sent a ripple of laughter through the crowd. Immediately, the attention focused back on the stage and Jen's discussion of how to make a perfect dry martini.

Although she'd thought calling mixology a science sounded a bit overblown, Bree was intrigued when Jen discussed temperature gradients, super-cooled barware, and other technical issues. Jen's science classes may have been unorthodox, but based on her talk, they'd been founded on sound principles.

Patrons were drifting away from the main stage and back to their tables when someone slung an arm around Bree's shoulders. "Hey, good lookin'." Matthew Tugood's voice poured over her. Between his sexy baritone and the woodsy-spicy scent of his aftershave, she didn't need to look to identify him.

"What are you doing here?"

"Using our cover to get a little closer to your friends." He nuzzled her ear. "You forgot to check in. I wanted to see if you were okay."

A shiver ran from her earlobe and shimmied down her spine, as if the caress had been real, not just a covert way of speaking to her.

Emotional warfare broke out in her mind. Her rebel faction welcomed his presence and his strength. Her old guard resented wanting, needing, or even appearing to need help with her mission. The old guard won the first volley.

"No offense, but aren't you a little old to be my boyfriend? Or did you forget I'm supposed to be twenty-three?"

"I can play the role if you can." Tugood steered her toward the table where her coworkers sat. "Pretend you like older men."

"How old are you, anyway?"

"Old enough to know how to keep my cover."

She perched on her stool, and he leaned on the high bar table, giving her the first good look at his face she'd had all evening.

Thank goodness, she'd recognized him by his voice and scent. He no longer looked like the confident Matthew-in-charge she knew. He looked like ... a gangly geek.

In place of his near precision military cut, long shanks of dark hair tumbled over his forehead. His gray eyes, distorted through the lenses of black plastic rimmed glasses, twinkled. His white button-down shirt lay open and rumpled at the neck. A narrow black tie—halfway undone—gave him the aura of a boy playing dress-up rather than a man of confidence.

The rugged cut of his jaw was softened by the day-and-a-half growth of whiskers and a slight stoop hid his height.

Bree's jaw sagged open. Talk about the power of make-up and illusion.

Matthew gave her a wink and a smile. "Aren't you going to introduce me to your friends, babe?"

She turned to her lab mates. "Everybody, this is my boyfriend—" she hesitated. The word felt strange on her tongue, as if saying it gave a ring of truth to their associations. Which it didn't. Couldn't.

"Matt," he said quickly covering her pause. "Matt Goodson."

A chorus of greetings followed his announcement. Emily gave Bree a thumbs up behind Matthew's back, then dragged her to the ladies' room. Tonya followed.

"Your boyfriend is hot," Emily said the minute the trio was behind closed doors. "I want to know everything. How you met. How long you've been together. If he kisses as well as I think he does."

Heat rose in Bree's cheeks at the thought of kissing Matthew for real. It flamed as Emily pressed for details, probing like a scientist yet gushing like the young woman she still was.

Bree started to mumble something, but Tonya saved her.

"Em, if you'd get out of the lab and into the world, you might have a boyfriend of your own."

"I have a life. And lots of companions."

"Four-legged companions." Tonya shook her head and asked. "Just how many flea-bags do you share your place with?"

"Three dogs, two cats, and a parakeet. No fleas."

"No men, either." Tonya fluffed her hair and pulled out a tube of lipstick. "Honey, at least take those dogs for a walk and try to meet someone. You need a little chemistry outside of the lab, too."

"Like you and Ricco?"

Before long, the three of them were bonding over boyfriend stories. They returned to the table, giggling, to discover Matthew deep in conversation with Ricco and Jackie. Tonya and Emily joined in immediately, accepting Matthew without question. For some reason, it irritated Bree that he'd included himself so casually in the group.

Before she could drag him away, he pulled business cards from his shirt pocket and passed them around, along with a load of nonsense. "So, I'm, you know, working for my dad while I set up my programming business. Virtual 3D animation gaming. I'm going to blow the lid off the industry. If I ever get capital, that is."

Jackie rolled her eyes and the others only expressed polite interest. But everyone took the card he offered.

"Meanwhile," Matthew continued, "I'm helping at my dad's car lot. He's running a promotion. A brand new, top-of-the-line car, winner's choice, just for signing up. All you have to do is put your name and contact info on the card to enter." He leaned forward. "I need to get a dozen or more signatures before the end of the night to get my dad off my back. Plus, the more signatures I get, the bigger my commission. Which means the better I can treat Cat here on date night."

He slung his arm over Bree's shoulder again and gazed at her with the same look Sherlock used when he wanted tuna. Dear God, she hated the fake sincerity in his eyes.

Time to play her own role.

"Oh, sweetie pie, that's so thoughtful of you," she gushed, pleased when Matthew winced at the pet name and her tone. She slid a glance to the others at the table "Isn't he the best? He was so sweet to surprise me by coming tonight."

She continued the adoring chatter while her friends busied themselves by filling out information in the business cards—likely to avoid having to watch her drool over Matthew.

He collected the cards and slid them into an aluminum case, his eyes darkening each time she called him sweetie pie or honey bear. Good. She'd prove she could play the role of adoring girlfriend.

They ordered a round of drinks and the conversation at the table turned to work. Matthew looked slightly befuddled when the team talked chemistry, but stuck to his role by passing out blank cards and reciting his silly story whenever someone new came to the table.

Edward Tinsdale stopped by to see Bree. "Young lady, your chicken strips were a hit. Sorry they didn't win the grand prize, but with your permission, I'd like to put them on the menu. Could you show our chefs your recipe and techniques?"

"I'd love to." The invitation would give her a chance to question the bar staff more closely. Edward and Bree set a time and he ambled off.

She looked to Matthew. "I'm so excited. Aren't you, honey-bea—"

He cut her words off with a fierce kiss, slamming his lips to hers and swallowing the rest of her pet name. Stunned, Bree struggled until the pressure of his lips turned gentle and searching.

He swept a hand down her back, the caress firm and warm. Soothing. She relaxed into the kiss, savoring the slight tang of beer and the warm taste of him in her mouth.

When he pulled away, the only word left in her vocabulary was a breathless "wow," which she exhaled on a sigh. Lethargy suffused her bones, until she looked in his eyes. Instead of affection, she saw cold calculation and a gleam of satisfaction.

Her body chilled, but her spirit reared up. If he wanted a fight, that's what she'd give him.

"Snook—"

Another kiss cut off her words.

She bit his lip.

Not hard enough because he growled and deepened the kiss. His tongue swept into her mouth, searching for weakness. Seeking dominance. She broke away before he could find either.

"I can play as long as you can, sweetheart. I've had lots of practice at this game." His words whispered across her lips.

She managed a shaky nod and turned back to the table. The conversation had shifted to the new lab set up. "The safety hoods are being tested next week, and the rest of the equipment is basically in place," Ricco said. He rattled off a list of typical analytical equipment. "Once the printer is working, we'll be ready to go," he added.

"When do we move?" Emily asked.

"As soon as you're finished with your work, we can go. So get those experiments done, schedule that thesis defense, and be ready to be Dr. Appleton."

Emily gave him a mock salute and turned to Bree. "I have about a dozen more mixtures to study. Most of the synthesis is done," she said. "If you and Jackie can run multiple columns at a time, I can finish the sample analysis and write up the rest of the results. We could be done in a couple weeks."

"Ricco and I will help run your analytical data," Tonya added. She turned to Bree. "If you need an example of how to make it through grad school, you couldn't do better than Emily. I swear she's been writing sections of that thesis since she proposed the research. I've never seen anyone so efficient."

"Amazing," said Bree. She meant it. It had taken her months to pull her data into a thesis draft and weeks to revise it before her defense. The *Naturalistics* team was more impressive by the moment.

If only they weren't suspects in a drug ring and maybe a murder.

The thought splashed over her like cold water, drowning the sense of camaraderie and reminding her none of the evening was real. She was undercover.

The colleagues weren't her friends.

Matthew wasn't a friend, either. Nor was he a love interest.

Reality lodged in her gut, as toxic as the suicide pills spies supposedly carried. The evening couldn't get worse.

Until her friend Kiki entered the bar and headed straight toward her.

Bree was about to be burned.

Chapter 14

A s Kiki and her husband neared the table, Bree did the only thing she could think of. She grabbed Matthew and pulled his head down for a kiss.

She threw herself into the action, curving her body into his and using him as a shield to keep out of Kiki's line of sight. Something in the desperation of her kiss must have gotten through to him, because he played along, letting her plunder his mouth with her tongue and explore his body with her hands.

His own palm, broader and hotter than she could have imagined, curved around her waist until it came to rest in the small of her back. A trail of sparks crackled in its wake.

His lips slid from hers to graze her cheek, her temple. "What's wrong?" he whispered, the sound low and ragged in her ear.

Nothing was wrong. The strength of his hands, the heat of his body, the heady mix of restlessness and languor that weighted her limbs—everything about the kiss was right. Everything except—

—except the reason they were kissing.

"Kiki is here." She sought his lips again, but he tucked her head under his chin.

"Grab your bag." Freeing one hand from their embrace he pulled out his wallet, peeled off some bills and tossed them on the table. "Let's ditch this place, babe," he said loud enough for the others to hear.

Next thing she knew, his lips locked on hers again and she gave herself up to the magic of the kiss. Worries about being discovered receded. Bree gripped the back of his shirt and held onto Matthew as he maneuvered them toward the back door.

She banged into an unoccupied table, sending half-filled glasses of beer onto their sides. Her steps faltered.

Matthew picked her up and murmured in her ear. Something—either his instructions or her instincts—urged her to wrap her legs around his waist and bury her head in the crook of his shoulder.

His body heat engulfed her. Flames licked her face at the thought of them locked together like lusty teens. Yet when he nibbled a path down her neck from jaw to shoulder, she forgot embarrassment. Forgot everything.

When Matthew eased them through the back door, a wash of cooler evening air hit her sweat-slickened skin, sending shivers down her back while his raging heat burned her from breast to belly—and lower. Adrenaline coursed through her veins unleashing pinpricks of awareness. Her fingers, toes, and everywhere in between tingled.

She sucked in a breath and kissed him again, not caring that they were in a dingy alley next to the dumpsters.

He complied, turning his kiss from frantic to slow and thorough, exploring the recesses of her mouth, searching out the hidden spots that wracked her body with shivers.

She tightened her legs around his waist and together they rocked into the solid wall of the metal dumpster. Bree flinched and tore her mouth from his as a whiskey bottle tumbled out near her shoulder. It bounced off her tote and landed harmlessly in a heap of empty plastic soap, rubbing alcohol, and bleach bottles spilling from a second dumpster.

"It's okay," Matthew said before giving her another long, slow kiss.

Bree unlocked her ankles, intending to stand, but Matthew had other ideas. He hugged her to his body, letting her slide to the ground by hot, friction-filled inches. By the time her feet hit the gravel her knees were too shaky to hold her. She clung to Matthew instead, accepting his help rather than fighting it.

"We're safe," she whispered. "Kiki didn't see us."

Matthew chuckled. "Oh, she saw us all right. She saw two people engaging in more PDA than she was comfortable with, judging from the look on her face. But you're right about one thing. She didn't see her best friend and a work colleague in a place where she didn't expect them."

He brushed a thumb along her cheek. In the dark corner, she couldn't see his eyes clearly, but his touch and his voice held warmth and a trace of humor. "You did good tonight. Most people would have panicked with their cover close to being compromised. Instead you improvised and found a way out."

The words of praise brought her back to her disappointing reality.

Somewhere between the panicked first kiss where she'd used him to hide her face and the smoldering last one where they'd celebrated their escape, she'd lost sight of the mission, her cover, and their professional relationship. She'd given in to passion, excitement, and a hunger for connection that drowned her common sense.

In those moments, she hadn't felt smart, capable, strong, or any of the other words she routinely used to describe herself. Instead she'd been desired, exciting, protected. All the things she'd buried when she decided to compete in a male dominated science.

She pressed her fingers to her lips—hard—determined to blot the feel of him from them. But even as she swallowed her disappointment, his taste—and her desire to be something more than a capable woman—lingered.

"If you think that was good, wait till you have our lab analyze this." She pulled the tequila-filled commuter mug from her bag.

"I'll drive you home while you debrief me on today's intel. We'll come back for your car tomorrow." Matthew took her elbow and guided her along the alley toward the parking lot. "Good work."

This time the praise severed her illusions that her Sci-Spy career was anything more than a job.

CHAPTER 15

Bree woke to the scents of alcohol and sweat. A heavy weight rested on her chest. She choked back her revulsion and levered herself up on her elbows to come face-to-face with Sherlock. As usual, everything from his wide, round-eyed stare to his mews and his twitching tail demanded she get out of bed and feed him.

Bree padded to the kitchen, fed the cat, started the coffee and tossed yesterday's alcohol-drenched clothing into the hamper. The tacky, bedazzled denim tote was also soaked, thanks to the times she and Tugood had knocked into tables on their way out of the bar last night.

She pulled her crime notebook from the bag. Its sturdy cover spared it any lasting damage. A mangled packet of Kleenex hadn't fared as well. Bree tossed the alcohol infused tissues into the garbage, wiped down her wallet and switched the ID inside from that of Cat Holmes back to Bree Mayfield-Watson.

At the bottom of the bag lay a dozen capped vials from the lab samples she'd taken yesterday.

Damn. She'd forgotten to give them to Matthew last night when she'd passed on the sample from Hannah's private bottle of tequila. She texted a message asking him to meet her at *The Barkery*.

She arrived early for the meeting. The muted sound of giggles, barks, and general revelry drifted out of one of the rooms to her right. A chorus of "Happy Birthday" indicated a doggie party was in full swing.

Horace stepped from the back of the store to greet Bree.

"Morning, Doc. What brings you by today?"

"I'm meeting a friend for lunch. He's going to pick me up here."

"He?" Horace grinned. "Anybody special?"

Bree shook her head. *Just a way to meet Tugood on neutral ground.* She bit her lip as a memory of their frantic, searing kisses surfaced. *Surely her imagination and hormones wouldn't get her into trouble at* The Barkery.

"I don't know," Horace drawled, with a smile. "You look pretty dreamy-eyed for a woman who's meeting someone who isn't a boyfriend." He stuck his hands in his back pockets and straightened his gangly frame, gawking at her.

"Really. He's just a friend," Bree said. "While we wait, why don't you tell me how Rookie is doing with his training? Or is that still a secret?"

Horace took the bait. He motioned for her to come behind the counter into a private room in the back of the store. Bree dropped her purse on a couch and followed Horace to where a computer monitor blinked on top of a desk in the corner.

"I been doing a bit of research," he said, waving at the screen. "See, dogs have a sense of smell that's about a thousand times more sensitive than humans. Humans have about five million whatch-ya-ma-call-its to sense smell."

"Chemical receptors?"

"Yeah, that's it. Receptors. But a dog has fifty times as many receptors, and like I said, a thousand times more sensitivity. Dogs can be trained to sniff out just about anything."

"You said Rookie was a failed drug dog. Is something wrong with his sense of smell?"

"Nope." Horace leaned back in the desk chair and rubbed his chin. "Rookie's nose is fine. The California lawmakers just voted him out of a job when they legalized marijuana. It isn't too hard to teach a dog to sniff out a scent, but it's dang near impossible to teach him not to smell it."

"So, Rookie is out of a job because his sense of smell is too accurate?"

"Pretty much." Horace's face lit up and his features became animated. Bree braced herself, knowing the look indicated a crazy idea about to be unleashed.

She wasn't disappointed.

"See, the thing is, just because a dog's been trained for a set of scents, don't mean he can't be taught to identify even more scents. I've been working with Rookie here to understand exactly how he was trained." He clicked to another site on the computer. "There's lots of information on how to do it. Turns out, it's pretty easy. Any breed of dog can learn to recognize scents and alert the owner to them."

Horace called for Rookie then turned back to Bree. "So, Wendy and me got the idea to train him to sniff out roofies and stuff."

"Roofies?"

"Sure. That and other drugs men like to slip into ladies' drinks. You know. Date rape drugs."

Bree bit her tongue to keep from pointing out that to train a dog to sniff drugs, you actually needed access to the drugs. If Horace had access to date rape drugs, she didn't want to know. Instead, she posed what seemed to be a more logical question.

"Even if you succeed, how will that help? Are you going to hire Rookie to stand by the door and sniff people as they walk into a bar?" The idea seemed a little out there, even for Horace.

He cackled with laughter. "Good one, Doc Bree. I hadn't thought of that. I was thinkin' more along the lines of training them over-bred, little designer dogs. You know—the kind the starlets like to tote around in their purses."

"Like Pocket Poodles?"

"Pocket Poodles, Min-Pins, Papillion, Chihuahuas—all of 'em. Posh girls carry their dogs everywhere, even in restaurants and fancy clubs. I bet they'd pay a bundle to get a chance to pamper a trained, drug-sniffing pocket protection system. First, we're going to train up some dogs as a trial run. Then we're going to work up a system to set up boot camps for existing pets. Trust me, it'll be all the rage."

Bree's mind filled with images of personal, pocket-sized drug dogs and she bit back a giggle. The idea was so crazy it just might work.

"I'll show you. I've already started training with Rookie to get the technique down." Horace called for the dog again, but Rookie didn't show.

A whimper sounded from across the room. Horace headed toward it and stopped in his tracks as he rounded the couch. "Doc Bree," he said in a shocked tone. "Don't tell me you've taken to smoking the whacky weed."

"No, of course not. I—"

"If that new boyfriend of yours is to blame, me and the boys will take him out and beat some sense into him. There's no call to be muddling a brain as smart as yours with that stuff."

"I promise, I'm not into drugs."

"Then why's he doing that?" Horace pointed to Rookie.

The dog sat staring at her purse, his floppy ears alert for once. While she watched, he wiggled his body and whimpered, trying to get Horace's attention.

Wendy bustled into the room a tray full of plates, cups, and half-chewed party favors in her hands. "Will you look at that?" she exclaimed as she stopped in her tracks to stare at Rookie. "Horace, he's actually alerting us."

A smile lit her face. She put down the tray and bent to pet Rookie. "Good boy." The dog's tail thumped on the cracked linoleum. She gave another command and Rookie stopped staring at Bree's purse and ran to greet her instead.

"Horace, he actually alerted us. Isn't that great?"

"It'd be great except it means Doc Bree's carrying something she shouldn't in that bag." He turned a sad gaze on Bree.

Wendy punched him lightly in the arm. "No, silly. Bree isn't carrying anything illegal. It means the training is working. He's already learned a new scent." She swiveled to face Bree. "Horace and I have been using a mix of cinnamon and other spices to train him to alert on new scents. He probably picked up on something you used while you were baking recently."

Horace's face cleared immediately. "Sure. That explains it. Sorry, I doubted you, Doc Bree." He winked at her. "And my apologies to the boyfriend, too."

"He's not a boyfriend," Bree protested automatically. The chime over the *Barkery* door sounded dimly in the background and Horace went to greet the customer while Wendy took her tray to the kitchen.

Bree absently stroked Rookie. She didn't have cinnamon in her purse. And she no longer needed the Sci-Spy crime lab to test the samples she'd stolen from *Naturalistics* for drugs.

Rookie had already confirmed her worst suspicions.

CHAPTER 16

"That alcohol sample was absolutely clean."

Bree paced the length of the Sci-Spy crime lab—a luxury RV outfitted with a plethora of high-end analytical equipment—as she listened to Nate discuss the methods he'd used to analyze the tequila she'd collected last night.

His graying hair stood in unruly tufts and dark circles rimmed his eyes. The eyes themselves were alight with excitement. "Matthew dropped the sample off here last night and sent me a text. I couldn't sleep, so I got myself in here early to check for contaminants. I've run every technique known to man and God, but I didn't find anything in the sample except high quality tequila."

He reached for the coffee pot and poured himself a cup. "I might-could save the rest and fix myself a drink later."

Might-could. Bree smiled, as she always did, at the southern phrase. It was something her grandmother would say and the thought warmed her. More than four decades living in the Chicago area hadn't severed Nate's Tennessee roots. She suspected he flaunted his accent, and his hunting, fishing, and camping skills just to vex his politically liberal neighbors.

Despite his prickly nature, Bree knew Nathanial Morris Rayburn, like her family, had her back in times of trouble.

As did the rest of the team, she thought as she looked around the RV.

Nate had been recruited to the team for his analytical equipment skills, razor-sharp mind, and ability to keep a secret. Her other colleague, Milt Shoemaker, had been recruited for his engineering, medical, and military skills. Bree still didn't know what the jack-of-all-trades technician/medic had done in his former life, but she suspected he had a Special Forces background.

Matthew Tugood and Luisa Cane, a colleague of Matthew who created deep-cover identities and supervised makeup, rounded out the team. Matthew seemed to have other resources, but Bree didn't know about them.

Everyone in the elite investigative team—except Bree—possessed some extraordinary or unique skill. She still wasn't sure what benefit she brought that one of the others couldn't have provided.

No matter. She shrugged off her insecurities and turned back to Nate. "Too bad the liquor was a dead end. Maybe analyses of these will shed more light on at least one of our problems." She handed the set of vials to him. "These fractions came off a separation column Emily was running in the *Naturalistics* labs. They are from a drug mixture of some sort."

"And how would you know that? Did she tell you?"

"I have my sources." Bree smiled at him and explained about Rookie alerting his owners to the scent.

"If that dog could talk, he'd save me a heap of prep time." Nate grinned. "I'll get started on this as soon as I finish my coffee. Don't expect quick turnaround time on this one, though. A man's got to sleep sometime. Besides, this kind of analysis takes longer than looking for poisons."

Bree checked to make sure she'd handed over all the sample vials then helped herself to some coffee while Nate logged the samples in.

Minutes later, Matthew swiveled from a computer monitor to look at Bree and Nate. "The three of us need to go over the details of our investigation so far and see what we've learned. Bree, why don't you bring Nate up to speed? Maybe going over this again will help us see it from a new angle."

Bree pulled out her crime notebook and flipped through the pages, getting her thoughts in order. Before she could begin, a knock sounded at the door.

Matthew tamped down his annoyance, ready to make a deal with whatever devil he needed to in order to accomplish his mission. He ambled to the door, giving Dr. Rayburn time to hide the analytical instruments behind fake fronts that disguised them as furniture in the second bedroom of the RV. Once the chemist slid into a banquette across the table from Bree, Matthew opened the door.

"It's about time you arrived, Detective." His reluctant truce with James O'Neil didn't extend to small talk and other social niceties.

"Nice digs, Spook." O'Neil shouldered his way past Matthew and flipped the blinds aside to look out the window on the opposite side of the RV. "Great view of the nature preserve. You should give up poking into other people's business and try camping like the decent folks out here."

"Thanks for the advice, Boy Scout." His version of camping consisted of hunkering in godforsaken caves gathering intel during sandstorms, enemy fire, and every other disaster man and nature could throw at him. All so people like

O'Neil could sleep safely. So people like Bree could choose to sleep next to them.

He swallowed a retort. His choice to enter covert service, and his choice to leave, were his own to live with. They weren't up for discussion.

Matthew focused instead on Bree. Her gaze darted between him and O'Neil as if she expected a fight to break out. Her face paled, her mouth pinched shut. A slight shift of her lower lip indicated she was chewing the inside of it.

The sight brought back a memory of last night when he was the one chewing on her lips. When she'd stopped trying to be strong and brave and had let him help her. Her trust then contrasted with her wariness now.

Damn. She deserved better than being dragged into his life, but he didn't regret having her as part of his team. She'd given him a glimpse of what he'd sacrificed so long ago. He owed her for that. Enough to put aside his animosity toward O'Neil and try to get through this investigation without tearing her apart.

"Let's get to work." He paced to the computer and retrieved a stack of printouts while O'Neil sat. "We have a drug ring to bust."

"No," said O'Neil. "We have a murder to solve."

"Actually, we have both." Bree had found her voice. With icy precision, she brought them both back to the investigation. "I was undercover investigating a suspected drug ring when Hannah died. I can't confirm—or deny—anything, but I suspect the two crimes are related." She summarized her work to date, bringing Dr. Rayburn—Nate—up to speed.

"What turned you on to the drug angle, anyway? That's not the sort of operation narcotics investigations or the DEA normally targets." O'Neil turned to Matthew and lifted his brows in question.

"It's need-to-know, Detective. And you don't." Hell, even he didn't know details. A friend of a friend asked for an off-book investigation. And when the Undersecretary to the Assistant of the Deputy Administrator of the DEA asked for an investigation to keep his granddaughter safe... Under those conditions, Matthew didn't ask questions to figure out what side he needed to be on.

Shit. Bree's pinched look was back. And he'd broken his unspoken promise to her already. "Sorry, O'Neil," he added, softening his voice for Bree's sake. "I'm not at liberty to share that information, unless it has some bearing on the case. Either case."

"And if evidence points to it having bearing on the case?"

"Then you'll need to know."

"Do we have the results of a tox screen on Hannah yet?" Bree addressed her question to James.

"No. Even under special circumstances autopsies take time. What I do have is a preliminary analysis on the liquid left in her coffee mug and the toast. They came back clean." He dragged a hand through his hair. She'd lost count of how many times he resorted to that gesture, but even so, the strands fell perfectly back into place. "What makes you so sure she was poisoned?"

"I'm not. But my gut tells me she was."

"That's your past experience talking," James countered. "When we met, your boss had just been poisoned. It makes sense you'd look for poison now."

Maybe he was right. Bree remembered how she'd tried to avoid eating or drinking with anyone at the lab the day after the murder. How she'd even wondered if poison coated the cups and plates in the communal kitchen. Maybe she was too focused on—

"It isn't only her past experience," Matthew insisted. "The brain is like a supercomputer. It stores thousands of tiny details every minute. Bree just happens to be better than most at remembering those details." He turned to her and offered a reassuring smile. "Close your eyes and walk through the day Hannah died. Which details stick out in your mind?"

Bree reached for her notebook, but Matthew stilled the movement by resting his hand on top of hers. Warmth from his palm surrounded her chilled fingers. "Not your note-book," he said staring into her eyes. "Your memory."

Rather than closing her eyes as he suggested, she grounded herself in his gray gaze and steadied her breathing.

"Tell me," he coaxed.

Slowly, she started to relive the morning. "Hannah was unsteady on her feet that morning. Her vision was blurry. She claimed it was mixing martinis with margaritas..."

Bree snapped her head toward James. "She'd couldn't read the menu at the bar. That's why she let someone else order food. Her vision was blurry at the bar and it was still blurry the next morning."

She turned back to Matthew and squeezed his hand. "She must have been poisoned at the bar."

"She couldn't have been," grumbled Nate from across the table. "I analyzed her special tequila and it didn't have any poison in it."

"She couldn't have been poisoned by the tequila," added James, "but what if—"

"—she was poisoned by something else." All four of them voiced the conclusion at the same time.

"So," Nate picked up the conversational thread, "what else did she eat or drink at the bar?" He grabbed a pen and listed everything Bree could remember.

Next, they identified items the group had shared. Tangerine Tango, chicken strips, and potato skins were crossed off the list. Margaritas, coffee, cream and sugar stayed on.

"The sugar and cream were in individual packets," said Bree, "so they should be at the bottom of the list."

"It doesn't matter." Everyone turned to James, who tapped his pen against a small notebook. "We don't have samples of any of those items. Poison could have been in any—or all—of them and we'd still be without a case."

Nate threw his pen on the table. "You're right. We can't tell if any of those had poison in them. But we can tell who handled all of the items."

"Miranda—the owner's daughter. And the mixologist. I'm not sure who brought the coffee." Bree briefly outlined her suspicions regarding Miranda and Elizabeth Tinsdale, citing the supposed affair between Hannah and Edward Tinsdale as a motive.

"Don't forget the bartenders," Nate added. "Drinks don't mix themselves."

"Anyone at the table could have put a hypothetical poison in her drink. I wasn't watching Hannah the whole time." Tension coiled between her eyes as Bree remembered retreating to the ladies' room to call Kiki. She rubbed her forehead trying to stave off the inevitable headache.

Matthew nodded. "Anyone halfway competent at misdirection and sleight of hand could have slipped something in her drink. I've done it many times."

"Not a ringing endorsement of your character," James observed. He turned back to Bree. "You said you talked with the Tinsdale wife and daughter. Who else did you question at the bar?"

"No one. But I've been invited back to show them my recipe."

James nodded. "Good. I'll run my investigation while you're on site. That way we can both listen and watch the suspects. And I can have your back."

"Agreed." Matthew leaned forward in his chair and pulled his folder close to him. "Now, one last piece of business before we go our separate ways. I've run prints of the lab personnel and most of the bar staff through AFIS."

James groaned. "Do I even want to know how you got access to the AFIS?"

"Probably not."

"AFIS." Bree searched her memory. "That's the Automated Fingerprint Identification System, right?" Both men nodded.

"But how did you get the prints?" Bree asked.

"Business cards." Matthew flashed her a smile. "The cards had a special coating to capture and enhance fingerprints. Once I added a developing solution and fed the prints into the system, we had results."

"And?" James reached for the printouts.

"Most of the bar staff had priors. Drunk and disorderly. Public nuisance. Low-level stuff. Miranda flirted with carjacking in college, but the charges were dismissed when it turned out to be a sorority prank.

"As for the *Naturalistics* staff, Jackie Torres—and Paul Bender for that matter—have a few citations for public protests in the '60s. Ricco Torres is the only other hit I got. He had some juvenile priors and a couple of brushes with the law in his twenties, but appears to have had nothing since. Not even a traffic ticket." He grinned. "That's more than

I can say for Tonya Cooper. If that woman gets any more points on her license for speeding, she'll be taking the bus."

"So, basically nothing." James collected the printouts and tucked them under his arm. "I'll see if I can pull up anything else through legitimate channels, in case we need it to hold up in court."

"Don't forget the tox screen on Hannah," Bree added as he rose to go.

"I'll try to rush it. With luck, we'll know before we return to the bar to question Edward Tinsdale." He pecked her on the cheek then turned to the door without saying good-bye to the others.

Matthew glared at his retreating back while the air between the two men crackled with barely restrained antagonism.

Bree massaged her throbbing temples while across the table from her Nate chuckled. "If both those boys make it through this investigation without killing one another, I'll be mighty surprised," he mused. "We live in interesting times. And if I can get some data out of those new samples you gave me, they might just get a lot more interesting."

Interesting or not, thought Bree, they'd at least have another piece in what was becoming an intricate jigsaw puzzle. One she hoped she could solve before Tugood and O'Neil came to blows. Or before she gave in to her baser urges and knocked off both of them.

CHAPTER 17

W hen Kiki met up with Bree at the salon for their weekend get-together, she handed her a long mailing tube.

"What's this?"

"A project for you." Kiki smiled. "Actually, it's a challenge. Everyone at the lab decided to challenge you to bake a cupcake flavor for each symbol on the periodic table." She nodded to the tube. "We found the largest periodic table we could so you can hang it in your kitchen for inspiration."

Bree took the tube and offered a smile in return. "I think the periodic table of cupcakes is just your way of getting me to bring in more treats."

"Guilty as charged," Kiki admitted. "Is it working?"

Cupcake flavors swirled through Bree's mind. Starting with the Pina Colada flavors she'd used in her chicken strips. "It is. For C—carbon—I can use the Chocolate Cherry Cupcakes I made a while back." Back when she'd been investigating her boss's murder. "Phosphorus—P—could be Pina Colada. Magnesium—Mg—could be Margarita…"

"Sounds like you need a drink more than you need a mani/pedi." Kiki sent Bree a questioning look.

"Fortunately, the spa serves both." Bree and Kiki let themselves be swept into the interior of the spa where soft lights and quiet music lent an air of serenity to the surroundings. Soon they were ensconced in luxury.

"I can't tell you how much I need this." Bree relaxed in a chair at the salon and plopped her feet in the steamy pedicure basin. She took a sip of iced champagne and turned to Kiki. "I don't know about your week, but mine has been hell."

Kiki shrugged. "My week's been nutty, but otherwise fine. I take it your special project research hit a snag?"

Bree took another sip of champagne to delay answering. Which fictional project did Kiki think she was working on again? Oh, yes. The fake energy company. "It's just been long hours and lots of conflicting data," she hedged. "I can't seem to see any patterns that make sense."

"Do any of the others you work with see patterns?"

"They are all off on completely different tangents." That much, at least, was true. No one at *Naturalistics* knew what she was really doing there.

"Listen, Bree, it's the weekend. We haven't gotten a chance to really talk or have fun for weeks. Maybe what you need is to forget about the projects for a while and have some fun."

"Agreed. So why don't you tell me the nutty parts of your week?"

"When it comes to nutty, we work with a mixed bag. One advantage to you being off at a special projects lab is that you don't have to listen to Troy whine and moan. He acts so much like my teen son that it's all I can do not to smack him."

Bree pulled her foot from the tub and the pedicurist scraped the rough, dry skin from her heels. She wiggled whenever he accidentally tickled her, which was often. "Troy's not handling his new responsibility well?" she asked through gritted teeth.

"He's got us filling out three—THREE—different forms to keep track of our time. Plus, there's the monthly report, the quarterly report, the semi-annual report and the annual report he's demanding we write. In between, he holds project update meetings with Powerpoint slides. I ask you, how many ways does one man need to receive the same data to keep him happy?"

Bree relaxed back in her chair as her newly callus-free feet were treated to a massage. "I'm lucky I can't disclose any of my special project work."

"Maybe that's why the rest of us have to keep filling his inbox with reports. He's compensating for not being able to control you."

"I'm not the only one he can't control. What's Norah's latest antic?" The pedicurist focused on a particularly tense spot and Bree moaned in appreciation. "This is heaven."

Kiki finished her champagne and waited for a refill before answering. "Heaven about sums up Norah. She's still dressing in black and purple with skulls, but now, she's added astral projection, numerology and astrology to her list of interests. Friday, she brought in a candelabra and lit it to illuminate her spirit path. I kid you not, that is exactly what she said."

"How's that working for her?" Bree almost missed seeing Norah doing whatever it was that astral projection, numerology and astrology meant to the girl. Norah's quirks, while a source of amusement for most of her colleagues, were actually distractions that hid the girl's tender heart.

"The point isn't how it's working for her. It's that she's driving Troy crazy." Kiki paused to consider her polish options, finally settling on bright blue.

While Kiki was older than Bree by at least a decade, her spirit seemed younger, wilder, and more fun than Bree's straight-as-an-arrow approach to life. Kiki challenged Bree to relax her need for control and generally acted as a big sister and best friend rolled into one. On impulse, Bree grabbed a bottle of bright green polish and passed it to her technician before she could talk herself into going with a traditional red hue.

"Driving Troy crazy?" she prompted when she and Kiki had settled back to have color applied to their toenails.

"Right. Well, Norah did some number hocus-pocus and determined Troy's name equates to an ancient evil, like Jack the Ripper or the Emperor Caligula. Last week, she burned sage and smudged his office to combat the evil."

"Did it work?" Bree asked between giggles.

Kiki flashed an evil smile. "I'll say. After the smudging, Norah concocted what she called a healing herbal mix—I swear she used Italian seasoning and garlic salt—and left sachets of it hidden in his office. Everyone in the lab could smell him coming. I managed to avoid him for most of the week."

"I almost feel sorry for Troy."

"Well, don't. Being named department manager went to his head like cheap champagne on an empty stomach. Speaking of which, Ed and I discovered a new pub on Friday. We should go there someday. Other than a couple of hormone crazed twenty-somethings about to get naked and nasty," Kiki shook her head, "it was an enjoyable evening. Good food. Good drinks. And the couple made it to the alley before any clothes came off."

Bree's face flamed as she remembered stumbling out of the bar lip-locked with Matthew. Kissing him in the littered alcove by the dumpsters amid liquor bottles and empty totes of cleaning supplies.

Instead of looking at Kiki, she focused on selecting the color for her fingernails. Despite the bright green on her toes—which she actually liked—she selected a neutral shade. As Matthew and the Sci-Spy makeup artist constantly reminded her, the less memorable Bree Mayfield-Watson was, the more memorable her cover characters could become.

If only I could stand out for once, she thought as she watched the stylist brush blue onto Kiki's nails. She took a deep breath, then sputtered and coughed as she inhaled a lungful of acetone. The sharp, stinging scent filled her nostrils and made her eyes water. The concentration of nail polish remover at the salon was worse for her health than any solvents used in the chem labs at work.

Someone offered her a bottle of water and Bree alternately gulped water and coughed until her lungs cleared. Once she settled back into the chair, the scent lingered. Clear, sharp and undiluted by other solvent scents, the smell triggered a memory of another time she'd whiffed acetone.

It was the scent she hadn't been able to identify on Hannah's breath the morning she died.

Bree headed to the Sci-PHi offices on Monday morning, a pan of Margarita cupcakes nestled on the passenger seat of her car. Whenever she was in town, Troy required her to attend the Monday morning group meetings.

To excuse herself from her work at the *Naturalistics* labs, she'd told Paul Bender and Tonya that she had a Monday morning graduate school class.

This morning, her schedule included reporting to Troy about her fictional work for the energy company then heading home to change into her disguise for her fictional work at the suspected drug lab. All while keeping the identities and stories straight.

Mondays gave her headaches that even cupcakes couldn't cure.

This Monday the headache started the minute she woke and reviewed the events of the past week. She'd begun her cover job and located the supplies for drug production at the lab on Wednesday. Thursday—the day Hannah died—she'd been recruited by O'Neil to investigate the death while working on the drug lab mission. Friday and Saturday passed in a blur of questioning suspects, analyzing data, avoiding detection, and watching Matthew and James trade insults.

On Sunday, she'd figured out how Hannah died.

But knowing the poison didn't make finding the killer any easier. Especially when the poison was available at every chemistry lab, drug store, and grocery in the country.

As she pulled onto the corporate campus, she dialed the Plainville PD using the hands-free sync feature Matthew had installed on her car. James O'Neil came on the line after the third ring.

"Bree, it's a pleasure to talk with you." As always, the cheerful warmth in his voice caused her pulse to flutter. Too bad they had business to discuss.

"James, I only have a minute. Literally. Have the ME test Hannah for alcohol poisoning, okay?" She steered into a parking spot.

"So, you agree she could have died from an overdose of alcohol rather than poison? She was pretty drunk according to everyone I questioned."

"Yes, she was drunk, but that doesn't mean she wasn't poisoned." Bree switched the call from her car speakers to her Bluetooth headset, grabbed the cupcakes, and walked toward the building. "Be sure they look for markers for methanol—that's wood alcohol—and isopropanol. I remember smelling acetone on her breath, so I think she could have been given something other than drinking alcohol. It's one of the chemical by-products of alcohol breakdown."

"Got it. Wood alcohol and what was the name of the other?"

"Isopropanol." She spelled it. "The toxicologist will know what to look for. I'll talk to you later."

She yanked the headset out and cut the call off as a group of researchers caught up with her near the door. Time to focus on keeping her Monday morning cover. She chatted and answered questions about her work at the fictional energy company as they headed down the hall.

After stashing her briefcase at her desk, and the cupcakes in the kitchen, Bree stopped by Norah's office. The first thing she noticed was that Troy's door was shut. A peek inside his window slits showed him staring at his computer while wearing earmuff style hearing protection.

Odd.

In the administrative assistant's office across from Troy, Norah sat cross-legged in her office chair. Flickering votive candles, in a rainbow of colors, scented the small space.

The new office arrangements now allowed Norah a cubicle to herself. Today the shelves were lined with bowls of crystals; jars of dried flowers and herbs; incense; extra candles—enough to light the entire building in case of a blackout—and a large oval mirror arranged above the computer monitor.

If Norah's eyes had been open and looking into the mirror, she could have seen Bree approach. Instead Bree stepped close enough to hear Norah humming—or chanting, she wasn't sure which—before the girl's eyes snapped open.

"Bree!" Norah hopped up and gave her a hug then turned to extinguish her candles. "It's good to have you back. When are you going to tell your boss that you should be running this department instead of him?"

Norah pointed a long, black tinted fingernail toward Troy's office. With her other hand, she swooped up a jumbo packet of bubble gum then headed to the conference room, chattering gaily. The scents of rose, bergamot, and patchouli which clung to her short black tunic were overpowered by grape bubble gum once Norah shoved a handful into her mouth.

As usual, Norah's exuberance and warmth provided a sharp contrast to her attire. If she expected people to be put off by her purple leggings, skull emblazoned tunic, and black lipstick, she'd have to work on appearing threatening. Or at least aloof.

Today, she was too interested in telling Bree how Troy had banned her from burning sage and tapers at her desk. "It's only a matter of time till the votives have to go, too," she added. A wicked smile curved along her lips, making the piercing on her upper lip glint in the light. "But as soon as he does, plan C goes into action."

"Why are you burning candles?" Bree asked. She took her seat at the conference table next to Milt Shoemaker while Norah positioned herself near the head of the long table.

"Isn't it obvious?" Milt asked, his eyes on Norah but his attention on Bree. He tilted his head and waited.

From the hallway, a series of sneezes, each louder than the other drifted toward them.

"Troy's allergic to the scents?"

She didn't need to hear Milt confirm her hypothesis. Troy yanked the conference room door open with a snarl. "Damn it, Norah. What did I tell you about lighting candles?" His eyes were rimmed in red and his nose looked raw.

"They can't fall over like the tapers. They're in glass holders." Norah's voice dripped honey and innocence. She blew a bubble and Troy flinched.

"No candles. Of any kind. If it burns, it can't be in your office. Got it?" He sniffled and fished in his pocket for a Kleenex. "Your candles are a fire hazard. And they give me a headache."

"What about paper? It burns. Should I remove my files?"

Bree tuned them out as Norah continued to bait Troy. The lingering scent from Norah's office clogged Bree's sinuses, too, but oddly her headache receded as she watched Troy's discomfort. Poor man. If only he'd be nice to Norah, she'd do anything in the world for him.

Her sympathy for Troy dried up as soon as he turned to her. "Bree, I've implemented a new recordkeeping policy." He outlined a plethora of reports and timecards each with iron clad due dates. "Since the Director of Special Projects won't keep me in the loop regarding your activities, you'll have to do it."

The sarcasm in his tone indicated that he'd tried—and had no luck—talking to Matthew. Bree jotted a note to herself. She'd need to consult with Tugood about ways to pacify Troy before his actions either threatened her mission or ate up more of her time maintaining cover stories.

The hour crawled along at a slug's pace. The slug in question being Troy. Clearly, putting him in charge of the department and keeping him out of trouble were two different things.

Bree scratched out another note to Tugood. Her fingers itched to page through her crime notebook and her mind raced, first proposing, then knocking down scenarios that involved someone slipping toxic alcohol into Hannah's drink.

Too bad Horace Clark couldn't train Rookie to sniff out bad alcohol. The image of Rookie sniffing bar drinks made her smile.

"When you were project leader, you didn't think safety was funny, Bree." Troy's complaint snapped her out of her daydream. Across the table, she saw Kiki smother a grin and remembered her friend had compared Troy's grumbling to a teen's whine. The comparison was spot on.

"Sorry, Troy, what were you saying?" Soon Bree added multiple safety inspection chores to her list of Troy-decreed nonsense. Tugood owed her for this. Big time.

All she had to do was figure out a way to make him pay.

CHAPTER 18

Monday night, Bree passed the nearly empty lot of *All Mixed Up* and drove around the block for the third time, her mind focused on Hannah's private $500 bottle of tequila.

Originally, she'd agreed to meet Edward Tinsdale and his family tonight so she could help them create a version of her Piña Colada Chicken to put on the menu.

Then James insisted on coming along to question the owners and staff regarding Hannah's death while she was there. He'd also admitted to wanting to watch her back.

Next, Matthew had demanded she don the hated earpiece and spy-cam necklace so he could be in the loop as she interacted with suspects. He adamantly told her that James was not to know about the spyware.

To top things off, James had just dropped another bombshell on her when he'd asked her to join him for a cup of coffee before going to the bar.

Bree had expected a strategy meeting. James had given her a complication—in the form of a flash drive discovered hidden among Hannah's belongings. The drive, as far as PD techs could tell, contained blackmail letters from Hannah to a list of undisclosed clients. One or two veiled threats to Hannah had also been located in the cursory review of the drive's contents.

Bree could feel the copy James had given her as clearly as if it were literally burning a hole in her pocket rather than resting peacefully beside her loose change.

Which led to the tequila. While the bottle was expensive, was it enough to constitute a bribe or a blackmail payoff? Or did Edward supply it to Hannah because she was his lover? Perhaps, it was simply a gesture of friendship. What exactly was the going rate for friendship in Hannah's set?

As she approached the bar again, she gave up her futile ruminations and pulled into the parking lot. Since the bar was closed on Monday nights the only cars in the lot belonged to the owners and a few staff members.

Bree reluctantly set up her communications with Matthew and did a series of routine sound and video checks.

"I was starting to worry," he said via the hidden earpiece. "You should have been in place half an hour ago."

"I was delayed." She hesitated, but decided to fill him in on Hannah's blackmail attempts.

A low whistle sounded in her ear. "That changes things. The list of suspects could easily double—or triple. Whatever you do, don't blind me tonight." It wasn't an order. It was a plea.

"Okay," she agreed. "I'll wear the necklace and earpiece at all times."

She exited the car and headed to the dimly lit entrance. Edward answered almost as soon as she had knocked and swept her into the warm, bright interior.

"Welcome, Cat. We're glad you could make it."

"Hi, Mr. Tinsdale."

"Oh, please," he waved her comment aside, "call me Edward. You're part of the *All Mixed Up* family now. I'm just sorry we got to know each other during such a difficult time."

Across the room, Bree saw Miranda's lips tighten. Because of the reference to Bree as part of the family? Or because of the veiled reference to Hannah?

Mrs. Tinsdale—Liz—hurried over. "I can't imagine how frightening the past days must have been for you. Miranda told me you found that woman. Dead." Liz wrapped her in a motherly hug and patted her back. "You have amazing presence of mind to deal so well with a crisis. I would have fallen apart."

Bree tried to channel the part of herself that still felt young, and uncertain. The part that should have been horrified at finding a dead woman sprawled across her desk. She was surprised to find it wasn't as easy as it would have been before she joined Matthew's spy team.

She forced herself to shrug her shoulders and stare at her toes, relying on the pose to do what her imagination would not. "It was awful," she muttered. "The paramedics, the police, the people asking questions and pointing fingers." She shuddered. "I didn't even know she was sick."

"Sick?" Liz asked. "Is that what they're saying?"

Bree turned to Liz, careful to stay in character. "I mean, she had to be, didn't she? If she died? It's not like anyone killed her or anything."

Horror washed down the older woman's face, turning her skin gray as it sagged into lines belonging to a much older person. "I should hope not." But the glance she snuck at her daughter made Bree's skin prickle.

"I'm sure they'll discover it was a heart attack or some unknown disease." Edward's briskness didn't shake the pall that had fallen over the group. "Hannah was a troubled young woman, prone to bouts of depression. There may have been a physical cause underlying both her troubles and her health."

"She caused a lot of her own troubles." Miranda took a step closer and turned hard, glittering eyes on her dad. "She specialized in making people feel inferior. I don't know how you ever let yourself get mixed up with the likes of her. Not as a friend. And especially not as a lover."

Miranda turned on her heel and strode to the kitchen. Her mother followed, her formerly sagging features now set in a marble mask of fury.

"You're doing great, Bree." Tugood's voice held approval. "See if you can keep the women talking."

A knock at the front door indicated James was in place. Edward excused himself to answer the door and Bree headed to the kitchen.

Inside, Miranda and Liz shouted at one another with raised voices.

"I won't stand for you talking to your father that way, young lady."

"Come on, Mom. Face the truth. Don't ruin the rest of your life for a man. Not even for my father." She clasped her mother's shoulders. "I know about the work conferences. The marriage counselor. The bouts of tears. The fits of anger. You think I didn't see or hear, but you're wrong. I know he was having an affair with her."

"Miranda, honey," Liz's voice softened and moved further into the kitchen, "you don't know as much as you think."

Bree edged into the kitchen, keeping far enough away from the pair to avoid drawing attention to herself. She pretended to study her recipe notes, making sure the necklace camera was trained on the women. Out of the corner of her eye, she saw Liz lean against the counter, defeated.

"I told your father it was a mistake to keep quiet." Liz dabbed at her eyes with a tissue. "But he insisted we try. He wanted you to finish school and have some fun. We did it for you."

Miranda shook her head. "For me? Are you telling me you let Dad sleep with that harpy? What about the ones before her? How many women does he have to fuck before you wake up? Maybe if you stood up to him, he wouldn't treat you this way."

"Miranda, stop." Liz's voice crackled with hidden fury. "You're talking about things that aren't your business. The issues between your father and I are exactly that. Our issues."

"But Mom, Dad and Hannah—"

"It isn't about Hannah. It never was. Your dad wasn't a saint, by any means. Neither was I, for that matter. And yes, he had a wandering eye when he was younger. But not this time. I swear to you."

"Mom?" The anger drained from Miranda's voice, leaving a quaver in its wake.

"Your dad," Liz gulped in a breath, "wasn't at work conferences during those weeks we told you he was traveling. He was at a treatment center. Fighting late stage prostate cancer."

"Oh, my God." Miranda froze for a heartbeat before throwing herself into her mother's arms.

Bree gave up trying to hide and simply watched the tableau unfold. The pair wouldn't have noticed an elephant storming through their kitchen at this point.

"He's fine, honey." Liz repeated the words over and over as Miranda dissolved into sobs. "He beat it. I'm sorry I didn't tell you. But you were in your last year of school and we didn't want to burden you with this. We didn't want you to worry."

"But if he ... If he'd..."

"He didn't. That's the point." Liz grasped Miranda by the shoulders and eased her back to look into her tear stained face. "Right or wrong, we kept the secret because we love you."

"Did she know?" Miranda asked in a small voice.

"She was your dad's protégé at work. He spent his time making sure she could take his place once he retired. She was the HR rep that handled his disability, his time off, and brokered his early retirement package. She knew."

Bree tiptoed away, leaving the pair in private while she digested the new information.

As Bree exited the kitchen, Jen appeared from the bar area.

"Cat, you look pale. Is anything wrong?"

"It's just—" Bree gestured helplessly. "Miranda and her mother."

"In another argument? It happens. I'm sure your mother and you have disagreed on a few things. Like boyfriends."

Bree nodded, distracted by wondering what her mother would think of Matthew and James.

"Hey," Jen said, bringing Bree's attention back to her current situation, "how about me showing you a few drink mixing tips while those two sort things out?"

They headed to the bar where Jen showed Bree how to use dry ice and liquid nitrogen to "super cool" barware to make an extra dry martini. Next she showed her how to use the ingredients to make frozen drinks.

"Most people remember water freezes at thirty-two degrees Fahrenheit. As a chemist, you probably know pure ethanol—drinking alcohol—freezes around negative one hundred seventy-three degrees."

"I also know drinking alcohol is a mixture of ethanol and water. You can't get alcohol more than about ninety-six percent pure without adding toxic solvents."

"You're a smart one," Jen said. "Most mixologists have to work to learn the science. You'd be everyone's favorite study-buddy since you know things like chemical azeotropes. Here." She handed Bree a thermometer and directed her to test the temperatures of a series of mixed and frozen drinks.

"You probably also know that the percent alcohol times two is called 'proof.' So, 100 proof alcohol is 50 percent drinking alcohol and 50 percent water."

Bree was mildly surprised at Jen's use of a technical chemical term like azeotrope. The woman would have made a good scientist. To hide her surprise, Bree focused on the mixed drinks in front of her, and was soon fascinated by the temperature variations in the frozen drinks.

Jen leaned on the bar and watched Bree. "The percent alcohol in a drink determines at what point it freezes. I don't have to tell you the science behind it, but you might be interested in some trivia."

"Sure. Fire away. I love chemical trivia."

As Jen talked about the early origins of distilling, she absently fingered her charm bracelet, a distant look in her eyes. Eventually she grew tired of the history lesson and brightened as she talked about the science of drink mixing.

Matthew yawned loudly in her ear. "Wake me when chemistry class is over." He gave a fake snore. Bree ignored him.

"The higher the alcohol content—the greater the proof—the colder a drink will be when served as a frozen variety. Twenty-four proof liquor freezes at twenty degrees, just a little colder than for water.

"But eighty-four proof liquor freezes at minus thirty degrees. So, if you put beer in the freezer, it will likely freeze and explode. On the other hand, you can store vodka and other aperitif alcohols in the freezer without problems."

"Cool." Bree grinned. "Literally. Thanks for the lesson."

"No problem." Jen turned her attention to cleaning the bar area while Bree helped.

Bree took the opportunity to learn a bit more about the bartender, relaxing and enjoying the conversation after her stressful time with Miranda and Liz Tinsdale.

"My mom used to have a charm bracelet like yours," she said. "She collected charms from her vacations with Dad—before I was born. Did yours belong to your mom?"

Jen shook her head. "Some of the charms were Mom's. The bracelet itself was a gift from my big sister."

"I don't have any sisters—unless you count sorority sisters. All they gave me was a hard time," Bree quipped. "They teased me for being a brain instead of a beauty."

"Teased? Past tense? What changed?"

Oops, Bree scrambled to cover her slip. "Nothing except a really tough prof for some of my sisters. Once I started tutoring them, my popularity soared. Even with the trend-setter girls."

"Smart of you to share your skills. Smarter still of them to take advantage of you." Jen wrung out a dishcloth and nodded to the kitchen. "It looks like Miranda and Liz are looking for you."

"Thanks for the bartending lesson." Bree left Jen and headed to the kitchen to continue her cooking lessons with the subdued mother-daughter team.

CHAPTER 19

As Bree showed Miranda and Liz how to make her crunchy Piña Colada coating, James stepped into the kitchen and offered the trio a professional smile.

"Sorry to interrupt, ladies, but I just have a few questions about Hannah Rogers' death. It's routine, nothing to worry about. But since she was here the night before she died I need to establish if there was anything odd or out of place about her behavior."

The Tinsdale women relaxed under his skillful patter and warm smile. Soon he led Liz aside. Bree turned to her dipping sauce and instructed Miranda on how to prepare it all the while itching to listen in on James's questioning.

When he interrupted them again and took Miranda aside for a few questions, Bree distracted Liz. She tried to open a conversation regarding Hannah, but the older woman stubbornly redirected the conversation back to the recipe.

"I've relived that night more than enough times." Liz gave Bree a warm smile. "I'm sure you feel the same. I can't imagine how many times you've had to deal with the police since you found the body."

"Lots," Bree muttered as she focused preparing a batch of chicken strips from scratch with Liz. Another hour passed before Liz, Miranda, and Bree finished the lessons.

Bree took a plate of food and a drink to a quiet booth while the Tinsdale women retreated to the back office.

As she sat collecting her thoughts, Bree heard Detective O'Neil's voice. She started to rise then realized he was talking to Edward Tinsdale. Bree huddled in the corner of her booth, hoping to remain unseen.

James and Edward, already deep in conversation, sat in the booth directly behind her. Their muffled voices were clear enough to her, but was her hidden mic picking them up?

"...she had a difficult childhood, from what I understand. Parents died young. She didn't talk about it much. Spent most of her time focused on the job. She was a bit of a loner."

Edward's voice trailed off and Bree held her breath, waiting for someone to break the silence. Finally, James spoke. "I understand Hannah was a regular at the bar."

The seat behind her back thumped, as if Edward had leaned back heavily. "Yes. Hannah was one of my first customers. She helped me get started. Not directly, you understand, but she knew I was fascinated with the science of beer and wine.

"I'd wanted to open a place like this for as long as I could remember. Hannah structured my early retirement package so I'd have the cash to buy the place."

"And in return you..."

"I did what I could to help her out. She'd taken a risk, convincing the company to give me both an early retirement and a severance package. I don't know how she did it. What I did know was that she'd committed to helping the *Elemental Fractions, Inc.* grow by acquisition.

"I kept my eye out for potential investment opportunities. When *Naturalistics* made its way onto my radar screen, I knew a merger between the companies was an ideal match. So, I introduced Hannah to the owners."

"Was Hannah bribing you?" The blunt question—more Tugood's style than O'Neil's—shocked Bree.

"No." Bree felt Edward shift as if starting to leave the table. She shrank deep into the corner of her booth as his shoe and sock came into view.

"But you knew about her habit of blackmailing others."

"I knew she liked to gather and hoard information. I always assumed it was because of something that happened in her childhood. Like I said, she was a troubled young woman. Underneath her hard shell, she was as frightened and vulnerable a person as you'll ever meet. I thought she could use a friend."

Edward shifted more and Bree saw him leave his seat and stand.

"What about the private bottle of tequila?"

"She claimed cheap tequila made her ill. The bar was doing well. The least I could do for a friend was to give her decent drinks." Edward took a couple of steps away from the table, his slumped shoulders curved under an invisible burden. He turned back to James. "I'm sure you'll want to check the bottle for prints and examine it. Follow me."

"Could I have a few minutes of your time, Miss Holmes?" James stood before her, notebook in hand offering a polite smile.

"Of course." Around them, the bar took on an eerie silence as Liz closed down the kitchen. One by one, the employees left until only the family, Bree, and James remained.

James turned to Mr. Tinsdale. "No need to keep the place open for me," he said. "I just want to clarify a few issues with Miss Holmes before I leave for the night. We can chat outside."

Bree took the hint and gathered her purse. She smiled up at James, hoping to give the impression of a girl with a crush. "I'll feel very safe if the detective walks me to my car," she gushed.

"Well, then, it's settled." Edward Tinsdale patted her on the shoulder. "Cat, you're welcome back anytime—as long as you bring a new recipe to try. And don't worry. The bar doesn't usually have this much excitement. Take care of her, Detective."

Bree let out a sigh of relief once she and James exited the bar. They rounded the corner to where he'd parked out of the line of sight of the windows and doors. She leaned against his car in the darkened, nearly empty parking lot.

The warm evening wrapped them both in a companionable silence. James slipped his arm around Bree's shoulders and she leaned into the embrace, drained from her evening undercover.

"It looks like you were able to get close to Liz and Miranda Tinsdale tonight. Did you learn anything?"

Bree filled him in on the conversations she'd had that evening and the two of them compared notes. "Should we leave and go somewhere else?" She cast a nervous glance at the bar. Tonight, it looked lonely and isolated, situated as it was on the edge of town, away from most of the noise and bustle of the main shopping areas.

"I've got my eye on the lights," James said, not moving. "If they go out, I'll walk you to your car before anyone leaves the building."

When she focused on the bar again, James turned her so she was facing him, her back to the bar. "Trust me," he whispered.

One calloused hand cradled her face. The look he gave her was softer, more intense than the teasing glances he'd shared with her before. Despite the dimness—or perhaps because of it, Bree saw his pupils widen, obliterating the normal green of his eyes.

"You did a good job in there." James drew his thumb along the line of her cheekbone and cupped her cheek with his hand. He wound his free arm around her waist, tugging until the inches between them disappeared.

Bree relaxed into his embrace, drawing on his solid strength as exhaustion suffused her limbs. His warmth surrounded her, protective, secure, comforting. She never worried about James lying to her or, worse yet, breaking her heart. No, he was exactly what he appeared to be. Strong, easy-going, predictable, caring. But tonight, something else wove itself through the comfortable, familiar warmth.

Bree's heart thumped erratically, sending tendrils of awareness surging through her veins with each beat as he leaned in, his lips claiming hers in an unexpected move.

The kiss started slowly. Sweet, with a restrained, aching tenderness. James nibbled along her lower lip while drawing slow circles on her back with his palm.

Plastered as she was against his body, she felt his every reaction. Each shift. Every unsteady breath.

He moved both hands to her head, cradling it as he pulled ever so slightly away from her lips. Just far enough to form words.

"Bree," the sound tingled on her sensitized lips like a butterfly kiss. "You have to know how I feel. That I want more. Whatever you can give."

A guttural noise reverberated in her head, breaking the sensual spell. Bree flinched. "My surveillance would be a lot more effective if your camera wasn't plastered against Romeo's shirt."

Tugood's voice doused Bree in ice water. How could she have forgotten that her camera necklace and hidden earpiece let Matthew hear every word, see everything, that she did?

Bree tensed and James loosened his grip. "It's all right," he whispered. Disappointment chased across his features. "We can take our time. Go as slow as you want. I'm a patient man."

She skimmed her fingers across his cheek, trying to tell him with her touch the things she refused to say while Matthew listened via the earpiece. She smiled, knowing only James could see her face. "It's complicated."

"It doesn't have to be."

Tugood snorted. "Don't believe him, Watson. That pick-up line is older than conflict in the Middle East. But, hey, you two kids have fun. I'm signing off for the night." A click sounded in Bree's ear.

Bree rose on her tiptoes and kissed James again, but the moment was lost. Tugood's interruption lingered in her mind, acrid, like the scent of burned rubber. Overpowering everything.

She dropped back to her feet and offered James another smile. "Let's take things one step at a time."

"Sure." His voice was thick with disappointment, his nod a bit too sharp. "I'll walk you to your car."

Bree's heartbeat had almost returned to normal when she slid behind the steering wheel of her car. She'd almost pushed the romantic encounter—and its abrupt end—into a quiet corner of her mind.

Until James wedged himself between her door and the car frame. He leaned in, blocking the last of the light from the bar and filling the car with the clean, light scent of his aftershave.

"I meant what I said." His breath wafted across her skin warming her lips and making them prickle with awareness. "I know what I want, and I'm patient enough to work and wait for it. So, unless you tell me to get lost, you'd better get used to having me around." Before she could respond, he closed the door gently and disappeared.

For a woman who didn't have a prom date in high school, the attention Matthew and James gave Bree left her mind and emotions swirling. The uncharted emotional territory loomed ahead, taunting her with questions.

Too bad deductive reasoning couldn't help her find the elusive answers. When it came down to it, dealing with facts—chemistry, drugs, murder, and crime—were easier than unraveling matters of the heart, any day.

CHAPTER 20

On Tuesday, after spending the day collecting samples for Emily—and sneaking a few for herself, Bree dropped by the *Barkery* to get Rookie's analysis of her samples before heading to the Sci-Spy mobile crime lab.

In preparation, she'd placed the lab samples in a series of paper bags which she lined up amid dog toys and other items in the store's main retail area. She'd told Horace and Wendy that some of the bags contained cinnamon and some didn't. They'd been delighted to let her blind test Rookie.

When the dog came into the room, Rookie stopped at half of the bags, giving his alert signal while Bree made notes of his behavior. She hid her grin when he walked past a bag she'd doped with cinnamon, just for fun. No, the Clarks didn't have Rookie trained to alert for spices. At least not yet.

When Rookie raced past a series of bags and came to her, tail wagging, Bree's laughter turned to puzzlement. She patted the dog while he soaked up the attention then collected her bags.

He'd alerted her to all the samples she'd collected from the columns she'd run for Emily. And none of the ones Jackie had run.

After a brief chat with the Clarks, Bree left the shop and headed to the nature preserve where the RV/mobile crime lab sat parked. Tugood and Nate greeted her at the door.

A pot of chili simmered on the stove, and Bree helped herself to a bowl before passing her samples off to Nate for analysis.

"What's the most recent result?" she asked.

"Well," he dragged the word out and eyed her until she put down her spoon. "Can you get me a sample of that media the girl's using?"

"I can try. Why?"

"I suspect it's some kind of chiral separation media."

"It is. She already told me."

"You might-could have told me that to begin with," Nate grumbled. "It would have saved me scratching my head over enantiomeric resolution for the past days."

Matthew cleared his throat and plopped into a chair. "Hello? Non-scientist here. Can we get that translated into English?"

Bree launched into an explanation of right and left handed molecules but Nate cut her short.

"Not important for him to know. Bottom line is these samples you gave me look a lot like drugs, but their spectroscopic signature is different."

"English," Matthew repeated.

Nate sighed. "Complicated molecules—like drugs—can exist in two forms. Basically, the chemical structure of one form is the mirror image of the other. They look similar, but not identical. The body reacts only to very specific forms. In the case of psychotropic drugs, only one of the two forms will get a person high. The other will pass harmlessly through the body. With me so far?"

Matthew nodded. "One form is active, the other inactive."

"That's it. The samples Bree gave me fall into a class of psychotropic drugs," he rattled off a list of several illegal

149

substances. "But each and every one of the drug samples Bree gave me is the inactive form."

"Didn't the dog confirm the identity?" Matthew wrinkled his brow as he addressed the question to the room.

"Sure." Nate pulled off his glasses and polished them with the hem of his lab coat. "But the sense of smell—human or canine—is less specific than the lock and key mechanism the body uses to metabolize drugs. The dogs smell both the inactive and the active forms as if it were the same."

"Why would someone want inactive drugs?" Bree asked. "Or are they using the purification method to make super-pure drugs?"

"The material they use to separate the drug mixtures isn't cheap," Nate replied. "In short, it makes no sense why someone would want to go to all that trouble to purify a simple street drug."

"It's about to make even less sense." Bree retrieved her newest set of samples and explained how the drug dog had only alerted to some of the alleged drugs, not all of them.

Nate's eyes lit up. "Ain't nothing I like better than a puzzle. Let's see what I can learn about these. Now that I got the equipment set up we could maybe get a sample run before you leave tonight."

He headed to the back of the RV where the equipment lab churned out samples.

A wave of exhaustion swept over Bree, leaving her feeling hollow, sucked clean like the empty straw in a Big Gulp after all the soda was gone.

She rummaged through her purse, pulled out her wallet and checked the driver's license to see who she was supposed to be today. Cat Holmes stared back at her. Like the mirror-image molecules, Cat both was—and wasn't—Bree. And tonight, Bree honestly didn't know who she'd see looking back at her if she checked a mirror. Herself? Her latest cover identity? Someone else entirely?

She dropped the wallet in her purse and stared at the food, no longer hungry.

Beside her, Matthew shifted in his chair. The hum of Nate working with his equipment in the back room sounded faint as if she and Matthew were alone. The air between them heated. Bree's stomach fluttered, killing what was left of her appetite. She pushed her bowl away and studied her cuticles as if her fresh manicure held answers to the dozens of questions crowding her mind.

Matthew rested his hand atop hers, breaking her concentration. "It isn't what you thought it would be, is it? The job," he clarified. "It gets to every operative sooner or later. Looks like sooner, in your case."

"I don't know what you mean."

Matthew didn't press. Instead, he curled his fingers around hers and drew her hand close. "Okay. Let me ask this. Now that we've confirmed the lab is making drugs, who is involved?"

She mentally checked off the names. "Emily definitely did the synthesis. Tonya and Ricco are helping with the analysis. Unless they're stupid—and they're not—they knew what she'd manufactured." She thought of the others and shook her head. "I can't say if Paul or Jackie know."

"Hmm. Now what about Hannah? Who had motive and opportunity to kill her?"

Again, Bree's lab mates flashed through her mind. "Tonya was jealous of the way she flirted with Ricco, but didn't give her anything poisoned the morning of her death.

"Emily hoped her death would slow down the acquisition. We don't know if the capsules she gave Hannah were tainted. Jackie might have tried to get rid of her because she thought Hannah was out to cheat Paul and hurt Ricco, but the food she gave her wasn't tampered with."

Bree paused from her dry monotone recitation and sipped some water. "Miranda thought Hannah was sleeping with her father. She had access to Hannah's drinks. For that matter, if Hannah was blackmailing people, anyone at the bar—but especially Edward and Liz Tinsdale—might have wanted to get rid of her. Although Edward seemed to like her."

She shrugged and raised her eyes to meet Matthew's gaze. "I honestly don't know. Maybe tomorrow everything will seem clear. I just need sleep." She started to rise, but he tugged her back down.

"Who do you want to be guilty?"

Bree stared at him, not comprehending.

"Who, Bree? If you had to pick one to be the killer, who would it be?"

"No—none of them," she stammered, remembering how each, in turn, had been kind to her. "I don't want it to be any of them. I want to discover she died of appendicitis, or heart failure, or something."

"And the drugs?"

"I want to believe they're doing legitimate research, not trying to kill kids with highly purified street drugs. But it's not true, is it? They are making drugs that kill children. And one of them might have killed Hannah because of it."

Matthew shifted until he sat beside her, hip to hip. He wrapped an arm around her and pulled her head to rest in the hollow between his shoulder and his throat.

She didn't fight him, just went willingly, absorbing his warmth and breathing in the scent of just-washed skin. His heart thumped beneath her palm as she curled closer.

"Every kid who ever picked up a superhero comic book or watched a TV spy talk his way out of a tight fix wants to join the CIA or FBI or maybe be the kid who brings down both." His voice washed over her, soothing, steady, and something to fix her weary mind on.

"The real job isn't about gadgets and high-speed chases. It's getting to know people, battering down their defenses until they trust you. Then, when they slip up, you betray them. It rots your soul."

"But the drugs," she picked at his shirt button, flicking it with her polished fingernail, focusing on the tiny click it made with each movement. "Drugs are bad. Murder is bad. It should be black and white."

"No." He pulled her closer and swept one hand down her back. "It isn't black and white. Good spies tell themselves it is; they buy into the idea of right and wrong. But it's a lie, and deep down we all know it. Every criminal, no matter how bad, justifies his actions. Just like we do."

He fell silent, and Bree let her hands slide down to rest near his knee. She pushed herself to a fully seated position and swallowed. "How do you live with it?"

"Sometimes you—" He broke off and stood, robbing her of his body warmth. "Focus on the greater good. Whatever it is. Even in a world filled with shades of gray, some are blacker than others. Betraying a friend is a lighter shade of gray than blackmailing an innocent. Or killing someone."

Bree grabbed her purse. "For the record, you give a crappy pep-talk," she said.

"Hey, at least it was worth what you paid for it." He offered her a weak smile. "You can leave any time. I promise."

In answer, she turned to the door.

Before she reached it, Nate rushed in from the back room, bristling with excitement. "You are not going to believe what I just discovered."

❧ ❧ ❧

"Face it, Emily, my printer is going to make your thesis work obsolete." Ricco's voice drifted from the office as Bree approached.

Bree cursed her luck. For days, she'd been trying to get a private look at Emily's notes to confirm the hypothesis she and Nate had constructed after his analyses of the recent lab samples.

"Only part of it," Emily replied. "Besides, without my work, your greatest discovery might never have happened." The banter continued in a friendly vein. "By the way, remember when you told me I'd never succeed at separating the isomers? Looks like you owe me lunch, since my data proved you wrong."

Ricco muttered something under his breath then addressed Emily in a tone that clearly carried into the hall. "I told you the process wouldn't be economically viable. No one is going to pay top price for your purified samples when a lower grade works just as well at a fraction of the price."

"They should," Emily replied sulkily. "It's safer and more responsible."

Bree walked past the office, trying not to be noticed.

"Listen, if it makes you feel any better, your work did contribute to the new manufacturing process."

"The one that costs way more than the current process? Now who's not economically viable?"

"Not true." The voices sounded louder as Ricco and Emily approached. "The initial set up is expensive, but the ongoing costs will drop dramatically. Besides, we're proposing it for high-end pharmaceuticals, not the junk you work with."

Did Ricco mean traditional pharmaceuticals—like medicine—or was he referring to illegal designer drugs?

Bree listened as they entered the kitchen, but the minute they saw her, the conversational thread dropped.

"Hi, Cat," said Emily. "Ricco and I were about to go to lunch—his treat. Want to come?"

"Actually, Emily owes me lunch, but since I'm a gracious winner, not a struggling graduate student, I'll buy."

"Gee," Bree gushed, "thanks, but I still have a ton of work to do today. I promised Matt I'd get home on time so we could go out for pizza."

They accepted her spur-of-the-moment excuse and went in search of the rest of the group. As soon as Bree watched the cars pull from the lot, she headed to Emily's office.

Using the surveillance tricks Matthew had taught her, she accessed Emily's thesis files and copied them onto a flash drive, then erased the electronic evidence of her activities.

Next she installed the spyware program—the same one Matthew had used on her when they'd first met and he suspected her of murdering her boss. The program turned the computer into a remote camera and listening device accessible to the Sci-Spy team.

The software, which had been updated since Matthew used it on her, now allowed the computer to be turned on remotely. The stealth mode feature assured the computer owner would not be aware of its recording and monitoring activities.

Unless the user was another spy.

Bree made her way through the offices, repeating the procedure on each computer. Too bad she couldn't access Paul Bender's files the same way. Unfortunately, his office was either locked or guarded by his admin, Alice, at all times. Bree gathered the security measures had been put into place around the time Hannah appeared.

No matter. She'd get what she needed from the rest of the team's data.

She holed up in her office and uploaded the data to her secure tablet. Disguised to look like a typical mass-market device, the ultra-portable, mini-computer contained scores of special features.

Tugood insisted the spy business wasn't about gadgets, but he seemed to have an endless supply of them. She'd have to find out where he got his hands on such great toys.

A quick scan of Emily's thesis draft confirmed Bree's suspicions. Emily had created a series of methamphetamine-related drugs as well as other common products. According to the thesis, the point was to discover how to purify and separate active and inactive forms of chemical mixtures, including drugs. No end use was specified, although Emily had cited several government resources and included grant proposals.

Grant proposals? Bree stopped scanning the document and paced the small office. No one working on illegal narcotics would write a grant proposal. What was Emily up to? Hoping to assist against the war on drugs in some way? The write-up was frustratingly unclear—and deliberately evasive.

Normally, Bree would appreciate the detail to science that Emily included. But today, all she could do was wonder if Emily had deliberately created illegal drugs for distribution, or inadvertently—and foolishly—created them for benign research. Surely any number of other chemical mixtures could have supported her hypotheses.

Drugs, both legal and illegal, often worked with a lock and key mechanism as Bree and Nate had explained to Matthew earlier. But so did biological enzymes and a host of other specialized molecules. So why did Emily focus so much work on drugs?

Something niggled in the back of Bree's brain and rattled around aimlessly. Her stomach growled and the beginnings of a headache—likely from skipping lunch—pounded behind her eyes.

Bree headed to the kitchen and grabbed her lunch, then rooted around in her purse for aspirin. She pushed aside the brown paper bag containing the vial of cinnamon she'd used to test Rookie's nose. Then the something that was banging around in her head crystallized into a series questions.

How did one train a drug-sniffing dog?

And what, if anything, did the process have to do with Emily's research?

CHAPTER 21

"If you want to know about dogs," Bree mumbled to herself "go to the *Barkery*." She pushed the door open, but the sound of its chimes was lost in the din.

She dodged past a couple too wrapped up in one another to watch where they were going, and headed toward the counter. At least a dozen people crammed around the display cases.

A harried clerk pushed her hair out of her eyes and scanned the crowd. "Can I help the next customer?"

"I want a dozen Pupcakes, two dozen Pig-Newtons, and a large scoop of People Crackers." The customer worked her way through the crowd to the register. "Don't these Pupcakes look good enough to eat?" She pointed at a luscious, creamy frosted treat with dog-bone sprinkles on top.

"They do." Bree said when no one else answered. She imagined biting into a pupcake hoping for chocolate and discovering liver. Ugh. For one evil moment, she also imagined presenting one to Matthew the next time he dragged her on a training mission.

Like the "fake out" where he'd forced her to spend hours observing the local UPS store while he lectured her on surveillance techniques, dead drops, the importance of Morse Code in the modern world and a host of other topics.

The first ten minutes had been fun. The next ten hours—not so much.

"Next customer, please."

Bree edged away from the crowded display case, to a basket of dog toys. She picked up a stuffed toy soldier dressed in camouflage, then stared at it, imagining Matthew's face during their training exercises.

He'd grilled her on her cover ID, needled her until she'd remembered every last detail of something she'd barely glanced at and demanded she think harder, faster, and more creatively than ever before. She resented him pushing her—yet she loved the challenge.

"No matter what you throw at me, I'm going to succeed at this, Matthew Tugood." She curled her fingers around the soldier and shook it. It responded with a high-pitched squeak. She glared at the toy "That's right. There's more to me than meets the eye. And don't you forget it!" Bree tossed the squeaky toy into the basket.

Her Sci-Spy training was hard, but with each obstacle she'd overcome, she became more sure of herself, more excited about her life and more…More what? More herself. The person she was born to be. The observations, the puzzles, the mechanics of the spy life suited her.

The relationships baffled and hurt her.

On her undercover missions, she'd learned to trust Matthew with her life—literally. But even so, he didn't trust her.

A dog snuffled up to the basket and grabbed the toy soldier, giving it a good shake. The basket tipped over, spilling toy firemen, police officers, and white-coat-wearing vets onto the floor.

As the dog's owner refilled the basket, Bree's thoughts conjured James O'Neil. On one hand, he and Matthew were the same: they both wanted to take on 'bad guys' and keep the world safe for decent people. But the comparison stopped there. Matthew lived a life of secrets and lies. James simply stood for justice and decency.

Both men would take care of her if she were in danger. Hadn't they both rushed to save her when her former boss's killer held her in a choking, bone-crushing grip? Hadn't both worried about her safety only days ago at the bar?

She'd shared a few dates with James—and a couple of careful kisses. The kind that started out sweet, gradually warmed, and built toward a slow fire. Kisses her grandmother would approve of.

Not the kind that battered her defenses, then flashed with explosive speed into a bone-melting inferno. Kisses Matthew had given her while posing as her boyfriend.

Caught between the warmth of a real relationship and the scorching passion of a fake one, the choice was obvious.

Neither.

Bree refused to settle for less than passion, trust, and honesty. Not one—or even two—out of three would satisfy her.

Giggles and raised voices drew Bree's attention to the party room where Wendy Clark, outfitted in a retro, flowerchild-inspired dress, floated between three tables of ladies, each apparently planning a pet party.

Bree was ready to save her questions for another day when Horace ambled out of the back room and worked his way around the counter. Or rather, Rookie led him around the counter. The beagle sniffed politely at the customers, then sat near one woman who'd been eyeing a display of catnip. *Both the woman and her cat are into recreational drugs.* Bree shoved the thought out of her mind. It wasn't her business.

She followed Horace and Rookie outside, not sure if the man or the dog was in control of the leash. "How's Rookie's training coming?"

"The young boy's got a nose on him, that's for sure." Horace choked on his laughter. "It's a risk letting him near the customers. Either a bunch of 'em are into cooking like you or they're into something else. My guess is he's not scenting cinnamon on all of 'em. But live and let live."

"I was curious," Bree continued, huffing a bit as the pair picked up speed. "How are you going to train the dogs to sniff out date rape drugs? Don't they run the risk of getting addicted?"

Horace paused and turned to her, his eyes filled with hurt. "Doc Bree, you know better than to think I'd have anything to do with hurting dogs."

"Of course I do. That's why you rescued Rookie." Said dog tugged at the leash and they all started walking again, although slower. "But how do they train dogs to sniff drugs without running the risk of them ingesting a dangerous substance?"

"There's places that makes training aids. The idea is to get the dog to associate the smell with a favorite toy. He thinks recognizing the smell is an invitation to play." Rookie stopped to sniff a nearby tree before lifting his leg to add to the potpourri of dog scents he apparently found there.

"The training aids aren't real drugs. They just smell like it to the dogs." Horace shrugged. "You'd know more about that than I would. Being a chemist and all."

She did. More than he knew.

Bree curled on her sofa, tablet in one hand and Sherlock on her lap. After initially hissing at her when he smelled

Rookie's scent, the big orange cat had finally settled. Of course, Bree had to shower, change, and bribe him with Tiny Tuna Treats she'd picked up at the *Barkery* before he came near her, but she'd take what she could get.

Now, his contented purrs rumbled through her body and soothed her as she reread information she'd taken from the *Naturalistics* computers. Buried deep within one file, which also contained a dozen photos of Emily's dogs, Bree had found a document filled with web links to sites about drug dogs. Beside each were typed cryptic notes.

Bree stroked behind Sherlock's ears while she read. "Now, don't get angry just because I'm talking about dogs." She shifted her attentions when he stretched his chin out, asking for her to rub underneath. "It looks like Emily hoped her work would result in a new way to purify training aids for drug dogs. She seems to think the chemicals sold for training were tainted with either active drugs or contaminants."

She heaved a sigh, packed with the tensions of the past days. "Maybe no one at *Naturalistics* is actually making drugs for sale."

Sherlock ducked away from her hand and stretched before showing her the back side of his tail and jumping off the couch with a disgusted mew.

"You're right," she said to the cat. "It can't be that simple. Unless I can prove they are safely destroying the drugs, no one is off the hook." Bree followed Sherlock to the kitchen, checked his food and water supplies then fixed herself a salad.

She plopped down at the kitchen table and had just pulled up the files from Ricco's computer when someone knocked at her door.

She opened it to find Nate holding a stack of pizza boxes. Behind him Matthew stood with several kinds of beer in one hand and a pack of Diet Coke in the other. They shouldered their way into her condo without waiting for an invitation.

"Now, isn't this better than having her drive all the way out to the RV?" Nate plopped the pizza boxes onto her kitchen table.

"Sure, if you don't want to get distracted by data and surveillance updates."

"Like you aren't toting more gadgets in your gym bag than most crime labs have in the county. You forget, Tugood, this ol' country boy wasn't born yesterday."

Matthew ignored him. He sat the drinks on the counter then opened the gym bag and pulled enough equipment out of it to build a mini Tech-Ops Center on her kitchen table. As he moved her tablet to make room for his setup, Nate sighed.

"Don't know which of you is worse," he grumbled, looking from one to another. "I'm the analytical scientist, but you two are so buried in data it's no wonder you can't see the forest for the trees."

"Meaning?" Tugood looked up from plugging in a monitor.

"It's time to forget the case for a while. Have a beer. Eat some pizza. Talk about something other than drugs and murders for an hour." He followed his own advice by taking a beer and one of the pizza boxes into the living room—as far away from the monitors as he could get.

Matthew continued to fuss with the equipment while Bree hovered, torn between her two friends. Finally, she gave up the struggle and took both her tablet and a pizza box into the room with Nate.

She considered the two choices, finally deciding on a thick, cheesy slice. The first bite made her forget the healthy salad she'd been planning to eat. The second bite nearly burned the roof of her mouth.

Before she could jump up, Matthew appeared at her shoulder and handed her a cold bottle. "I don't like beer," she told him, still holding her hand in front of her burning mouth.

"I know." He pointed to the label. Instead of beer, he'd given her fermented cider. Bree took a sip. Cool and crisp, it slid down, easing both the pain in her mouth and the dryness in her throat.

She looked at him as he settled into a chair with a slice of meat-laden pizza. "How did you know? That I don't like beer?"

"Questioning my observation skills, Watson?"

"No. I'm just," she hesitated, "impressed."

"Don't be." He turned away from her but not before she saw a spark of pleasure in his eyes. "It's part of the job."

"Unless we're on a stake out, bringing pizza and drinks for me isn't part of your job," she pressed. "It's more like what friends do for one another."

"Don't get sentimental on me, Watson. So, what if I brought pizza? You think better when you're not hungry. And a little alcohol helps the creativity flow." He paused and grabbed a second slice of pizza. "But I'm glad you like the cider, because I wouldn't be caught dead toting any of the other girly drinks you order when we're out."

"I am a woman."

"You're a wimp." He softened the words with a wink and a smile. "But one with potential. I'll make an operative out of you, yet. When I do, we'll share a shot of whiskey to toast the occasion."

"I'm already your operative."

"In training," he shot back. "With a long way to go."

"And who bugged the *Naturalistics* computers today while you were sitting miles away in an RV?"

"Someone who should have done it days ago. A pro would have planted the program while the office was occupied. A trainee waits till the entire lab is empty."

"And how many times does a pro have to read a research thesis before he understands it?" she asked sweetly.

"So? You're a trainee with special skills. Don't get cocky on me, Dr. Watson."

Bree gritted her teeth. "It's Mayfield—"

"—Watson. I know that, too."

Nate brought the teasing argument to a halt when he straightened in his chair and banged his empty beer bottle on the coffee table. "Enough. Stop fighting like a passel of cats tied in a sack. Get yourself another beer—or whatever it is you're drinking—and let's get to work. If we can't have a simple social evening, we might as well discuss the case."

Once everyone had fresh drinks, Bree explained what she'd overheard in the labs. Then she outlined Emily's research, including the girl's fascination with creating what appeared to be new training aids for drug dogs. She was detailing how the dogs were trained when Nate interrupted.

"You're telling me the girl separated street drugs using top-of-the-line chiral chromatography and a handful of other expensive techniques to make a safer pseudo-drug for training DEA dogs?" He shook his head. "I've heard of frivolous research, but this takes the cake."

"Actually, her thought process was elegant and the experiments were well planned. It's no crazier than a lot of other graduate studies I could name."

Nate shrugged, conceding her point. "I take it this *Nature* company sponsored her work?"

"It's *Naturalistics*. And yes, the company—and Paul Bender—sponsored the work."

"What about the mask?" Tugood leaned forward, his beer bottle dangling between loose fingers as he posed the question. "Didn't you say she'd created a chemical compound that masked the odor of the drugs?"

Nate nodded. "That was in the last batch of samples Bree brought us. Based on her observations, it fooled the drug dog. But when I prepped the samples for analysis, the complex fell apart, giving me two chemical compounds instead of one."

"The two chemicals fit together like," Bree paused, searching for an example to explain it to Matthew. Finally, she held up her hands and pantomimed as she talked. "They fit together like two Lego blocks. While they were chemically connected, neither part was active. Nate's prep pulled them apart, making the drug active—and detectible—again."

"For the record, I checked the complex without the prep to verify it's a single compound. I also managed to grow some crystals to create a three-dimensional image of the molecules."

"It wasn't supposed to be part of the work," Bree said, picking up when the others fell silent. "Emily discovered the scent masking agent by accident. It was—"

"It *is* something that could get her killed. A chemical like this could open the door to mass imports of illegal drugs, all slipping in past every detection method we have." Matthew let out a long, low whistle. "Then they either break the complex apart, or sell the drugs and the digesting agents separately, and—Bam! Detection-free drugs and more money for the drug boss."

A shiver raced down Bree's spine as she envisioned the impact of such a technology. Yes, drug kingpins would pay handsomely for such a product. And even more handsomely to keep knowledge of it out of the hands of the government.

"Do you think Emily and the rest of them are in danger?" Matthew shook his head. "Not yet. Someone at the DEA got wind of her plan to cook meth or fake meth. That's why they pulled me in." He took a swig of his beer before racing to his computer.

When Bree and Nate joined him, half a dozen windows were open on the desktop and blinking status bars indicated his programs were cross referencing data. He stared at them until an audible ping drew his attention back to the screen.

"Here's the connection." He pointed. Half of the screen held an organizational chart. The other, a genealogy. "Emily Appleton is the granddaughter of Dick DuBois. The Undersecretary to the Assistant of the Deputy Administrator of the DEA."

"That's a lot of unders, assistants, and deputies," said Nate. "How'd you dig through all that?"

"The same way you separate chemicals. Because I know my job." Matthew flashed a quick grin. "Bree, pull up the government and grant references from Emily's thesis."

"On it, boss." She loaded the documents and passed her tablet to Matthew.

"Granddad knew because she'd pumped him about his work. When her application for the DEA to fund her graduate research hit his desk, he must have guessed she was getting close to trouble. That's when they brought me—us—in to investigate. What DuBois doesn't know is that his granddaughter discovered this masking agent. The feds would be all over her lab if they had wind of this."

Bree pulled out a chair and sank down, giving in to the effects of the alcohol she'd chugged earlier, along with another, less comfortable feelings. "Is that it? The end of our mission?"

"It's the end of what *we* were hired to do," Matthew said not taking his eyes off the screens. "But now we have bigger problems. If this technology gets out, the effect on national security could be unprecedented. If you can mask the scent of drugs, it's a small leap to mask the scent of—"

"—explosives," interjected Nate.

Dread coiled in Bree's stomach crowding out the pleasant effects of the alcohol and leaving her chilled. "What do we do next?" she whispered into the thick silence of the room.

"Brew a pot of coffee," said Matthew. He cast a longing glance at the remainder of the beer, then his eyes turned dark and hard. "We're going to erase every scrap of data—paper and electronic—that points to this masking agent."

CHAPTER 22

T orch the lab. Matthew's instructions to her whispered through Bree's mind like a nightmare. But nightmares only happened when she was asleep, and neither she, Nate, nor Matthew had slept.

After they'd wiped everything they could from the *Naturalistics* staff's computers using the remote feature in the bug she'd planted, the team had headed back to the RV to gather the remaining bits of data and samples. They'd secured them in the vaults at the Tech-Ops Center in the former executive offices of the main Sci-PHi complex.

Then they'd planned a way to destroy the rest of the data. Including paper copies and samples that might exist in the labs. At least, Bree had convinced Matthew to let her email a sanitized copy of Emily's thesis to the girl's university.

The document, minus any references to the masking agents, now sat in her professor's inbox. It didn't cover all her research, but Bree was convinced it contained enough to let Emily pass her doctoral defense.

That small act of kindness somehow made it easier for Bree to slip into Emily's office and place one tiny explosive charge in the case of her computer and another in her file cabinet.

As for the rest of the researchers, Bree regretted that their data needed to be lost as well. But they, and whatever new corporation Paul Bender founded, would survive. She didn't doubt that Tonya and Ricco could replicate their critical experiments from memory. Besides, the staff was almost ready to vacate the university labs. In a way, Bree and Matthew were doing them a favor.

By the time the *Naturalistics* staff wandered in, Bree lounged at the kitchen table cradling a mug of coffee. Her hands shook from the excess of caffeine she'd already consumed. Or maybe it was from the adrenaline surging through her body in never-ending, nauseating waves.

"Someone's up early," Ricco teased, his accent growing thick. "Sleepless night with the boyfriend, *chica?*"

"You have no idea."

"Ah, to be young and carefree." He poured a cup of coffee for himself and another for Tonya who followed him into the kitchen. "Compared to this one, you and I are old. We wasted our night watching the news and turning in early, while Cat, here, was busy all night long."

He topped off Bree's cup. "Better drink up. You have a long day ahead of you. Emily's processing the last of her samples and any mistakes on your part will set her back. Mess with her research and she'll chop you up for dog food."

Little did he know how much Emily's research had already been compromised.

At noon, just as planned, the campus alarms went off, forcing evacuations of all the buildings. Bree waited till her colleagues were out the door before gathering her own belongings. Then, she tipped bottles of organic solvents onto the lab benches and floors. She tossed a small charge into the puddle and hurried out of the labs.

While the firefighters and university officials worked their way through the crowds, Paul gathered his team and did a head count. Once everyone was accounted for, Bree pushed a button on the key-fob sized detonator in her pocket.

The small charge made no sound, but her phone vibrated. A glance at Matthew's text told her the fire had started successfully. Less than a minute later, the sharp, crystalline ping of shattered glass sounded.

The team turned to see smoke and flame pouring out of one of the lab windows. Emily shrieked, her voice piercing Bree's ear as Paul and Ricco kept the girl from running toward the building.

"My data," Emily wailed over and over again.

Bree's heart twisted. *Better to sacrifice Emily's data than to put her life in danger.* The thought settled Bree's mind, if not her conscience.

Once she was sure the team was a safe distance from the building, she pushed the second button on the detonator. A high-frequency pulse reached first one, then another, and another of the explosive charges she'd planted in the offices, rocketing the small labs and throwing up a wall of flame.

A good spy completes his mission at all costs. A better spy eradicates sentimentality, personal loyalties, and any other threats to the mission. The best spies don't have happy—or long—lives.

Matthew had been an excellent spy. Yet in the years since he'd left the agency, he'd discovered burying passions in the darkness of his soul wasn't the same as killing them.

As he watched Bree run from the explosion, an inconvenient emotion slithered free and wrapped around his chest. He fought the tightness, struggling to suck in air that caught in his throat.

171

Bree's face, chalk-white and drawn, reflected terror as she raced toward him. Except she wasn't really running to him. The high-powered field glasses gave the illusion she was as close as the python squeezing his heart and lungs, not half a mile away, fleeing the blast.

Matthew gritted his teeth till his jaw ached and turned from Bree to examine the building. The fire raged, incinerating both the data in question and the evidence of the explosives they'd planted.

A siren pierced the air.

When firefighters and emergency personnel flooded the scene, Matthew packed his field kit and evacuated. The practiced moves didn't fill him with his usual calm. Instead, sweat trickled down his back and his hand shook despite efforts to steady it. He blamed the coffee he'd drunk last night while helping Bree erase all electronic evidence of the masking drug.

But when he'd swept Emily Appleton's apartment this morning, clearing away copies of her research documents, his hands had been steady, his breathing even. Watching Bree in the path of an explosion had stripped away a decade or more of training.

He shivered. For a second, his vision blurred and he was sixteen again. Ash rained from the sky, dropping to the smoldering earth. His hopes, his dreams, and anyone who'd given a damn about him perished that day. The boy he'd once been had died, too, leaving behind a shell. A shell he'd filled first with anger, then vengeance.

Years of training dried the vengeance into a different kind of shell—harder, blacker, more impenetrable, filled with lethal skills and duty.

He'd turned his back on the rest of the memories the day he took his new name. Matthew Tugood didn't have a past. Didn't dare hope for a future.

A faint hiss of water on the burning lab reminded him that today was a different day. He should pick up his gear, arrange for someone to take his place, and abort what was left of this mission. He'd done what he set out to do—uncovered and eliminated the drug threats from the *Naturalistics* labs.

So what if there was a murder to solve? The murder had never been more than a complication. It wasn't his job. And it sure as hell wasn't Bree's.

When her image flashed through his mind again, he knew he couldn't just walk away. Not after he'd seduced her into joining his world. He'd made her his responsibility. His duty.

And he didn't shirk duty.

Matthew stood so still and quiet, not even the cat paid him any attention. Waiting. Longing. Footsteps sounded in the hall.

Bree squealed—not a power-filled shout, but a frightened scream—the moment she walked through the door and saw him lurking in the shadows of her apartment. Her reactions—too slow and weak—didn't stop him from swooping her into his arms and kissing her roughly, thoroughly.

To hell with finesse. Matthew needed connection, to feel as if he belonged somewhere, linked to someone, even if only for an hour. She'd learn soon enough that sex was a passing hunger to be assuaged. Every spy did.

But as she melted against him and responded to his kiss, something shifted. Slight, like a weapon being put into safe mode, the change signified danger. Yet, he couldn't resist gentling his kiss. A tiny crack opened in the casing around his heart and a piece of his long-forgotten soul slipped into the kiss.

He'd repair the damage later. Now he softened under her touch, tension seeping from his shoulders, and accepted what she offered.

Blissful minutes passed until, far too soon, he eased away. "We've got to work on your awareness and upper body strength," he murmured into her hair.

Her only response was a sigh.

"I could have hurt you."

"You didn't."

"But I will."

Silence.

He untangled himself from her arms, regretting the chill that replaced her warmth, yet glad for the numbness that followed in its wake. He forced himself to sling an arm over her shoulders and inject his voice with crispness. "It's just a cover story, Watson. Don't forget."

She bristled, ready to correct his misuse of her name, just as he'd expected. Good. He'd be less likely to hurt her if she focused on fighting him.

"It's Mayfield-"

"Whatever." He shrugged. "Names aren't important in this business. Now that the lab situation is taken care of, let's get back to work solving the murder. What have you learned about Hannah's blackmail schemes?"

CHAPTER 23

*D*amn *the man.* Bree bit her tongue to keep from snapping at Tugood and his games. Sleeplessness made her irritable. Or maybe it was blowing stuff up that irritated her. Destroying data? Ruining lives? Lying to the police—especially her friend Detective James O'Neil—about the lab fire?

No, it was all of that. But mostly it was being scared out of her wits by a spy lurking in the shadows, kissing her senseless, then pretending nothing happened.

The only murder she cared about now was the one she would commit if Tugood didn't stop messing with her emotions.

"What's the matter, Watson? Didn't you analyze the flash drive the detective gave you? You've had it for days now. I would have—"

"I need to sleep, Tugood. And eat. And go to my undercover job to blow stuff up. Only one of which I've done in recent memory."

As if to accent the point, her stomach growled.

Tugood laughed, the sound grating on her nerves like steel wool. But when he spoke, his voice was soft, kind. At odds with his words. "You look like hell, Watson. You smell like smoke. Clean up. I'll be back in half an hour. You can practice our cover as lovers when I take you to dinner."

With that he sauntered out the door, leaving her alone with Sherlock. The cat eyed her from across the living room, eyes narrowed. Bree crouched down and held her hand out to him. Likely he'd been as scared as she had when Tugood surprised her at the door. The big orange ball of muscle and fluff—she refused to call him fat—was a softie under all his yowling, growling, and bluster.

Sherlock crossed the room cautiously, flinching when a draft of air stirred the curtains on her French doors. He came close, sniffed her fingers and jumped back, hissing. His hair stood on end, making him appear double his already hefty, twenty-pound size.

Maybe she did smell like smoke. And whether or not she looked like hell, she felt like it. Bree locked up and headed to the shower. Twenty minutes later as she shimmied into slim-fitting black slacks, ballet flats, and a dressy summer blouse, she considered turning out the lights and going to bed rather than letting Tugood in.

She nixed the idea. He'd already broken into her house once today and wouldn't hesitate to do it again. Unlike chemistry, espionage work didn't have set hours or any concept of private time.

The doorbell rang, right on schedule. Bree marched to the door and yanked it open, still stinging from his earlier behavior. "Let's get this over with." She shouldered past him, pulling her door closed.

"We really do need to work on your awareness and self-preservation skills."

Bree turned, ready to snap off a retort, and stopped, mouth half open, the words frozen on her lips.

He looked stunning. Not handsome, work-a-day Matthew in polo shirts and khakis. Not her sexy, undercover, rumpled-white-shirt-and-torn-jeans boyfriend. Nor even her hunky tee-shirt-clad partner. But gorgeous, in a GQ-billionaire-playboy way.

"Surprised?" He cocked his head and studied her. "I have been known to clean up on occasion."

"You look," she paused, torn between honesty and her residual anger, "dressed to kill. Metaphorically speaking." She hoped.

He smiled slowly and captured her gaze, searching her eyes until she could feel the air between them smolder. "Don't underestimate me." He stroked a thumb along her jaw. "Partner."

He leaned close. Bree had just enough self-control to pivot away and walk down the hall. "Not now," she said with a nonchalance she didn't feel. "You promised me dinner while we discussed the case."

"Actually, I promised you dinner and a chance to practice our cover relationship while we discussed the case." His voice, dangerously close to her ear, held a hint of amusement that put her on edge. His fingers wrapped around her elbow. "Keep it up and the world will think we've had a lover's quarrel. Which, of course, would require make up sex."

"Fake make up sex."

"Would you know the difference?"

She paused and let him open the corridor door for her. No, she admitted, she wouldn't know the difference. "How do you do it? Pretend to be interested in someone when you're just using them for a cover story?"

He shrugged. "There's a grain of truth in everything I do."

"Even fake sex?"

"Everything." The cool night air wrapped around them as they exited her building and headed to his car. "Even this." He leaned in and kissed her cheek before handing her into the car.

Just then a pedestrian rounded the corner and smiled at her, leaving Bree questioning Matthew's motives. Had he kissed her because he wanted to? Or because they were being observed?

"One more time," he whispered. Matthew's breath shivered along the sensitized nerve endings in her neck and his hand cradled hers.

Bree knew everyone in the restaurant saw an amorous couple snuggled together in a booth, sharing chocolate mousse and coffee. She struggled to remember it was an illusion.

"Hannah kept files dating back to her college days. She analyzed them for *SIGN*s of weakness: Secrets, Information, Gossip and News they didn't want the world to know."

"Sounds like MICE."

"I suppose if the bar had rodents in the kitchen that would be cause, but she didn't have a file on the Tinsdales."

Matthew chuckled. "A mouse in the kitchen is one thing, but MICE is quite another. It stands for Money, Ideology, Compromise and Ego—the tools we use to recruit foreign agents and others. For example," he paused and held a spoonful of mousse out for her while twining the fingers of his other hand in hers, "you joined Sci-Spy partly for ideology and ego."

She took the bite and swallowed, struggling to keep in character despite the revulsion his words caused. Beneath the tablecloth, she tugged against his grip, but he wouldn't let her hand go.

"Don't get offended, Bree. I just categorize the world that way. You liked the idea of making the world a better place by solving puzzles. Plus, you wanted to be recognized for your unique skills. Ideology and ego."

Matthew dropped the spoon and with a warm caress turned her face toward him. "And liking. A new recruitment method—RASCALS—includes liking. I liked you and wanted to work with you. I'm just enough of an egoist myself to think you liked me, too." He offered a tentative smile.

"So, liking me is what gives a grain of truth to our cover?" she asked, irritated by the entire evening.

Instead of fading, both the warmth in his eyes, and his smile, deepened. "Exactly. I like you. A lot." His thumb traced a circle on their entwined hands. "If I were a different kind of man, it could be more than a cover for me."

"What kind of man would that be?"

Matthew swallowed. Emotions chased one another across his features—fleeting softness followed by a tightening jaw, a hint of sadness, obliterated by the cold darkening of his eyes, and other emotions she couldn't name. Eventually he broke the silence.

"A man like your detective, O'Neil. Someone capable of commitment. Of love. Not damaged goods."

"Matthew, you're not—"

"I am." He leaned his forehead against hers, the very image of a lover, but his soft words were icy. "I've spent almost half my life keeping secrets and telling lies. Watching friends die for a cause. Be smart, Bree. Trust me with your life, but not your heart."

This time when she pulled away, he let her go. She drew in a shuddering breath, aware of both what he'd said and the myriad of things left unsaid. Her imagination spun in a dozen directions, trying to save him, and herself.

Eventually she reined in her chaotic thoughts and focused on something tangible. Their investigation.

"Speaking of Detective O'Neil, he's taken the lead on the blackmail angle. Hannah's bank accounts show deposits that correspond with times she made contact with various victims. James is investigating the victims, but so far, no one stands out as a suspect in her murder."

"But..." he prompted when her voice trailed off.

"I'm not convinced she wasn't blackmailing the Tinsdale family, even if she didn't keep notes on it. I still think the bar is the key to solving this mystery."

Matthew regarded her carefully then nodded. "I trust your instincts. Tomorrow we go back to the bar to see what we can learn."

"Same cover?"

He nodded. Bree's stomach knotted. She couldn't blur lines the way he could. Pretending to be his girlfriend might not put her life in danger, but the same couldn't be said for her heart.

On Saturday, Bree woke early, thanks to Sherlock the Alarm Clock. She'd resigned herself to rising on his schedule months ago. While she made breakfast for herself and the cat, she mulled over Hannah's blackmail file.

She didn't have the technology or the skills to pull bank records and other relevant data. Even if she did, questioning the suspects—some of whom might be in the chemical industry or patrons of the bar—didn't fit with her cover as a college student.

So what could she investigate? James had brushed off the few college files on Hannah's flash drive as being too old and too sparse to warrant detailed analysis. Yet Bree wasn't convinced the files were irrelevant.

Matthew's words came back to her. *I trust your instincts.* It wasn't the first time he'd told her that. And if Matthew trusted her instincts, maybe she should learn to trust them, too.

Bree grabbed another cup of coffee and booted up her computer. She clicked the link to Hannah's files. An hour's worth of searching yielded exactly nothing. Her mind—usually so fast to access data and make connections—insisted there was something more, but Bree couldn't put her finger on it. Frustrated, she pulled up the background files the team had gathered on Hannah.

The section on her college days revealed a student with a respectable GPA and a full social life. Bree scanned the list of organizations and activities Hannah had been involved in. Midlist, something caught Bree's eye. Kappa Zeta Rho Sorority.

Excitement zinged through Bree's body and she abandoned the files to pace the length of her condo. Bree—at her mother's insistence—had joined the Kappa Z's during her freshman year in college. As a legacy candidate, the group had welcomed her with open arms. She'd made lifelong friends.

She shook her head, remembering how, at the time, she'd fought the suggestion. She'd been wrong, just as she'd been when she fought her mom's suggestion to join the high school drama club rather than signing up for advanced physics. In both cases, her mom—a professional psychologist—had been right. Working at Sci-Spy demanded Bree push the limits on her knowledge *and* her people skills.

Regret wormed its way into her mind. She'd never told her mom how much those life skills had helped her. Now, thanks to the Sci-Spy code of silence, she doubted she'd ever be able to fully express her gratitude. Losing the chance to connect with her mother after years of being her father's protégé left a bitter taste in her mouth. She swallowed it and focused on her work instead.

Bree dug out her Kappa Z alumni directory, looking for familiar names, finally deciding to contact a local sorority sister and friend who hailed from Northwestern. Lindsay Morgan picked up on the second ring and agreed to meet Bree for lunch at Hugo's Frog Bar in downtown Naperville.

Next, she steeled herself for a confrontation and dialed James's cell phone. "I'm sorry I didn't call back last night," she began when he answered.

"I was worried about you." His words—and the concern behind them—were the opposite of what she'd expected. Clearly, she'd been dealing with Tugood and his prickly attitude too much.

"Bree? Are you okay? Do you want me to come over?"

"I'm fine," she reassured him. "I mean, not fine, exactly, but I'm dealing with it."

"The fire in your lab scared the crap out of me, Bree. As soon as I heard the first 911 call, I raced out. I was halfway to campus when I heard about the explosion. Thank God you called to report you were safe."

Guilt washed over her and lodged in her gut. Should she have ignored Tugood's directive and told James about the plan to destroy the lab? Would he have tried to prevent them from going through with it? The national security risk had seemed a real and credible threat when she, Tugood, and Nate had come up with their mitigation strategy. But was it?

"Bree?" O'Neil's voice held a sharp edge of panic. "I knew I should have checked on you last night. You're not anywhere near fine. I'm heading there now."

"I appreciate your concern, but I'm meeting a sorority sister for lunch. Maybe we could meet for brunch tomorrow."

"All right. I'll pick you up at eleven. Promise me you'll call if you change your mind or want company." A heavy sigh punctuated his words. "Meanwhile, I've got a hornet's nest of issues to deal with. The university had just gotten the parents calmed down after Hannah's death.

"The lab incident riled everyone up again. President Jenkins is worried about losing students, and funding and Mayor Greenwood is accusing the police department of bungling the case."

"But the lab fire didn't have anything to with Hannah's death or the investigation."

"I didn't say the complaints made sense. Emotions are high and it's up to me to calm them. But you raise an interesting point. Could the fire have been set to cover up some clue as to the murderer's identity?"

Bree flinched at the question. If an investigation into the lab fire pointed to arson would Tugood be able to cover it up? She rubbed her forehead, trying to massage away her out-of-control thoughts.

Thank goodness James hadn't called on a video chat. She tried to redirect the conversation. "I doubt the fire had anything to do with Hannah or the murder. Your techs wouldn't have missed any evidence."

"Even good crime techs miss evidence. I wonder..." his voice trailed off and Bree held her breath. "Much as I hate to admit it, your spy may be onto something with his drug ring theories. Could the explosions have resulted from a bad meth cook? Or an attempt to cover up meth production?"

"I think the lab was old. A spark could have lit solvent vapors and caused a chain reaction."

"Maybe." *Damn.* He didn't sound convinced.

"Speaking of investigations," she said, trying to disrupt his thoughts, "did you ever get the autopsy results on Hannah?"

"Actually, they came in late last night. Turns out you were right. Hannah died of alcohol poisoning." Bree heard him shuffling papers. "Here it is. Isopropyl alcohol is indicated due to presence of ketones and other metabolic byproducts. I have no clue what that means."

"It means I was right when I thought I detected acetone—that's nail polish remover to you—on her breath the morning she died. If I'd thought of it sooner, I could have searched the labs for large quantities of the poison alcohol."

"Too late now. Listen, I want you to back off investigating. That fire could have been a warning from the killer to you. Don't do anything until we can talk."

Bree crossed her fingers behind her back and solemnly promised to do as he asked.

Then she cut off the call and headed out to break her promise.

CHAPTER 24

"Hi, Lindsay. It's great to see you again." Bree hugged her sorority sister when she walked into the restaurant. Soon, the two of them were ushered to a table.

Adjusting to the light in the dark interior after being in the sun took a few minutes, but Bree didn't mind. The dark cherry stained woods coupled with the quiet of their booth reminded Bree of an old-fashioned library. The ambience soothed her and she relaxed against the high back of the booth.

Once they'd put in their orders for bowls of bookbinder soup and salads, they chatted, catching up on news and gossip.

"I heard your company was sold," Lindsay said. "How is the transition to the new owners going?"

"It's complicated."

"I'm sure. When I was still in corporate law, I handled plenty of mergers and acquisitions. The worst part was dealing with employees who lost their jobs due to consolidation." Lindsay shuddered. "I'm glad to be out of that world."

"Speaking of which, how is your start-up business going?"

Lindsay brightened. *"Mom's the Word* is doing better than I predicted. Despite the start-up stresses, I've loved every minute. I've even had time to rejoin the Kappa Z alumni association. I'm serving as secretary for the local chapter.

Besides being fun, several of our sisters contracted me to help start businesses."

Lindsay flashed a smile at Bree as she buttered a slice of raisin bread. "If you ever want to leave your corporate stress and establish that bakery you've been dreaming of, I'm at your disposal."

"I thought you geared your business toward helping young mothers start their own businesses."

Lindsay waved the comment aside. "I work with people from all backgrounds. Even the occasional man. Don't let the company name fool you."

Bree took a spoonful of soup and enjoyed the rich melding of tomato broth, vegetables, and white fish in the stew while Lindsay talked about her new customers. Eventually Bree steered the topic back to the Kappa Z alumni association.

"My job has me learning a bunch of new skills, too. I think I met some Kappa Z alumni at one of my consulting gigs." She paused as if in thought. "Did you know a Hannah Rogers? She was about your age and from Northwestern, like you."

"Hmm. Let me think. She sounds familiar."

Bree described Hannah.

"She isn't someone I've met recently, but I'm sure I know that name." After what seemed like an hour, she snapped her fingers and turned to Bree. "Now, I remember. Trust me, you don't want to get close to her."

"Why?"

"She's been subject to so many disciplinary actions that she should have been kicked out of the sorority. For some reason, she keeps her status, despite everything."

Bree was sure she knew the reason. The blackmail list. But how Hannah had managed to keep the disciplinary actions out of her student files remained a mystery.

"It all started back in college," continued Lindsay. "She pulled a prank on a pledge that nearly shut the chapter down. We were lucky to get off with a stern warning and probation."

"Were you on campus when it happened?"

"Actually, I was spending a semester abroad. I heard about it from some friends. Believe me, you can't require a pledge to steal a diamond bracelet and expect to get away with it, even if the theft is a setup."

"What?"

"Exactly my reaction. I'm all for having new members demonstrate loyalty to the sorority, but not by breaking the law. Even if Hannah and her cronies knew it was a prank, the pledge didn't. From what I heard, she was a sweet, shy girl. I can only imagine the pressure Hannah's gang must have put her under before she caved in."

"Who was the girl?"

"That, I don't remember. I heard she transferred to another university. After I returned from my semester abroad, I had to focus all my attention on graduation. Having the sorority under investigation kind of cast a pall over my events, but at least, being busy kept my mind off things."

Bree digested the information, wondering if Hannah had used blackmail to get the pledge to steal for her. It wasn't out of the realm of possibility. The thought both disturbed and depressed Bree.

If anyone deserved to die, it had been Hannah. Bree almost felt sympathy for the killer.

For the second night in a row, Bree sat across from Tugood, pretending to be his girlfriend. His giggly, twenty-something girlfriend. For once, she was grateful to be in the guise of Cat Holmes. Playing the role helped her remember her relationship with Matthew wasn't real.

She didn't want it to be real.

Except…Every time she thought she'd put him back into the emotional box labeled "do not touch," something happened. Like last night, when he'd slipped and referred to himself as damaged goods. Why couldn't she resist trying to repair the damage and bring him into the light?

Her mom would probably accuse Bree of reaching for the unattainable—thereby avoiding a real relationship. Her grandmother, on the other hand, would simply say Matthew needed a good meal to fill those gaps and make everything right again. Which reminded Bree that her grandmother was sending her family recipes. Maybe tomorrow she could…

Matthew kicked her under the table.

"Hey!"

"You're about twenty seconds from blowing our cover. Get in the game."

Her warm feelings for him evaporated. Before she could think of a suitable reply, Edward Tinsdale came over to the table to greet them. "Hi, guys. Cat, how are you holding up? I heard about the lab explosion yesterday. Thank God everyone was outside when it happened."

A shudder slipped down Bree's spine at the memory of the flames. She blinked as unwanted tears stung her eyes. Setting the explosions only added a layer of regret to the terror. "It was horrible. I keep seeing it over and over in my mind." Her voice shook.

A warm hand covered hers. Bree looked into Matthew's face, surprised to see worry—and something else—etched there. She curled her fingers into his and turned back to Edward. "How did you hear about it?"

"Seriously? It's been all over the news. Besides, Tonya and Ricco came by for dinner and drinks last night. They were both shook up. If there's any bright spot to the whole thing, it's that Paul and the team had the new labs almost ready to go. Will you be moving there with them?"

"I don't, that is, I—"

"Cat can't stop talking about how much she loves working with the team." Matthew squeezed her hand. "She hopes Paul will offer her a job."

"If she's as good in the lab as she is in the kitchen, she shouldn't have a problem." Edward placed menus in front of them and pointed. "See? Your Piña Colada Chicken is a customer favorite. I'll set you up with a complimentary appetizer plate of them and you can tell us if we need to modify the recipe. And Miranda will be over to take your orders. Don't worry. Everyone has trouble in life, but tough, smart people like you find a way through."

When Edward was out of earshot, Bree turned to Matthew. "What do you mean I hope Paul will offer me a job? Aren't we done investigating them?"

"We were—until I heard about the new lab. What do you know about it? Could the team be trying to replicate Emily's work with the masking agent?"

"From what they told me, no. Ricco—or maybe it was Jackie—called Emily's work a bridge between the work *Naturalistics* did and the research the new lab was focused on."

"Until we understand this link between masking scents and the new work, I can't stop the investigation. You need to get into the new labs and see if you can get your colleagues to talk."

"They've been secretive so far. If it's something they're trying to patent, I may not be able to get them to share anything."

"Sure, you will. You've just been through a tragedy—people bond and open up under shared stresses. I'll teach you how to use the explosion to get them to talk to you."

She sagged against the booth and tried to avoid his eyes. "Don't you ever get tired of using people, Matthew? I used to have friends. Now, I have a series of people I pump for information. I hate it."

In the ensuing silence, Matthew loosened his grip on her fingers and pulled away, leaving a chill. Bree fisted her hand and buried it in her lap, still not looking at him.

"If you hate it so much, you need to leave," he said eventually.

Did she imagine the hint of resignation in his voice? The breath that might have been a sigh? She risked a glance at him. His clenched jaw didn't give her any clues.

"Finish the mission and I'll find a way to give you back a normal life," he added. "Or as normal as you can be after working for me."

"We both know it won't be that easy."

As if to illustrate her point, Miranda approached with a plate of appetizers. Bree plastered a smile on her face and turned to Miranda, toying with the Kappa Zeta Rho lavaliere she'd worn for tonight.

Miranda placed the platter in front of them and took their orders. Instead of hurrying away, she lingered. "Can I talk to you for a minute?" she asked Bree.

"Sure." Bree slid from the booth and followed Miranda, aware of Tugood's eyes on her back the whole time. Miranda led her from the bar into the back-alley entrance. The same one where Tugood had kissed her senseless a week ago. Bree pushed the memory aside.

Unfortunately, it was replaced with thoughts of how isolated the entrance was. The dumpsters loomed over her, a perfect place to hide a body. Bree mentally slapped herself. The dumpsters still overflowed with empty liquor bottles and jugs of cleaning supplies. There was no room for a body. She hoped.

"You heard a lot of things you shouldn't have last week," Miranda said.

Was her voice colder? Without the overtones of friendliness? Or was Bree's imagination playing tricks on her? A shiver skittered across Bree's arms and neck before washing down her spine. In the dim corner, Bree couldn't see Miranda's eyes clearly. The alleyway took on a sinister edge.

Miranda could easily have added tainted isopropyl alcohol to one of Hannah's drinks without having poisoned the pricy bottle of tequila.

"What do you mean?" Bree asked as she toyed with her necklace. Miranda wouldn't kill a sorority sister, would she?

Dumb question. Hannah had been a sorority sister.

"Don't play stupid with me, Cat." Miranda's gaze flicked toward the necklace and back. "I noticed your Kappa Zeta Rho letters. I was a Kappa Z, too. I don't want a sister thinking the worst of me without knowing the whole story."

"I don't understand." Bree cast about for a potential weapon, wishing she'd worn her earpiece and camera necklace. "I didn't hear anything."

Miranda snorted. "Of course, you did. When you came on Monday, you ended up in the middle of a family feud. The Hannah situation had all of us on edge. Mom. Dad. Me. Things had been brewing for years. You just happened to be in the kitchen when everything boiled over."

"I didn't hear that much."

"You heard enough. But you kept quiet about it. Thank you. We—that is Mom, Dad and I—had a long talk. We're getting our issues out in the open and talking for the first time since I can remember." She raised her hands then dropped them helplessly to her sides. "I hope you don't think badly of us after all that."

Bree ducked her head and dug her toe in the gravel before answering, ashamed of her earlier suspicions. Still, the prickle of gooseflesh on her arms didn't fully recede. But at least for now, it appeared Miranda only wanted to talk. "I know what family arguments can be like," Bree lied. "That's why I value my Kappa Z sisters so much. I can always turn to them when things get difficult."

"True," agreed Miranda. "Most Kappa Z girls are great, but even the Kappas make mistakes. Hannah was a Kappa Z and part of the reason I pledged with them—before I knew what she was really like. Later, I learned she was on probation more than she was off. It's a wonder she didn't get dropped. I almost ended up on probation myself because of her."

"But wasn't she much older than you? How could she hurt you?"

Miranda turned back to the door and waited for Bree to follow before answering. "It wasn't her directly. Just a stupid pledge prank that dated back to her time. It doesn't matter. The point is, trust your sisters, but watch your back."

When Bree made her way back to the booth, annoyance replaced the fear she'd felt in the alley. Instead of coming to her rescue, Tugood sprawled across his bench, flirting with Jen Stands. Hadn't he worried about her at all?

Then she saw the slight tension in his pose. Signs most people wouldn't notice—like the way he looked over Jen's shoulder instead of at her, or the way one hand toyed with the cutlery while he scanned the room.

The minute he saw her, his fingers relaxed and his eyes returned to Jen's face. Bree slid into her seat, watching Jen as Matthew continued to flirt with her. As the woman leaned closer to him, Bree saw her in the light of the table sconce.

Heavy makeup caked her skin. Bree felt a flash of sympathy. She'd used the same trick to hide acne when she was in high school. How awful to be plagued with the problem throughout life.

Jen picked up a card from the table and turned to Bree. "Hi, Cat. While you were in the ladies' room, your boyfriend tried to sell me a car. I'm not likely to get a luxury vehicle on a mixologist's salary, but I put in for the drawing, just in case." She tucked the card into her pocket.

So, Matthew was using the business card ploy to collect more fingerprints. No wonder he'd been plying his charm on Jen. "I'll need that card back," he said.

"If Matt collects enough entries, maybe his dad will let him drive something other than that beater car he uses." Bree flashed a smile at both Matthew and Jen.

"Don't worry, babe. Once my gaming business takes off, I'll be able to provide all the luxury you deserve."

"Oh, Matt." She batted her eyes at him, hoping she looked like a lovesick college girl.

"Okay, you two. Knock it off," Jen scolded, shaking her finger at them with mock severity. The cheery tinkling of her bracelets contrasted with her words, making Bree giggle.

"You can laugh now," Jen continued with a smile, "but we still get customer complaints about your make-out session at the 'Mix Your Own Cocktail' party. If you're going to get hot and heavy, at least do it in the comfort of a bedroom."

"No sex on the table?" Matthew asked.

"Not unless it's a drink. But speaking of drinks, I have just the thing for you. How about a round of my 'Voodoo for

Two-To-Do'? It's a love spell in a glass designed for sharing. Tasty going down, and guaranteed to stir up heat between the sheets." She rattled off a list of liquors that had Bree's head spinning. "If you promise to take a cab home tonight, I'll send one over."

Later, Jen returned and handed Matthew a slightly damp business card with her name and—unknown to her—fingerprints on it. "Sorry about that" she said as she placed a colorful glass bowl etched with geometric symbols on the table between them. "The bar was wet."

She hurried off, leaving them to contemplate the bowl, and the glowing purple drink inside. Matthew dipped a straw into the concoction and sipped.

"Not bad. But once you drink this, we should leave. Something tells me this is a truth serum in a class of its own."

"Worried I'll blow my cover, cuddle cakes?" Bree drew satisfaction from the way his eyes narrowed at the pet name. "Or that you'll blow yours?"

"Both." He motioned to her straw. "Drink up and we'll see how resistant you are." The smile he gave her had a touch of evil in it and Bree sensed another training exercise coming on.

"Shouldn't we focus on our current case?"

He waved her comment aside and took another drink. "We're done here. Unless there's someone else you want to question." Matthew raised his eyebrows and waited for her reply.

"The staff?"

"Your detective has already verified everyone's alibis for the night in question. He's also spooked most of the bartenders and servers. We won't get anything of value out of them tonight."

"Then why are we here?"

"You had a hunch. We were following it. Now we're finished." He motioned toward the cocktail. "Drink up," he repeated.

Bree took a sip. Like the other drinks Jen mixed, the purple liquid slid over her palate without a harsh or bitter alcohol bite. The deceptively smooth connection went down easily as promised. She glanced at Matthew to find him staring intently at her.

A flash of heat warmed her, settling in her belly. And lower. If the drink tasted as good as Jen promised would it also heat up the sheets as she promised?

Another wave of heat pulsed through Bree's body and she met Matthew's gaze directly. Did she want to heat things up with him? To see—in his words—how resistant she was to him?

Or follow her wiser instincts to leave and never look back?

CHAPTER 25

Instead of driving Bree home to explore where 'Voodoo for Two-To-Do' led, Matthew took her to the RV crime lab where he plied her with more drinks. Followed by interrogation about her various cover identities. For hours, she fought the effects of his 80-proof version of truth serum while he developed fingerprints from the fake business cards he'd passed out at the bar.

"So, are you going to give one of them a car?" Bree asked, fighting the alcohol-induced brain fog. "It might compromise your cover if you didn't." The notion struck her as funny and she giggled.

"You don't hold your drink very well, Watson."

"Who?" She giggled again.

"Watson."

"Holmes," she shot back, her manufactured outrage cleared a bit of the fog. "My name is Cat Holmes. Undergraduate chemistry student. Or Dr. Catherine Holmes, Energy Researcher."

He grunted in response.

"And you're James Bond. Or Jason Bourne." Bree sat up and frowned in concentration. "Or maybe Maxwell Smart. He's the kind of guy who'd try to defend himself with a table knife while Agent 99 kicked some serious butt."

That got a reaction from him. "You think I couldn't?"

"I'd like to see you try." The alcohol—and memories of a self-defense class she'd once taken—made her bold. She stood and faced him. "Defend yourself with a table knife."

Before the words were out of her mouth, Bree tipped, whirled and found herself plastered against Matthew's body, her back to his front. One strong arm looped around her middle and the other held a sharp edge against her throat.

Her heart thudded, heavy as the beat of a kettledrum against her ribs. She gasped for breath, but the air seemed thin, the only reality the knife resting against her windpipe.

"Still worried I can't protect you?" Matthew's breath brushed her ear. Despite the lethal weapon he held, she relaxed into the makeshift embrace. "Or do you want to try kicking butt?"

Instead of kicking butt, she wiggled hers against his groin, eliciting a groan. She wiggled a second time, enough to distract him while she stomped on his foot with all the force she could muster.

He must have moved his foot because her heel came down hard on the trailer floor. Pain sliced across her throat but she didn't fall. Instead, she was turned again and caught in Matthew's embrace.

"Good try, Watson," he murmured into her hair. "If I hadn't been trained by the best, you might have bruised a few toes before you died." He rubbed her back, soothing the sting of his words. He waved a business card in front of her face. "If this had been a real knife, that is. Even a table knife from *All Mixed Up.*"

She'd been threatened by a business card? Her hand went to her throat where a slight tingle remained. Her face flamed at the thought of how weak her defense had been.

"I'm serious," Matthew said as he eased her hand away from her throat and tipped her chin up. He moved into the space he'd created and placed a soft kiss where he'd held the card.

This time her heart sped up, and not from fear.

He kissed a trail from her throat to her chin and finally claimed her lips. His mouth, both gentle and hungry moved against hers. Giving. Taking. Melding.

He framed her face with his broad palms and pulled back far enough to look in her eyes. "You're learning. Half drunk and pushed to your limits and you still manage to keep your cover while having wits enough to try to defend yourself."

"From a business card."

"You're good at this. But I'm better. If all I had was a business card, I'd make sure to do some damage with it."

"Teach me."

"I thought you wanted out."

His words hung in the air between them. A question? A challenge? She honestly didn't know. "Maybe. Teach me, anyway."

An hour later, alone in her own bed, she cursed the part of her that always responded when he riled her. Cursed her inebriated weakness. Cursed her ambition.

And cursed the fact that—like it or not—she'd agreed to work with Matthew for a least one more mission.

Sunday morning Bree woke early with less of a headache than she'd feared, given her experiences from last night. She'd even woken before Sherlock. She stroked the orange fur-baby curled at the foot of the bed and bent to listen for a response. A soft purr, punctuated with a kitty-sized snore assured her he was still alive.

Once she'd showered and dressed in a spring-green dress and cream pumps, the cat was his usual grumpy morning self—yammering for his breakfast. She fed him and gulped down a cup of coffee. Her conscience nagged at her, and to appease it, she decided to attend the early morning service at her local church.

Besides, she'd promised Gram she'd start attending again. Whether Gram was interested in Bree's soul—or her ability to meet marriage-minded men at the services—she wasn't sure. Either way, the decision felt right.

The tiny local church with its white clapboard siding and traditional steeple held a couple dozen people—no single men, unless she counted the over sixty crowd—when she entered. Founded over a century ago, the church sanctuary was the antithesis of the more popular mega-churches. No multimedia screens filled the walls. Instead, organ music— Bach, she thought—drifted through the congregation.

The aura of quiet that wrapped around Bree settled her mind. She put aside thoughts of murder, drugs, investigations, and the men in her life. After she sang some of her grandmother's favorite hymns, listened to a short, uplifting message and walked home, she felt more relaxed than anytime during the previous two weeks. Or two months, for that matter.

Once at home, the feeling of calm lasted through a call to her parents, one to her grandmother, and the arrival of James O'Neil.

Sure, her heart sped up a bit at the sight of him in a button-down shirt, tie, and jacket. Whose heart doesn't speed up at the sight of a handsome man? When his lips curved into a smile, the memory of their last kiss flashed through her mind. His smile deepened as if he read her private thoughts.

For a breathless second, she thought he'd kiss her again. Instead, he merely escorted her to the car. Yet, something in his manner—maybe the curve of his lips, the heated twinkle in his eyes or the way his hand lingered on hers as he helped her into the car—told her this was his way of drawing out the moment. Making her want his kisses—and him.

Soon they were sipping coffee at the local Hilton where the Sunday brunch was reported to rival any country club. James ignored the lure of the laden buffet tables and turned his focus to Bree. His earlier, gentle teasing was gone. The intensity of his gaze startled her, but held a measure of reassurance as well.

"You look like you're either ready to book me or to propose to me," she blurted. Immediately her cheeks heated and she tried to backpedal. "Not that I expected you to ... that is, I didn't mean that the way it came out."

He smiled and a dimple popped out in his cheek. "I did consider taking you into protective custody. If I thought you'd let me, I'd shadow you and sleep on your couch to keep you safe. Unless—"

The unspoken question hung in the air. "No," Bree said, covering the silence, "I won't let you shadow me and sleep on my couch. And no, no one else is sleeping there, either. Unless you count Sherlock."

"How is your monster cat? Still hissing at you and destroying your house?" James had given Sherlock to her when the cat had been discovered in her murdered boss's house.

"We've come to an understanding. I don't buy breakable knickknacks and he doesn't bat them off my shelves." She grinned, relaxing as the banter took the edge off their date. "Of course, he spends most of his time sleeping. On the couch. In the chair. On the bed. Even in the bathtub."

James sipped his coffee while she relayed stories of Sherlock's antics. When she paused to drink her own coffee, he interrupted the tales. "Sherlock isn't much of a security system. Would you let me get you a dog for protection?"

"That's sweet. But I still travel for work, so a dog isn't a good fit for me right now."

He sobered. "How is the spy business?"

"The same as always." She scrambled for a way to change the subject. She didn't want to think—let alone talk—about her espionage work or Matthew Tugood. She wanted to enjoy a stress-free afternoon with James. "Let's get some brunch before we get distracted. The omelet station looks yummy."

He took her cue and together they made their way through the lines, ordering omelets then filling plates with fruit, warm muffins, and an array of other breakfast items. Once back at the table, James dug into his food while Bree ate at a more leisurely pace.

"Are you having any luck following the leads from Hannah's flash drive of blackmail victims?" she asked.

He shook his head. "I've run into dozens of dead ends since we found the evidence. I can correlate bank deposits with her blackmail demands, but most of her victims didn't live nearby. In short, every one of her victims has the motive for murder, but few have the opportunity."

"And the few who were local?"

"Had alibis for the night before and the day of her death. Unless one of them hired a contract killer, the flash drive is a dead end." He spread cream cheese on a muffin and took a bite. "What about your hunch? You asked me to look for alcohol poisoning and we found it. Does that give you any idea who the murderer is?"

Bree shrugged. "Isopropyl alcohol is common in every chemistry lab in the country. It's also sold as rubbing alcohol in the drug store. People use it for everything from disinfecting thermometers to massaging sore muscles."

"Does that 'everything' include murder?"

"That part puzzles me. Most people don't understand its toxic effects."

"A chemist does."

"Exactly." Bree reached for the coffee pot and refilled her cup. "Any of the chemists at *Naturalistics* could have reasonably been expected to know about its toxicity. With all the noise and distractions at the bar, any one of them could have slipped isopropanol into her drinks. I can't rule them out, and I can't prove they did it. I'm stuck."

"With the lab out of commission, it's going to be hard for you to gather more information on the suspects." His eyes darkened and he reached for her hand. "I'm glad you're safe. Of all the worries I had about you being undercover, a lab explosion wasn't even on my list."

"We were lucky," she agreed. "Did you learn anything more about what happened?"

"No. The fire department wrote it off as an accident. They're saying it could have been electrical or perhaps caused by a gas leak from one of the supply lines to the lab."

"We used canisters of flammable gas for some of our analyses. It's a shame, though. Paul Bender was going to donate those labs to the university."

James gave her a smile that sent a pleasant zing through her body. "Paul did better than that. Remember the firestorm of negative publicity from the parents and university officials? Yesterday, before we could get the situation under control, Paul hosted a news conference. He donated enough cash to build several state-of-the-art labs. I'm surprised you didn't see clips of his speech on the news."

Bree had been so distracted with her investigation, she couldn't remember the last time she'd watched an entire news report. She muttered something about being busy.

"Anyway," continued James, "the donation seemed to calm most of the controversy. I guess the parents think newer is the same as safer and the university was simply glad to have the cash."

"That's good. But speaking of the suspects, I will be able to talk with them further. Paul is sending the whole team—including me—to work at the new labs starting next week."

"I still don't like the idea of you working undercover with suspected drug makers." James crossed his arms and glared at her. The friendly boy-next-door disappeared into the persona of implacable cop. "I would like to know you're safe."

Bree reached across the table to touch him. The tense muscles of his forearm relaxed a bit under her palm. "I have to do this. You said yourself that the murder and the drug ring may be connected. But I should let you know that I looked into as much of the research as I could before the fires.

"For the record, I think the team was working on a way to make pseudo drugs to be used to train canine teams. They weren't into actual drug production." She left out the information regarding the masking scents.

"Thank God." His face relaxed into familiar, comfortable lines and James cupped his hand over Bree's. "For the record, I hated every minute you spent working on that foolhardy investigation. Please, for my sake, give up playing spy—or sleuth—and go back to chemistry."

The concern in his eyes tugged at her heart. Unbidden, an image of her grandmother flashed through her head. James was exactly the type of man Gram hoped she'd find. Strong, ethical, stable, someone she could imagine as a husband and father. Hadn't Gram already suggested she stick close to him? Bree assessed his lean frame. Gram would love to help her fatten him up.

Yes, James was the kind of man she could settle down with. Except she didn't want to settle for a comfortable husband, family of 2.5 children and safe job. She wanted...something. And until she knew what that something was, she had no business leading anyone on. Especially not someone as kind and considerate as the man who currently held her hand.

"I can't make a decision right now," she said.

"About chemistry? Or are we talking about something else?" A frown furrowed his brow and he cocked his head in question.

Oh, Lord. Had she wandered off-topic? Where was her common sense? "About my job, of course. I committed to helping you find Hannah's killer. No matter what I do, I have to live up to that promise." She tugged her hand free. "Would you excuse me for a minute?"

Bree strode toward the ladies' room as fast as her heels would allow, feeling her face heat as she went. Instead of acting like the smart, professional scientist she was, she'd descended into acting like a love-struck adolescent at every turn.

She blamed her cover ID as Cat Holmes, chemistry student, for that. Living undercover for so long was destroying her sense of separation between her true self and her false self.

She brushed past a woman exiting the room and found herself alone in front of a row of sinks. Bree splashed cool water on her hands and held them to her face, careful not to disturb her makeup. When she looked up, she saw a woman with pink cheeks and shining eyes staring back at her. Not

Bree the scientist. Not her college student persona, either. But a woman full of life, energy, and enthusiasm.

Bree looked critically at her reflection. Was it also the face of a woman falling in love? Two men had woven themselves into the fabric of her life in the past months. Which of them caused the look? Patient, courteous, romantic James? Or daredevil Matthew?

Or perhaps neither. Maybe Bree was in love with the idea of love. After spending her childhood as a chubby wallflower, her adolescence as a confirmed geek, and her professional life in a lab coat, a handsome, sexy man—make that men—were pursuing her. Her—Gabriella Catherine Mayfield-Watson: brainy, curvy, headstrong, and definitely not your typical girlfriend.

More importantly, for the first time in her life, she had an exciting, glamorous career. A place where she could be the star, not just a brainy sidekick. And if working closely with sexy men was part of the package, who was she to complain?

An odd sense of déjà-vu came over Bree when she approached the table to find her date talking to another woman. The sense grew even stronger when she recognized the woman—from her six-foot height and lean frame—as Jen Stands from the *All Mixed Up* bar and lounge.

The pleasant excitement she'd felt a moment ago curled and twisted into a case of nerves. Of course, Jen knew James from the investigation. She didn't know Bree. But she did know Bree's alter ego, Cat Holmes. Bree wasn't sure her disguise—or lack thereof—could hold up under close scrutiny.

She backed away from the table and looked for an escape route, but before she could make use of it, Jen turned. "Oh, don't mind me," she said, looking Bree directly in the face. "I know James from—" She floundered for a second. "— from work. I was just stopping to say hello."

When she lingered, James made introductions. Bree kept her tone cool and professional while trying to look the polar-opposite of Cat Holmes. Still, Jen's forehead wrinkled and she gave Bree a puzzled look.

Bree resisted the temptation to look away, knowing the gesture was one she used when playing the role of Cat. Instead, she studied Jen's face, noting the fine lines around her eyes, the colors and tones of her highlighted hair and the pinched look of her lips.

Without the clunky jewelry, tight clothing, and heavy makeup she wore at the bar, Jen looked older. Bree felt a surge of sympathy. Jen obviously thought she had to appear young and trendy to keep her job. Bree knew how exhausting putting on a show like that day-after-day could be.

After a few tense moments of exchanging pleasantries, they parted and Bree sank into her seat.

"It's not as easy as it looks on TV, is it?" James asked. Bree caught a mild note of censure in his tone, but passed it off as residual nerves on his part.

"I hope she doesn't put the pieces together."

James studied her, sweeping his gaze from her head to her toes before responding. When he did, his tone was thoughtful, but ever-so-slightly distant. "Don't worry. She's not likely to remember meeting you. She's probably more interested in currying the favor of someone who can help her out with her next parking ticket."

A twinkle popped into his eyes and warmth returned to his tone as he shared stories of his days stopping traffic violators when he'd first joined the force.

When they left the restaurant, Bree had a spring in her step. An hour of laughter had chased her cares away and restored her spirits.

Plus, she had learned two dozen ways of getting out of a speeding ticket and one really important thing about herself: she needed more laughter, and fewer complications if she was going to survive her new life.

CHAPTER 26

Monday morning's staff meeting dragged on, eroding the sense of goodwill Bree had experienced yesterday. The coffee was bitter. Her friend Kiki was out with the flu. The other undercover scientists were off on missions that didn't involve her. And Bree was the primary target for Troy's attention.

"Let me see if I understand," he said to her, voice dripping with sarcasm. "You can't tell me a single experiment you did last week. Or the week before. You can't reveal the projects you're working on. You can't take calls to support our product lines while you're working with the off-site customers. And you can't even give me the name of a single person at the energy company that will vouch for your work there."

Bree took a sip of the bitter, tepid coffee. "The consulting contract signed by our Special Projects Division was very specific. I can't talk about my work to anyone other than the customer—that's *Energy Unlimited*—and Mr. Tugood."

"The energy company isn't the only customer who relies on you." Troy waved a stack of memos at her. "These are calls from other customers wanting your advice. Calls that haven't been returned because you're always *working off-site*." He spat the last words out with a sneer. "As far as I can tell, you could be drinking coffee and watching TV during all those hours you aren't at your desk."

Bree took the stack of notes from Troy. "I'll make sure someone handles these customers in my absence." She scanned through them. Each contained issues Troy could have handled, if he wanted to.

A ding from her phone indicated an incoming text. She glanced down to see it was from Ricco.

"By all means, Bree, don't let my staff meeting interrupt your social time. Norah," Troy turned to his assistant, who was busy inspecting her manicure. "Norah," he repeated more loudly, "get Tugood on the phone and arrange a time for us to speak. The special projects crap is getting out of hand. Follow up the phone call with an email to me, Tugood, and his boss."

With that, Troy turned and stomped from the room. No one at the table said a word. Tension mounted until Norah, with impeccable timing, popped a large purple bubble. As if released from a trance, everyone laughed and looked around the table. When they dispersed to their offices, Norah waylaid Bree.

"Here," Norah said, shoving a small cloth bag into Bree's hand. "I made you an amulet for protection."

"From Troy?" Bree laughed.

"It can't hurt. I read a book on charms and amulets this weekend. With the way Troy's obsessing about you being off-site, I figured you could use a little good mojo. Even if he can't make personnel changes without approval from the higher ups, he can make your life difficult."

Bree opened the bag to find a necklace with a tiny vial attached. She immediately distrusted the rusty red color of the contents. "What's in it?"

"It's a secret." Norah tried to look mysterious, but a grin spread across her face and she gave into laughter instead. "Okay, it's mostly salt, which is supposed to drive off evil spirits." She jerked her thumb in the direction of Troy's office. "I also added some chili pepper, since I figured you could use a little adventure—or some hot romance. You work too hard."

Little did Norah know. Between her long-term mission to get close to the international terrorist Zed, her short-term mission investigating the suspected drug ring, and trying to find a murderer on the side, her life had plenty of adventure.

And between Matthew and James, the potential for hot romance soared off the charts. Maybe what she really needed in the amulet bag was courage. When it came to moving either of those relationships forward, Bree chickened out. Going forward with one—in a romantic sense—meant giving up the other. And she wasn't sure she could stand to lose either.

Bree shoved the amulet bag and necklace in her pocket and thanked Norah again.

"No problem. And don't worry about work. I'll do my best to listen in when Troy and Mr. Tugood talk. If Troy tries to get you into any trouble, I'll stick up for you."

The earnestness in the girl's voice tugged at Bree's heart. So many people wrote Norah off as a nutcase because of her unorthodox dress code and strange hobbies. Yet, even before Bree had helped her out of a sticky situation involving the murder of their boss, Norah had confided in Bree and watched over her. The young woman had a loyal heart and a fighting spirit beneath her Goth attire and devil-may-care attitude.

Bree's phone dinged again. She ignored it and squeezed Norah's arm instead. "You're a good friend. But don't worry, I doubt Troy and Mr. Tugood are going to gang up against me."

Still, Tugood would rant at her after having to deal with Troy and his combination of delusion and insecurity. Originally Matthew advocated for putting Kiki into the position of department head. Bree had vetoed the suggestion, arguing Troy would be easier to manage. In truth, she hadn't wanted to lie to her friend any more than necessary.

But if Troy insisted on monitoring and controlling Bree's schedule, he would have to be removed from his position, leaving Kiki as the next logical candidate. Bree shuddered at the thought of the additional lies she'd have to tell if Kiki was her supervisor.

"Hey," Norah shook Bree's shoulder. "Don't look so worried. It will work out all right. You'll see."

"Thanks." Bree hurried away before she could get caught up in conversation. Once alone, she checked her text messages.

Paul Bender had officially invited her to join his new company, starting work in their private labs—as early as tomorrow morning if she wanted.

And Ricco Torres had asked to see her.

Tonight.

And he'd asked her to come alone.

The skin on the back of Bree's neck prickled and a shiver wracked her body as she climbed the stairs to Ricco's apartment.

She felt Matthew's eyes on her, but took no comfort from it. He was across the street in an unmarked van, watching her through a telephoto lens and the array of cameras she wore. She needed someone at her side.

Compared to the dark stairwell in a deserted part of town, contacting a suspected terrorist at a crowded chemical conference was a piece of cake.

Sweat trickled down Bree's back and she paused on the stairs, her hand clutching the railing.

"You're doing fine, Bree." Matthew's voice sounded through her hidden earpiece and she clung to the sound, drawing courage from it. "I'll be with you the whole time. Remember the signals."

"Right." Bree reviewed the code words they'd agreed on. "If I sense danger, I say I forgot to call my mother. If I need you right away, I say I need to call my dad."

"Good." Matthew's voice sounded calm. Bree wondered if she'd ever feel calm going into a situation like this. "Mother equals danger. Dad equals rescue. You've got this."

She'd better have it. She was already at the door.

Bree knocked, her hands shaking so violently she could barely control them. Her stomach twisted at the sound of footsteps within.

Instead of Ricco, Tonya opened the door. Bree's nerves instantly calmed and she chided herself for stereotyping Ricco as a Latino gang-banger. His youthful arrest records were more related to pranks than to anything nefarious. Nothing he'd done justified her fears.

Unless he'd murdered Hannah.

Bree silenced her inner monologue.

"Thank you for coming tonight," Tonya said as she led Bree to the brightly lit kitchen. Ricco stood at the counter, his back to them. "We wanted to talk to you before you met with Paul tomorrow morning."

"Hi, Cat. Welcome." Ricco flashed her a smile and headed to the table, three mugs in his hands. "I made some spiced Mexican cocoa. Tonya's favorite. But I give you fair warning," he skewered Bree with a look as he put the mug in front of her. "It isn't sweet."

Bree glanced at the stovetop and assured that the mugs of cocoa all came from a single pan of heated milk, took a cautious sip. Immediately the taste of chili pepper warmed her tongue, followed by the bite of dark chocolate and a hint of—she sipped again—vanilla. The barest touch of sweetness rounded out the flavors.

"This is great," she said. "Can I have the recipe? Or is that a trade secret?"

"No, you can't have my recipe." Ricco gave a dismissive shrug. "Not because I don't share, but because I don't know it. I just mix and pour. It's different each time."

"I keep telling him he needs to keep a lab notebook in the kitchen," Tonya sent Ricco a warm smile. "But he's a man; he doesn't listen to me."

"I keep a kitchen notebook," Bree said. "It helps me reproduce my recipes."

"Cat's perfect," Ricco said to Tonya. "She'll make a great addition to the team once she graduates at the end of the semester."

"Paul, Ricco, and I talked it over. We've decided to offer you a permanent lab position with the new company, if you're interested."

"We?"

Ricco nodded. "*Naturalistics* was Paul's concept. But for the new idea, he suggested Tonya and I join the corporation." He covered Tonya's hand with his own and she smiled up at him. The picture of domestic tranquility calmed Bree's nerves.

"Can you cut through the love fest and get me some intel?" Matthew grumbled in her ear.

"Why do you want me?" Bree asked.

"You're a good scientist. We think you could contribute and grow with us. Just look at what Emily's done." Ricco ticked off a dozen accomplishments from Emily's lab work.

"Where is Em, but the way?" And why wasn't she asked to join the new venture?

"She's taking some time off. After the stress of losing so much of her data, she's drained." Tonya shook her head in sympathy. "The poor girl's so stressed, she didn't even remember sending a draft of her thesis to her professor last week. Thank goodness she did it before the lab accident. I think that's the only reason she's not a total basket case."

Satisfaction at convincing Tugood to save at least part of Emily's thesis work filled Bree with a warm glow. The group chatted about Emily for a bit longer until Tugood prodded Bree again.

"Paul already sent me an invitation to join the new company, so why am I here tonight?"

At her question, Tonya left the room.

Ricco stared across the table at Bree. "You're here tonight, because, as I've told you before, chemistry is as much about business as it is about science."

His gaze seemed to look beyond her exterior, trying to penetrate her soul. Sweat beaded on her neck and ran in rivulets down her back as her nervousness returned. She steeled herself to meet his gaze without flinching.

"How much do you know about drug production?" he asked at last.

"No-no-nothing," she stammered. Through her earpiece, she heard Tugood suck in a breath. "Should I?"

"If you're joining us, you'll need to know." Ricco leaned back in his chair.

214

"My mom told me to stay away from drugs," she muttered, hoping Tugood picked up on the reference.

Ricco's body went rigid. His stare, cold where it had once been friendly, turned the sweat on her back to ice. "Is that what you think? That I'm involved in something illegal? I didn't take you for a racist, Cat."

Tonya appeared in the doorway, a sheaf of papers in her hand. "Ricco, you're overreacting."

"Am I?"

"Yes," Tonya snapped. "You play on the tough guy stereotypes when it suits your purpose—like with Hannah—but balk when someone buys into your illusions."

"H-Hannah?" Bree's voice trembled. Had Hannah reacted in a way Ricco feared was racist? Had he killed her for her assumptions? But poison was a crime that took planning. Ricco's anger over an implied slight would have resulted in a crime of passion. Wouldn't it?

"Baiting Hannah was Ricco's favorite pastime. Or at least that's what I think he was doing with her."

"Tonya, we've been over this. I was not sleeping with her. Nor did I want to. I was just yanking her chain." Ricco dragged a hand through his hair and angled his body to shut Bree out as he addressed Tonya. His once threatening tone turned wheedling. "You know I didn't think of her as anything but a pain in the ass."

"She was unpleasant, but a good part of it was her reactions to your prodding."

"She was a bitch from day one. That's why I baited her. Not the other way around." He rolled his eyes and heaved a sigh. "Mom's already dragged me to confession about a dozen times over Hannah. I've done more penance over being thankful someone killed her than if I'd been doing it for killing her myself."

"If I were Catholic, I'd be doing the same." Tonya put her hand over Ricco's. "I feel guilty over being relieved she died."

Bree analyzed the pair as they discussed Hannah's death, trying to match body language to words. Either Tonya and Ricco were great actors or they hadn't killed Hannah.

"I didn't kill her, either," Bree blurted, breaking into the conversation.

"Good to know," said Ricco, turning his attention back to her. "I don't want to be responsible for hiring a murderer. So, back to the topic at hand. Tonya's right. I overreacted. What I intended to ask was, what do you know about pharmaceutical drug manufacturing? From companies like AstraZeneca, Pfizer, and Bayer?"

"Nothing."

"Here's the short version. Development of new pharmaceuticals takes lots of time and money. And clean, reliable production takes even more. That's why the products are so expensive."

"Ricco and I came up with an idea inspired by some of Emily's research." Tonya took up the conversation as she sat. "One of the biggest expenses is the need to do multiple purification steps on pharmaceuticals."

She passed a stack of papers to Bree. "These are the patent applications we made for the new process. Without giving away anything that isn't public knowledge, we've essentially come up with an alternative method of manufacture that doesn't require purification."

Bree scanned the patent document. She assumed the assignee, a company called *Pharmicopia*, was Paul's new business. "What's your process like?"

"We developed a kind of molecular template for the drugs," Ricco explained. "It's a little like the way your body replicates DNA in cells, if you remember your biology. Anyway, when the template is combined with a molecular version of a 3D printer, you get a new manufacturing process."

Tonya passed her another stack of documents. "If you agree to join us, we'll need you to sign confidentiality waivers before we can divulge more about the process. Read over these tonight and we can answer your questions tomorrow."

"I do have one question now," Bree asked, going out on a limb. "Did you ever manufacture drugs other than pharmaceuticals? Maybe by accident?"

"God save me from observant women," Ricco muttered. "You understood more than you let on about Emily's research, didn't you, Cat?"

Bree waited for him to continue instead of answering.

"Her original research proposal centered on making safe training aids for drug dogs. She had some wild ideas about how to do it. Paul helped her turn the idea into a viable research project focusing on chemical separations. He also set up a procedure and a checklist to make sure no active, psychotropic drugs were released."

"But you—I mean Emily—made them?"

Ricco shrugged. "Don't worry. If the Feds come knocking, every last milligram of the product we made—no matter what—was documented and accounted for through *Naturalistics* and Em's university."

Ricco scrubbed his hands across his face and sagged in his chair, shoulders slumped and weary. "I'm almost glad the lab was destroyed. I worried night and day about Emily's research causing problems. We didn't do anything illegal, but that's no protection if someone wants to twist the truth."

He summoned a smile for Bree and gestured to the pile of papers. "For what it's worth, we'd be glad to have you join us after your graduation. Think about it and get back to me, Tonya, or Paul."

Ten minutes later, as she made her way back to Tugood's van, Bree crossed Ricco and Tonya off her list of suspects in Hannah's murder. As the list of those who didn't kill Hannah grew, Bree wondered, whom—if anyone—she should add to the list of those with opportunity and motive.

CHAPTER 27

As it turned out, Bree didn't go to the *Pharmicopia* labs on Tuesday morning. Instead, she called Paul and asked if she could have some time to consider his offer and carefully read the legal documents Tonya and Ricco had given her.

When Paul agreed to wait for her decision, Bree went about her normal routine. Not that anything she did qualified as normal these days. She'd hurried away from Tugood last night as soon as they'd done a quick debriefing on the encounter with Ricco and Tonya. Matthew agreed that they were no longer near the top of the list of suspects in Hannah's murder, although he didn't take them completely off.

He also agreed to dismiss any further investigation of the alleged drug situation and offered to write a report wrapping up their investigation for his client.

Still, after their hasty good-byes last night, Bree wasn't surprised to find a message on her phone summoning her to his office on Tuesday morning.

She was surprised to find Troy sitting in Matthew's office.

Warning bells sounded in her brain. Especially when Matthew shot her a terse look over Troy's head. Part annoyance, part apology, the look also conveyed a message: *keep your cover no matter what I do.* Especially when Matthew pinched the bridge of his nose and shook his head in slow motion in a signal they'd agreed upon long ago.

Bree swallowed and nodded. "You wanted to see me?"

"Actually, Troy has some concerns about how the Special Projects Division is using his resources. I've invited Mr. Townsend to join us."

Matthew moved from behind his desk to a small conference table at the other end of the room. Troy followed. Bree took a seat as well, reviewing the tangled corporate structure in her mind.

No wonder Matthew had a tightness around his mouth and eyes. Aimsley Townsend—Director of Toll and Temporary Projects—was, at least in theory, at the same level in the organization as Matthew. Aimsley, a long-time employee of Dolinski Incorporated—their corporate owners—was also Troy's direct boss.

He wasn't, however, part of the inner circle who knew the Science Professionals for Hire—known as Sci-PHi—was actually a front for the spy work of covert company owners, Matthew Tugood and Gary Dolinski.

For that matter, only Matthew, Bree, and a handful of others including "Shoe" and Nate knew about the covert nature of their business.

Bree's head, brimming with cover stories and alternate identities, pounded at the thought of adding another strand to an already thick web of lies.

By the time Aimsley Townsend joined them, Bree's gut was in knots. If she slipped up today, would it bring down the whole Sci-Spy organization?

After exchanging a few pleasantries with Matthew, Aimsley turned to Troy and asked about his concerns.

"The thing is, I'm worried that Bree is spending too much of her time on 'Special Projects' for Mr. Tugood and not enough on the projects our group is supposed to handle." Troy linked his fingers and rested them on the table, but Bree could see his knuckles were white with tension.

She felt no sympathy for him, especially after the way he'd made Special Projects sound like something dirty. He'd called this meeting, now he would have to deal with the consequences.

"Are some of your projects falling behind?" Aimsley asked Troy. "Are you understaffed? From your reports, I wasn't aware of any issues. Clearly, if you're having trouble meeting all the project obligations, we need to address it."

"It's not that," Troy's voice faltered a bit. "But with Bree being off-site so much, it sets a bad example. Not everyone who works off-site actually works, if you get my meaning."

Aimsley glanced at Matthew. "Are you satisfied with the work Bree is doing for your Special Projects customers?"

"Bree is doing an amazing job with the special projects. My only concern is that she's being spread a bit thin due to her obligations to your division."

Aimsley nodded. "That is an unfortunate issue. If your Special Projects Division justified having a permanent staff, I'd recommend Bree transfer. But as things stand, we have to continue to share her time."

"Share? She spends almost all of her time with his projects." Troy glared at Matthew. "It makes me wonder what's really going on with these two."

Before Matthew could respond, Aimsley took control of the conversation. "I'm sure you're aware," he said to Troy, "that the decision to make Special Projects work the highest priority comes from the CEO himself." He paused and in the pause, Troy paled. "If you wish to challenge that decision, we'll have to raise it to Mr. Dolinski."

"It's not just the way her time is allocated," Troy muttered. "It's her." He pointed an accusing finger at Bree, bringing her fully into the conversation for the first time. "She resents me. She thinks she should run the department because she has a PhD. She can't handle that I was promoted over her."

"That is not true." Bree straightened and looked Troy in the eye, pleased to see the widening of his pupils that indicated fear. "I fully supported your appointment. The last thing I want to do is run your department."

"The last thing you have time to do," interjected Matthew, "is run a department. Frankly, it would be a waste of your skills."

"He's in on it, too." Troy turned his accusations on Matthew. "He wants to monopolize her time for his own reasons."

"For my own, *project-related*, reasons."

In the steamy silence, Troy and Matthew glared at one another. Bree could hear the seconds tick by on someone's—maybe Aimsley's—watch. She turned her gaze to his wrist, mesmerized by the slow tick of the second hand. Fifteen seconds. Twenty. Twenty-five—

"Enough." Aimsley broke the staring match between the other two men. "We all need to calm down. Some deep concerns have been aired. Now, that they're in the open, we can move forward."

The calmness in his voice soothed over some of the tensions. "Our CEO's directive makes it clear where Bree's project priorities lie. As for the rest, I'm sure we can sort through the issues. Troy, why don't you and I chat a bit more and discuss some strategies? Bree, I'll meet with you later and do the same."

Bree watched Aimsley and Troy leave the office, taking much of the tension with them.

"Do you still think he was the best candidate for the manager's job?" Matthew's tone was light and his eyes glinted in what would have looked—on anyone else—like a twinkle.

"Actually, I still do. Although, how I'm going to deal with his insecurities is a mystery to me."

Matthew simply closed the outer door and headed to the hidden elevator leading to the Tech-Ops Center. "He's trouble. But we have other issues. I got some new hits on my fingerprint analyses and background checks."

"From the bar? Or from the *Naturalistics* labs?"

"The bar." He gestured for her to enter the elevator. "And I need you to help me understand if any of it makes sense."

"Mrs. Tinsdale was arrested for what?" Bree couldn't believe the dossier Matthew had given her. "Are you sure?"

Matthew clucked his tongue and shook his head as he regarded her. "How did you get through graduate school and remain such an innocent, Bree? For that matter, how did you get through the last four months and keep your rose-colored glasses intact? You've embroiled yourself in two murders as well as some undercover missions and you still manage to be shocked when people do bad things."

"But—prostitution? Liz seems like such a nice, motherly woman."

"Nice people can do all sorts of not-so-nice things if pushed. Elizabeth Silverton—that was her name then—was the first of her family to go to college. She worked multiple jobs trying to make ends meet. Can you blame her for taking a single, high-paying job instead?"

"That's how you look at it? She sold her body for money."

"Rented, actually." Matthew shrugged. "Sex is the ultimate in bartering chips. Women trade it for money, status, marriage and that feeling they call love. Men trade it for bragging rights, bolstering sagging self-confidence and the high of conquering a challenge."

"Still, I don't—"

"Spies trade it for information."

Bree squirmed at the coldness in his eyes and the set of his mouth as he inspected her. Was that why he could kiss her and remain cold and aloof? He'd traded sex for information—and all those other things he listed—for so many years he no longer felt anything?

She turned away from him and pretended to read the background information in front of her, but her heart wasn't in it.

After a few futile minutes, a warm hand settled on her shoulder. "Not always," Matthew said quietly.

"Not always, what?"

"Sex isn't always about information. Or bartering. Or even scratching an itch. Sometimes it's about more." She met his gaze. His eyes, no longer cold, ice-gray, reflected an inner turmoil. "Or so I've been told."

"It should be about more."

"In any case," he replied, his voice brisk, "it wasn't for Liz. Her defense attorney did some fancy deal making and sealed the documents for her prostitution charge. Officially, that is."

"And you have unofficial ways of reopening those documents."

He nodded. "I'll summarize the rest of the background check for you. After college, Liz returned home to care for her parents. Poor health and poorer living conditions took a toll on them and they died early. Liz returned to university life when she took a job as a sorority house mom. It's a kind of chaperone and—"

"I know what it is. I was in a sorority."

"Then you know the house mom is supposed to live an impeccable life. Or at least a gracious one. She's not supposed to become a Madam, pimping out the sorority sisters."

"Liz? Tinsdale?" Just when Bree thought she couldn't be more shocked, Matthew—or Liz—managed to shock her.

"It doesn't make her a murderer, but it does make me want to do a deeper investigation."

Bree dragged her attention back to the printouts and flipped through them. One name stood out. "It says she was employed by the Kappa Zeta Rho sorority. At Northwestern University. Can you tell me the dates she worked there?"

Bree flipped through the pages, scanning for dates while Matthew punched a few parameters into a search engine on the Tech-Ops computer. He found the dates first.

"Okay, cross reference the dates with the years Hannah went to Northwestern. Kappa Z was Hannah's sorority."

"And you know this, how?"

"The sorority alumni directory. And a Kappa Z sister."

"Maybe I should check your background for skeletons in the closet. Between house mom turning Madam and allegations of pranks involving theft, these sorority girls seem to have a lot of dirt."

"Not funny, Tugood. Besides, I didn't go to Northwestern. From everything I've learned, that chapter of Kappa Z is lucky they weren't barred from the Panhellenic society for all the infractions they committed."

Matthew swiveled in his chair, ignoring the computer screen in favor of giving Bree another unnerving once-over. "So, if I researched you, I wouldn't find prostitution charges? Or petty theft? What about academic probation? Did your straight-A record ever slip?"

"*If* you researched me?" Bree snorted. "We both know you did—or you wouldn't have trusted me to become part of your operation."

"So, no dark secrets for me to ferret out?"

Bree raised her hands, palm up and shrugged. "If you haven't found them by now…"

"A challenge." The corner of his mouth lifted in a half-smile. "I do love a challenge."

A ding on the computer saved Bree from answering.

"Bingo," Matthew said. "Turns out Liz was working as house mom until the end of Hannah's senior year. Later that same year, Liz married Edward Tinsdale. He'd been widowed. Liz adopted his young daughter and spent the next twenty or so years living life as the perfect wife and mother. As far as we know."

"Run Hannah's financial records," Bree said, moving to peer over Matthew's shoulder at the screen. "If money was tight for Hannah when she was in college—"

"—and Liz offered her a job—"

They looked at one another. "Motive," they said in unison.

After hashing out various scenarios involving Hannah, Liz, blackmail and murder, they'd agreed that Detective O'Neil needed to be in the loop. Bree had arranged for the three of them to meet at the Sci-Spy RV, which served as a kind of neutral territory for the ad-hoc team. She glanced at her office clock. Just over three hours until the meeting.

Instead of staying in her cubicle, Bree headed home, hoping to clear her thoughts. Troy glared at her as she passed him in the hall, briefcase in hand.

"Cutting out for another *special project*? Or for something else?"

"I'm on assignment. Ask Matthew Tugood if you need confirmation."

"Who am I to question the almighty Director of Special Projects? One day he'll overstep his bounds then all hell will break loose. You'd better watch yourself, Bree." His lips pursed as if the words were bitter.

In a moment of pity, Bree wondered if she should ask Norah to cook up a confidence spell for him. Or given the whipped puppy look he was currently wearing, maybe she should pick up a treat for him from the *Barkery* instead. She bit back a laugh and earned another glare.

Okay. Neither the confidence spell nor the *Barkery* treat. Bree settled for a good-bye and hustled out the door, annoyance quickening her steps.

Starting the day with Troy griping to upper management about her and ending it with Tugood and O'Neil sniping at each other—which they would—grated on her nerves.

A glimmer of cheer lightened the day when she picked up her mail and saw a letter from her grandmother. Filled with tiny, curving script, the letter carried information about her cousins in Chattanooga, her Aunt Lucy—whose recent trip to Nairobi was the talk of the block—and as Bree expected, advice on how she could find a man and settle down.

Included in the advice was a recipe for her grandmother's macaroni salad. Bree scanned the ingredients. Between the pasta, meat, cheese, veggies, egg, and sweet dressing, she couldn't decide if it was a side dish, a main dish, or a dessert. But no matter what, the handwritten card deserved a place of honor in her antique recipe box.

Her grandmother's advice about sweetening up a man by feeding him might not be as quaintly old-fashioned as she'd thought. Maybe if she took food to the meeting between Matthew and James, she could bring some harmony as well. Or at least, mute their arguing while they chewed.

She sorted through her recipe box, searching for instructions to make her grandmother's oatmeal cookies. As soon as she located the card, she transferred the basic recipe to her kitchen notebook and began thinking of ways to modify it.

Oatmeal. Brown sugar. Flour. Shortening. Raisins. She checked off the ingredients and lined them up on her counter. On a whim, she grabbed a packet of mixed dried fruit and one of dried cranberries. She'd use them to supplement the raisins for a different taste.

After pulling together the batter and tasting the mix, she added a bit of walnut and orange extracts and a pinch of salt until satisfied with the taste. Soon the kitchen smelled of baking cookies. If that didn't sweeten the male tempers, she didn't know what would.

Sherlock ambled into the room and plopped down by the oven, giving a pitiful meow. He swished his tail as he looked at the dishes stacked in the sink, as if to say, "All that mess and no food for me?"

"I came home early today, you big baby," Bree said as she squatted to pet him. "It's not even your dinner time yet, so don't think you can fool me."

Another meow was the only reply.

"At least wait until I change out of my work clothes." She looked down at her slacks and flour-covered dress shirt. "If I hadn't been so distracted by those men, I would have done it earlier."

She changed into jeans and a pullover while the first batch of cookies baked. While the second batch baked, she reluctantly filled a bag with a "costume change" consisting of the clothing, makeup, and hair accessories she wore in her Cat Holmes persona. She had a sneaking feeling she and Tugood would have to stake out the bar again tonight.

Bree hated these pseudo-dates with Matthew. Her logic insisted they were just a cover, not the real thing. Yet her emotions disagreed. If she never spent time with him outside of their cover identities or work, how would she ever get to know the real Matthew?

The image of James with his easy smile and lighthearted charm hovered in her mind alongside the image of dark, enigmatic Matthew. Could she date one and maintain a friendship with the other?

As always, the thought of having to choose between them made her scramble for an alternative. Today the alternative was to keep a professional friendship with both.

Or neither—depending on how they acted when they met this afternoon. The oven timer sounded again. With luck, Bree thought, Grandma's cookies would work their magic and she could avoid choosing for another day.

CHAPTER 28

"How many times do I have to remind you that you're not a special agent with government backing anymore," James grumbled as he looked over the reports Matthew handed him. "Unsealing records could be construed as a criminal act."

"Construe all you want, Boy Scout, but this change gives Liz Tinsdale a motive for murder." Matthew shoved a cookie in his mouth and chewed. After a minute, he continued, his tone somewhat less abrasive. "If Hannah was blackmailing Liz Tinsdale, that could be the evidence we need to question her."

"Only if it's obtained legally. That's the problem with your brand of research." James sighed and grabbed his second cookie. With each bite, the men seemed to be getting along better. Bree silently thanked her grandmother for the advice.

"But it's worth checking out. I can comb through the blackmail data again and try to trace some financial records to connect Liz and Hannah. Assuming they exist." James glanced at Bree, then Matthew. "Is there any way the two of you could get Liz to open up? Maybe incriminate herself?"

Matthew threw out possibilities and James countered with others. Bree, meanwhile, tried to remember anything that could have bearing on the case. While the men ate and planned, she reviewed her notes from the past weeks. Someone had said something that could help, she was sure of it. She just couldn't sort through the jumble of information in her head to pull out the relevant data.

She flipped back to the day she'd met Hannah and replayed the scene at the bar in her head, occasionally referring to her notes. Hannah had irritated everyone until... until Miranda had arrived with drinks. All the talk had centered on work, not her college days. Except...

Bree sighed in frustration. She hated not being able to find a meaningful pattern. Chemistry was so much easier than dealing with people. She gave in to temptation and grabbed a cookie for herself. Maybe a burst of sugar would clear her muddled brain.

The cookie flavor—complex, chewy, and not overly sweet, was one of her better recipe modifications. Bree took another nibble, focusing on the individual flavor components to deconstruct her recipe. The slight acidity of the orange flavoring brightened an otherwise heavy cookie. Good choice. Orange would...

Orange. The night she'd been at the bar with Hannah, they'd met the mixologist, Jen, and tasted her Tangerine Tango cocktails. Jen and Hannah had discovered they'd taken the same science class at Northwestern. Bree scanned her notes from that night. Hannah had also talked about fraternity parties and learning to drink high quality alcohol. Had the lesson occurred because she switched from dating fraternity boys to being a paid escort?

"I have an idea." Both men looked up at Bree's announcement. "Let's not talk to Liz first. I want to get a better feel for what Hannah was like at school." She outlined the possible connection between Hannah and Jen.

"It's a long shot," said Matthew.

"But not impossible."

"Didn't one of you say the sorority had been in trouble for something?" James pulled out a small notebook and scribbled in it. "I could try to get them to share historical data with me. If I go in person, I might be able to charm someone into sharing information without having to get a subpoena or search warrant."

"Careful, Boy Scout, or you'll be operating in my territory." Tugood flashed a cocky grin and the next thing Bree knew, James and Matthew were planning an intelligence gathering mission like they were old army buddies.

Bree sighed, knowing it was just as well they'd stopped paying attention to her. She picked up the gym bag and headed to the back of the RV.

Time to transform into "Undercover Cat" as she was beginning to think of her disguise. She had one more mission to run before the night was over.

"Hi, Jen." Bree slipped onto a stool and looked around the quiet bar. "Not busy yet, huh?"

Jen smiled at her, friendly as always. Thank goodness she hadn't recognized and connected Cat Holmes with the woman she'd seen with James at brunch. "It usually picks up in an hour or so. I was just playing with some new drink recipes to share with Mrs. Tinsdale tomorrow, but it can wait. What can I get for you tonight?"

"I, um," Bree hesitated. A plan popped into her mind and she improvised. "I was wondering if you could show me how to mix a few more drinks. I volunteered to tend bar at a sorority function, but I don't know as much as I should."

Jen's gaze darted to the door and back. "Sure. I have a few minutes. Which sorority are you in again?"

Bree told her.

"I never joined a sorority myself."

"Too busy studying?" Bree asked as she slipped behind the bar and donned the apron Jen offered. "I really wish I could have had some science classes like the ones you told me about. What was the one where Hannah got sick?"

A frown crossed Jen's face as she pondered the question. "I think we were talking about the *Physics of Amusement Parks* class and Hannah getting sick on a ride. I don't remember the rides being especially bad—unless maybe she was drunk."

"She did mention learning not to drink cheap alcohol. But seriously, what other kind can we afford? I mean, in college, right? Once you get a job or a rich boyfriend, maybe."

"Speaking of boyfriends, did I win the car?"

Damn. Jen kept navigating away from the subject of Hannah. But it did remind her that Matthew hadn't been able to get a clear print off the wet card Jen had given him. Bree pulled another card from a case in her purse, careful to handle it only by the edges. "Why don't you fill out another one? I'll slip it into the drawing and you'll get two chances. It's the least I can do to thank you for your help."

Once Bree had secured the card, Jen gave her a tutorial on martini making. "Is there really a difference between shaken and not stirred?" Bree asked.

"If you use a potato-based vodka," Jen said, starting to shake her martini, "shaking is better for dispersing the potato oils—which can ruin taste. If you use a grain-based vodka—Oh, crap." Jen abruptly stopped the shaking as her charm bracelet caught in a strand of her hair.

"Wait. Don't pull. I can untangle it." Bree grabbed the hair and began to gently untangle the charm. She bit her lip to hid her surprise when she saw the offending charm was a Kappa Zeta Rho lavaliere. Did Jen lie about not being in the sorority? Or had the charm belonged to her mother?

"There. I've got it. You almost lost the Eiffel Tower," she said naming another charm on the bracelet. "Or a hank of hair."

"Thanks. Why don't you try your hand at shaking the cocktail while I tie my hair back?" She handed Bree the shaker and fished in her pocket for an elastic band. "In any case, shaking a martini is more about show than taste these days."

"Anything that makes the drink taste better will help. My sorority chapter is small and can't afford pricey alcohol." She put the shaker down, feeling the burn in her arms from the unfamiliar move. "So, why didn't you join a sorority? I hear the chapters at Northwestern are great."

Jen turned away and sprayed the counter with a solution that caused Bree's nose to sting. She wiped it clean and moved on to washing up the barware. When she finally answered, her voice was nearly drowned out by the sound of rushing water.

"They may be good today, but when I visited, they were a bastion for bullies. Can you imagine people calling a poor girl *Her Royal Horkness* and *Barfy Betsy* because a senior sister threw up on her?" Jen shut off the water and shook her head as she dried her hands. "What Hannah described was cruel. I hope your house isn't like that."

"I wouldn't be a member if it was. They'd laugh a science geek like me right out of the house."

"Unless they wanted to use you for free tutoring."

The comment struck a nerve. Bree had had her share of friendships that were just as Jen described. "I don't think I could handle being ridiculed like Hannah's poor sorority sister."

Jen compressed her lips into a tight line and Bree steeled herself. Her mother wore the same look before delivering unwanted news. "Life isn't easy, Cat. Only the strong survive. There will always be bullies. You can't change them, but you can choose how you will react. Crumble, fight back, or simply walk away—the choice is always yours." She softened the words with a smile. "Now, I've shared enough drink mixing and life lessons for today."

A sense of failure nagged Bree as she stared at Jen's retreating back. Her search for information on Liz Tinsdale's past connections to Hannah had turned up empty. But at least she knew how to mix a good martini.

One failure followed another. Bree dragged herself to bed after her undercover "date" with Tugood, exhausted. At least Sherlock was so glad to see her home that he forgot to be miffed. He curled next to her and promptly went to sleep.

When she reached her office the next morning, she'd put yesterday in perspective. Not all experiments yielded good data, she reasoned as she poured herself a cup of coffee. And sometimes, even with seemingly poor data, a deeper look could lead to significant discoveries.

"Look who's here for the third day in a row," said Kiki from behind her. "I was starting to think we'd never see each other."

"Technically we could have had coffee together on Monday if you hadn't been sick." As far as Bree could tell, Kiki was still a bit pale but otherwise doing okay. "Are you feeling better?"

"Much. The bug kicked my butt, but I'm finally getting over it." Kiki reached for a tea bag and filled her cup with hot water. "I'm still not sure about corporate coffee, though. It could send me into a relapse. What about you? Is the energy project finished?"

Kiki sat and Bree joined her. Not long ago, relaxing in the corporate kitchen could have earned them a black mark from their vindictive boss. Now that the company had been acquired by Dolinski Incorporated and turned into a technical think tank and temporary staffing agency, the oppressive atmosphere had mellowed. Even Troy's overbearing nature was little more than an annoyance most days.

The not-so-pleasant odor of burned garlic—tainted with something slightly fishy—tickled Bree's nose. She looked up to see Troy entering the kitchen, a frown etched on his face. "Forget the open-door policy," he grumbled. "I need a lock. Norah keeps filling my drawers with her damn bags of stinky crap. Someone needs to tell her we run a science based company, not a voodoo shop."

He leaned against the counter and stretched his legs out in front of him, clearly not in a hurry to leave. Across the table from Bree, Kiki turned slightly green.

"Was there something you needed, Troy?" Bree hoped he'd come out with his request and leave before Kiki's stomach rebelled.

"Yeah. I needed to tell you that your *Special Projects* supervisor is looking for you. Apparently, I'm his errand boy now, too. If he keeps you working off-site any more, maybe I can convince Norah to put her charms in your office instead of mine." He gave her a curt nod then straightened and left as abruptly as he'd come.

One look at Kiki and Bree made an executive decision. "You're still not well. Go home. There's nothing you can do here. I'll let Norah know you're out for the rest of the day. Or the rest of the week if you need."

When her friend didn't argue, Bree knew she'd made the right choice. After Kiki left, Bree drained her coffee and headed back to her desk.

The blinking message light on her phone indicated messages—three of which were from Tugood. A check of her mobile phone showed more of the same. Just as she was lifting the receiver to call, he slipped into her office.

"You okay?"

"Of course, I am. I just—"

"You didn't return my messages. I had to call that," he glanced over his shoulder, "idiot, Troy, to see if you were here."

"What, no hidden locator bugs on my clothing to alert you to my every move? You're slipping, boss."

Matthew rounded the corner and dropped into a chair in her office. "I deserved that. You don't have to tell me everything. But I was worried. You weren't yourself last night."

"I'm just tired. This case seems never-ending."

"We caught a break. Your detective O'Neil asked Liz Tinsdale to come in and clear some things up for him. She agreed. He wants us at the police station in an hour so we can observe."

"I only have an hour to transform into Cat?"

He shook his head. "No, we'll watch through the one-way mirror. O'Neil wants extra eyes and ears. Can you be ready in twenty minutes? I'll drive."

Half an hour later, they arrived at the police station. James ushered them into the observation side of the inter-rogation room. At the sight of the room, Bree's skin tingled. A vision of the night she'd sat in the interrogation chamber laughing and dining with James flashed through her mind. It seemed a lifetime ago.

James must have remembered too. He tugged at his collar and a dull red colored his neck. But he remained professional. "I'll bring Mrs. Tinsdale inside in a minute. You two stay put. If you want to talk to me, send a text. I'll have my phone on vibrate. Ready?"

Once Mrs. Tinsdale and James were in the interrogation room, he greeted her pleasantly.

"I supposed you asked me here because you know," she said.

"Know what?"

Mrs. Tinsdale folded her hands and placed them on the table. Her erect posture and prim bearing looked exactly like what Bree expected from a sorority house mom, not an ex-prostitute-turned-Madam.

"You know Hannah Rogers and I had words the week she died. And you wonder if I killed her." She glared at James, daring him to disagree.

"Have you come here to confess?" James's tone was mild, his manner calm.

"I didn't kill that woman. I simply asked her to leave my daughter alone. She was a bad influence."

James sat, taking notes, until Liz spoke again. "My husband gave that woman her first job. He mentored her, grooming her to take his place when he was gone. She never appreciated him. Not really.

"Yes, she brokered him a good retirement deal, but that's it. Since we opened the bar, she's used it for her own private networking and blackmail center. She's benefited from their association far more than he has."

Silence again. Mrs. Tinsdale clamped her mouth shut and stared at the wall. Finally, James posed a soft question. "Was Hannah blackmailing you, Mrs. Tinsdale?"

"Me? If you call a private-label fancy tequila a blackmail payoff, then yes. She was too cheap to even buy her own drinks."

"Nothing else?"

Mrs. Tinsdale's eyes skittered from James to the corner of the room and back. Her fingers came unlaced and she slid them into her lap. One eye twitched. As she fidgeted, James watched her, pen dangling from loose fingers. Eventually, he spoke again.

"Was she blackmailing you about something from your past?"

"I don't know what you mean." One hand fluttered, as if batting away a fly—or an inconvenient truth. "I'm a devoted wife. A mother. An upstanding citizen."

"A former house mother?"

Liz sagged against the metal chair. "Yes. I worked at the Kappa Zeta Rho sorority house when Hannah was there. I met Edward when he came to a sorority sponsored career day. That's all."

"Not quite." James leaned forward, invading the woman's space. His voice had chilled and Bree knew—even though his back was to the observation window—that he was giving Liz an unnerving stare. "While you were at the sorority, you also headed up a very different kind of house, didn't you? A house of prostitution."

A sharp intake of breath crackled through the speakers. Even through the one-way glass and bad lighting, Bree could see Liz's skin turn ash gray.

"How did you learn of that?" Her voice trembled. "I left it all behind when I married Edward."

"Does he know? Was Hannah threatening to tell him? Did Hannah work for you?"

"No, Hannah wasn't threatening me. She worked for the escort service and pocketed a good wage for her time. And it was an escort service. Women were paid for their time—on dates—not in bed."

James leaned back in his seat, uncurling his tense posture. Warmth returned to his voice when he spoke. "Mrs. Tinsdale, your past doesn't matter to me. Northwestern University is out of my jurisdiction and this all happened a long time ago. What I want—need—is honesty. If you have any information about Hannah that could help us find who murdered her, please, tell me now."

Silence descended on the interrogation room. Liz fingered her handbag, opening and closing the clasp on it, staring into space. Finally, she spoke. "The trouble with blackmail, Detective O'Neil, is that it only works if a person has secrets to keep. Edward knew about my past. Knew and accepted me. Forgave me, even. He and I have no secrets."

"But your daughter didn't know."

"I hope you'll keep it that way. When I met with Hannah, I made it clear to her that I held as many secrets about her as she did about me. She and I reached an understanding." Liz closed the handbag with a snap and stood.

"In return for her silence, I promised Hannah not to expose evidence of her academic misconduct and the cover up she engineered to hide it."

"Cheating on exams? I don't see how that would damage her after so many years."

"Trust me. Once a cheat, always a cheat. Hannah didn't move up the corporate ladder for her business skills. My husband saved her from a number of indiscreet actions. We all knew my allegations could jeopardize the patent acquisitions, mergers, and other deals she brokered for her employer."

"One last question, if you will, Mrs. Tinsdale." James paused. "Did you kill Hannah Rogers?"

The thin smile Liz sent him chilled Bree to the bone. "Why would I kill her when ruining her would have been so much more satisfying?"

CHAPTER 29

"How about pizza and a movie later tonight?" Bree shifted in her seat to get a better view of Matthew's face as he drove her from the station to her car.

"Is this another training session?"

He threw her a baleful glance. "No. I'm hurt that you think everything is about work."

"That's because everything is about work with you. Name one time when it wasn't."

"Easy. There was the time when—" His brow crinkled in thought. "Okay, not then, but how about—" He clenched his jaw. "Not then, either, but remember when we—" He sighed. "Oh, damn. Maybe you are right. But it's different this time. I promise."

Which was exactly why she should say no. So why did the word yes pop out of her mouth instead? When a grin split Matthew's face, she couldn't regret her decision.

"Great." He shot her a mischievous look. "You want to pick the pizza or the movie?"

"I thought we were doing both."

"It's a game. As kids, Mom let one of us pick the snacks and the other the video on movie night. That way everyone won and no one monopolized the evening."

He hadn't been an only child. It was the first personal thing she'd learned about Matthew. Bree bit her tongue to keep from asking questions, not wanting to alert him to his slip. "I'll pick pepperoni, extra cheese and bacon," she said lightly.

"Thick or thin crust?"

"Thin. New York style."

"A girl after my own heart. Looks like I win on both counts. Great pizza and my choice of movie. I'll be by at eight." He pulled next to her car in the company parking lot and glanced at his watch. "Knock off for the rest of the day. You've been working almost nonstop. It isn't good for you."

"I should put in some face time to appease Troy. It isn't even noon yet."

"Watson," a stern note entered his voice, "for once, just follow orders. Go home. Relax."

"Yes, sir!" She snapped to attention—or at least as much as she could while still belted into the car.

For the second time in an hour, Matthew smiled.

Bree considered visiting the *Barkery* to visit with Rookie and the Clarks or spending the day shopping along the pedestrian mall located on her street.

But nagging questions about Liz Tinsdale wouldn't leave her alone. On impulse, she picked up the phone and invited her sorority sister, Lindsay Morgan, to stop by for afternoon tea. Lindsay's sorority days had overlapped with Liz's tenure.

To make the impromptu tea seem special, Bree pulled out an easy lemon bar recipe. A quick check of the fridge showed she had limes, but not lemons.

"One citrus fruit is as good as another," Bree mused as she opened her kitchen notebook and started a page for

Lime Spritz Bars. She pulled together a basic flour and butter crust and popped it into the oven. While it baked, she whipped eggs, sugar, flour, and a drop of green food coloring to form a light filling. Once she'd baked the filling into the crust, she sprinkled a mixture of grated lime zest and sweetened coconut flakes over the top.

While the treats cooled, Bree searched her crime notebook, focusing on the people, events, and conversations associated with the bar. But even reviewing them in light of Mrs. Tinsdale's secret didn't give her the new insights she'd hoped for. Maybe Matthew was right. Her brain was too tired to see the connections between events.

Good thing she'd taken his advice—sort of.

When the doorbell rang, Sherlock scooted past Bree's ankles and disappeared to parts unknown. Coward.

After showing Lindsay around the condo, Bree placed a tray filled with tea and treats on the coffee table and the two settled into comfy chairs for a chat.

"This looks lovely," Lindsay said as she reached for a lime bar. "And tastes yummy, too. Are you ready to start that bakery?"

"Not yet." Bree poured herself a cup of tea. "This reminds me of my college days. Did your Kappa Z house ever host afternoon teas?"

"When I first joined, they did." A wistful smile crossed Lindsay's face. "I remember dressing up for tea and dinner a lot that first year. Then things changed. The year I graduated, they were more likely to host a pot-brownie bash than high tea."

"You said they were a rowdy bunch. My house mom would have pitched a fit if we didn't behave like ladies." Bree watched Lindsay's reactions as she took up the topic of house moms. A shadow crossed her face and her wistful smile became a frown.

"My first house mom was great. But her successor had favorites who could get away with anything. I wasn't one of them." She reached for another lime bar. "Actually, that's not quite true. No one said it out loud, but we all thought she separated us into either the 'brains' or the 'beauty' categories."

"What about women who had both?" Bree asked, miffed that the world still believed pretty woman couldn't be smart and vice-versa.

"They pledged to different sororities." Lindsay's laugh sounded forced. "After all, who wants to spend their free time tutoring sisters without getting anything in return? Someone needed to teach those so-called beauties how to say thank you."

"It's a wonder you're still active, given how awful it sounds."

Lindsay offered a smile. "It wasn't all bad. I made some life-long friends and learned valuable skills. It just irritates me when I think about how the manipulative sisters got away with murder."

A chill raced down Bree's spine and she shivered at the innocent expression. A sister had been murdered. Another...

"Of course, the worst was a story I've already told you." Lindsay's cup clinked as she set it in the saucer and poured herself more tea. "I was so glad I wasn't in the house the semester they pulled the bracelet stunt."

"You mean the pretend theft?"

Lindsay nodded.

"I was talking to some other sisters recently," Bree said, playing a hunch. "They mentioned something similar that took place years later. A sister was nearly accused of stealing a car."

"Good heavens. I'd love to see a prosecutor look into those allegations. The sorority shouldn't be besmirched by the acts of a few self-centered—" Lindsay grimaced "—bitches." She spat the word without apology. She pulled out a notebook and scribbled something down. "Pranks like that condition people to go on to lives of crime. It's the opposite of everything the Panhellenic council stands for."

"For what it's worth, I agree."

"Do you remember where you heard it?"

Bree shook her head. "Sorry, but I don't."

"If you remember anything later, let me know. Meanwhile, I'm going to get in touch with one of my lawyer friends to follow up and see if anything can be done to assure these pranks never happen again."

They chatted a bit longer, moving on to general topics until Bree looked at her watch. With a start, she realized it was nearly five. Time to get ready to meet Tugood.

"I hate to cut our afternoon short, but," Bree leaned close, "I have a date tonight."

"You can't drop a bomb like that on me and expect me to just scoot out the door, sister. Who is he? Where are you going? And what are you wearing?"

For the next hour, they giggled like college girls again, as Bree fielded dozens of questions and found herself being drawn in to the real world, away from spies, murders, and the mess her life had become.

It was nearly seven-fifteen when Bree jumped from the shower and pulled on skinny jeans and a flirty top. She glanced in the mirror, satisfied with her hair, makeup, and general appearance.

On a whim, she clasped Norah's amulet around her neck. A little mojo—especially the spicy kind—wouldn't hurt tonight. Besides, she could sprinkle it on the pizza, if necessary.

Excitement pinked her cheeks and made her eyes sparkle.

If Tugood wanted a date instead of a working evening, that's exactly what he was going to get.

When Lindsay had learned Bree's date was with a coworker, she'd peppered her with advice on managing office relationships. Then she'd demanded details. Bree had given her the edited version of the steamy kisses she'd shared with Matthew in the alley behind the bar the night she'd nearly been burned.

Although, to be honest, she had been burned—by the kisses if not in the sense of having her cover blown. She'd been blown away, too. By the kisses.

Bree's face warmed at the memories. If she didn't get her thoughts off that night, she might attack Matthew the minute he came to the door.

She didn't need a repeat of the hot and heavy make out session by the dumpster. Amid discarded liquor bottles and cleaning supplies.

Including empty bottles of rubbing alcohol. Isopropanol. The alcohol that poisoned Hannah.

Bree grabbed her crime notebook and turned to the sections relating to Mrs. Tinsdale, no longer sure that she didn't murder Hannah.

The manipulative sisters got away with murder. Lindsay's words—and the chill that had accompanied them came back in full force. A sister...

Bree's pulse raced as a thought crystallized in her mind. All along, she'd assumed Hannah had been killed for some recent action or blackmail scheme she'd started. But what if she was killed for something else? Bree flipped the pages, searching for clues, testing her hypothesis.

If she was right, someone else was in danger.

She looked at the clock. Seven-thirty. Matthew would be here in half an hour. She dialed his number. When it went to voice mail, she left a terse message.

"Change of plans. Meet me at the bar. Undercover. With Detective O'Neil."

She quickly layered a Cat Holmes-style peasant top over her shirt, grabbed a hair band, and scooted out the door, forming a plan as she went.

One critical piece of information stood between her and the identity of the killer.

And only Cat Holmes could ferret out the truth.

Chapter 30

"Shit!" Matthew cut off Bree's message and stared at the printout in his hands. He jammed his Bluetooth headset into his ear and dialed the police department, then raced to the back room of the RV while waiting for his call to connect.

He checked his weapons. A revolver in the ankle holster. A Sig semi-automatic in the shoulder holster. A backup knife in his pocket, just in case. He slid his arms into a leather jacket to hide the shoulder holster. If his suspicions were right, Bree was walking into a death trap.

The minute O'Neil picked up, Matthew briefed him while racing for his car. The PD was farther from the bar than the RV, but Matthew needed official backup. With Bree's life at stake, he'd work with the devil himself—or in this case with Boy Scout Detective O'Neil.

Matthew cut off the call and spun out of the parking lot, spewing gravel and burning rubber.

He gave the voice command to call Bree. When she didn't pick up, he floored the car, not caring that he'd run a red light and caused a near collision in his wake.

He had to get to her before her questions led to her own death.

❧   ❧   ❧

Bree's hands shook as she locked her car and headed to the bar. Adrenaline? Fear? She wasn't sure. She wound her way through the lot, skirting cars haphazardly parked on the gravel. Whatever was going on tonight packed the house. Or was this the usual Wednesday night crowd?

At the door to the bar, Bree hesitated. When a group pushed ahead of her, she ducked behind them and entered. A tall, broad man clad in a leather jacket and sporting an earring gave her adequate cover. Peeking from behind him into the bar, Bree could see the Tinsdales—including Miranda. Jen worked the bar along with a host of other bartenders.

Satisfied everyone was safe for the moment, Bree slipped back outside. She was halfway back to her car when a vehicle slid into the lot, fishtailing on the gravel as it jerked to a stop. Matthew jumped out and raced to the bar.

Bree moved to intercept him and they nearly collided. At the last minute, Matthew pivoted, grabbing Bree in a bear hug as he did.

"What have I told you about waiting for backup?" The rough words washed over her, one part censure and one part relief. "Never, ever," he paused and tightened his grip on her, "EVER, go into a situation without backup. Understand?"

"I'm fine, Matthew. I was waiting for you." Bree slid her hands beneath his leather jacket and around his ribs, then stopped short when she reached a barrier. "Are you armed?"

A hint of humor crept into his voice. "I could say I'm just happy to see you. But I don't think the joke works well with a shoulder holster."

"That's lame, Tugood."

"Why didn't you answer your phone?" He released her and scanned her face, as if memorizing her features. "I thought you'd rushed ahead and gotten into trouble. I thought I'd lost you."

Bree stared at him, stunned. What happened to Matthew Tugood, super spy? The panicked person in front of her almost looked like a man who cared about something more than a mission.

"Don't worry," she quipped, trying to lighten the mood. "I'm not so highly trained that I'd be difficult to replace."

He gripped her shoulders, fingers tightening as if desperate to imprint himself on her. "You're irreplaceable. Got it? Irreplaceable. Not because of this mission. Not because you're a damn fine operative in training. Because you're you. You."

His voice shook with uncharacteristic emotion. Bree's reply froze in her throat and she simply nodded. "Got it," she managed after a few tension-laden seconds.

"Good."

The beam of a flashlight, barely noticeable in the dusk except for the way it shone in her eyes, cut the rest of his words off. James O'Neil switched the light off and stepped close. "Unhand her, Tugood."

Matthew dropped his arms to his side. "About time you got here, Detective. We need a plan before she goes in to that bar."

Ten minutes later, Bree slipped onto a stool at the end of the polished bar and ordered a Diet Coke with lime. Behind her, someone else elbowed his way in and shouted for a draft beer.

The clink of glasses and call of orders mingled with general conversation, forming an impenetrable wall of sound around Bree. Her phone vibrated in her pocket, but Bree didn't take it out. The pre-arranged signal was simply to let her know Matthew was in place.

Because he'd come without his typical disguise, they'd decided he'd pose as just another customer. Bree knew he'd set himself up in a position so he could watch her.

She also knew that James waited outside. Since he was well known as the officer investigating Hannah's death, he'd elected to keep watch until Matthew and Bree obtained some actionable information.

What I'd give to be wearing an earpiece and hidden camera now, Bree thought as she sat—seemingly alone—at the bar sipping Diet Coke and trying to catch Jen's eye. After her third glass, she finally succeeded.

Jen gave her a friendly smile. "Hi, Cat. If you're back for another bartending lesson, you're out of luck tonight. We're swamped. I only have a minute to chat. By the way, I like your new hair style."

Bree returned the smile. "I have a special date tonight."

"So, that accounts for your new look. If you don't mind some advice, you need to hook up with someone other than the used car salesman. That kind of man is trouble and heartache. Find yourself someone with higher aspirations."

Bree saw her opening. "Now you sound like my sorority sisters. In return for tutoring, they give me fashion and dating advice. I guess that's fair." She shrugged. "Isn't it?"

"All I ever got in return for tutoring was the chance to do more of it."

"That stinks."

"I wouldn't have minded so much," Jen fiddled with a charm on her bracelet, "if they'd just ignored me. Being ignored isn't so bad. It's being singled out for ridicule that stings."

"I'm sorry. Like I said, it stinks." Bree captured her hand and squeezed it. "Hey, isn't that a Kappa Zeta Rho charm on your bracelet? Did you belong to the sorority?"

Bree held her breath, hoping Jen would forget that she'd denied membership in a sorority.

"It was a long, painful time ago. Wearing this reminds me that, for some people, promises are cheap." She gave Bree a sharp, assessing look. In a flash, the assessment was replaced by a breezy smile and an easy attitude. "Listen, I've got to get back to work. I'll send something new over for you to try. The 'Arctic Orange' is a frozen version of my 'Tangerine Tango' that I think you'll like. I'm anxious for feedback on it."

With that, Jen hurried away to the other end of the bar.

Bree sipped her soda and put the pieces together in her mind, forming a scientific hypothesis about who killed Hannah. She tested the hypothesis against the facts.

If only Matthew could have heard Jen's part of the conversation. He—and even James—would agree that she was the prime suspect.

One. Jen and Hannah went to the same school. Although she tried to deny it, Jen also belonged to the same sorority as Hannah.

Two. Jen kept a reminder of what she referred to as a painful time. Jen's brains—and her own admission—indicated she'd had the skills to help academically challenged sisters.

Three. Liz Tinsdale had separated the sorority sisters into groups—brains vs. beauty. That, coupled with her knowledge of Hannah's academic misconduct—cheating— was consistent with Liz using smart sisters to tutor—and cheat for—the attractive girls Liz hired for prostitution.

Four. In addition to slipping tonight and admitting to being part of the sorority, Jen had slipped up other times. She'd talked about the girl in Hannah's sorority that was teased after being humiliated in the *Physics of Amusement Parks* class. But Jen had referred to the girl by names Hannah hadn't used. Was the girl really Jen? Or a friend of hers? What of the other sorority pranks the chapter had participated in? Had Jen's life or career been affected by those?

Bree constructed several scenarios in her mind—each featuring Jen as the killer. All of them stood the logic tests she threw at them. Jen had opportunity. And now, Jen had motive.

When a server placed a complimentary frozen drink in front of her, Bree hesitated. She scanned the bar, looking for Matthew, James, or someone else, but no one was in sight. Even though she knew they were close by, she felt utterly alone and vulnerable.

Absently she stirred the orange drink. Something about it didn't seem right. She sniffed but couldn't detect anything out of the ordinary amid the mix of orange and alcohol that greeted her. Yet, the texture didn't look so much icy as syrupy.

Her mind went back to the first night she'd been at the bar. *Miranda must have skimped on the ice.* Hannah had complained about her drinks that night. Bree stirred the drink, watching the sludgy orange liquid drip down the straw when she pulled it out.

Something wasn't right about this drink. *The percent alcohol in a drink determines at what point it freezes.*

Bree's nose twitched involuntarily as she remembered Jen swabbing down the bar, disinfecting it with isopropyl alcohol.

Didn't isopropyl—rubbing—alcohol—freeze at a higher temperature than regular alcohol? The difference might make a drink less slushy and more like syrup.

The back of Bree's neck prickled with icy awareness. Whatever happened, she didn't dare drink the concoction. She cast about trying to find something to put a sample of the drink in. Nate could surely analyze it to determine if it contained rubbing alcohol.

Bree pulled out her phone and sent a quick text to Matthew. *Getting sample. BRB.*

Drink in hand, she made her way to the ladies' room, which was blessedly empty. Bree searched through her purse, finally coming up with a bottle of eye drops. She emptied and rinsed the bottle then carefully filled it with the contents of her cocktail glass. The sample was small, but it should be enough to determine the type of alcohol used. She threw the rest down the drain and left the room.

Jen intercepted her before she could make her way back to the crowded main room of the bar. "What did you think of the 'Arctic Orange' cocktail?"

"Great," Bree replied. "How did you make it?"

"That's a secret I can't share. At least, not yet."

Was it Bree's imagination? Or was Jen's light tone forced? Were her suspicions of the woman right—or was she letting her imagination run wild? The dark, narrow hallway seemed to shrink and Bree suppressed a shudder.

"I'll get you another." Jen disappeared through a door leading to the back of the kitchen before Bree could decline.

Bree moved slowly cautiously, focused on the main room and the front door far ahead of her at the end of the long, dark hall.

She didn't make it. Jen—who must have cut through the kitchens and doubled back—entered from the dining room, blocking Bree before she could escape the confines of the hallway.

Bree whirled and headed to the back door instead. Jen grabbed her wrist from behind and twisted. Pain shot up Bree's arm until she stopped resisting. Jen dragged her into a storeroom, cluttered with crates of alcohol and assorted boxes. The woman was more than just tall—she had the strength of an Amazon. Bree wished she'd paid more attention when Tugood had given her self-defense tips.

Jen thrust a large glass into Bree's hand. "Drink up, Cat."

Bree threw the contents on the floor and raced toward the door. Jen, with her longer stride, overtook Bree immediately and gripped her throat in a wrestler's hold. "Didn't you hear that curiosity killed the Cat? You're too smart—and too nosey—for your own good."

Bree instinctively tucked her chin into the crook of Jen's arm, keeping the woman from cutting off her air supply. She tried to drop her body weight, counting on her heavier frame to be able to break the hold. But Jen countered effectively.

Her superior height and strength still threatened Bree—especially when Jen used her other arm to brace the chokehold and ease her way around Bree's defense. The bracelet, with its charms, bit into the side of Bree's neck

"You just had to keep asking questions." Jen's voice slithered along Bree's skin. "I did everyone a favor by getting rid of that manipulative liar, Hannah. She promised our friendship would last forever. We were going to visit every city represented by those stupid charms. But she broke that promise. Worse, she didn't even recognize me no matter how many hints I gave to jog her memory. If she'd only remembered..."

Jen dragged Bree deeper into the room. "Trust me," Jen said with a bitter laugh "the world is better without her."

Black swam before Bree's eyes as her air was cut off. Her strength wasn't working. Would Matthew realize she'd been away too long? Would he think to look for her in the storeroom? Would he arrive in time? She couldn't just wait for him to rescue her. She needed something else.

Her hand flew to her throat to claw at Jen's arm. Instead she touched Norah's amulet. *Mojo,* she thought as black filled more and more of her vision. *I need mojo.*

Bree planted her feet and yanked on the chain from her neck. She pulled the cork and spilled the contents—salt and hot pepper—into her hand. The glass vial tumbled to the ground.

Bree threw the irritating mixture over her shoulder.

Into Jen's eyes.

When the bartender howled in pain and Bree dropped her weight again. The hold broke, sending Bree to the floor. She rolled, scrambled to her feet, and jerked the storeroom door open.

Jen grabbed her hair, jerking Bree backward. She bit back a cry of pain and turned to her attacker. Instead of shrieking for help, she shouted a single word. "NO." Power filled her as she took control. "No." She kicked Jen's shins keeping her blows low to maintain balance. "No! No! No!" Each shout ended with a kick.

Jen's grip loosened and Bree twisted away. Her foot landed on the glass vial of her necklace, shattering it and causing Bree to stumble backward—into the arms of Liz Tinsdale.

"What on earth is going on here?" the older woman demanded.

In answer, James O'Neil rushed past them. He subdued Jen, slapping handcuffs on her. Tears streamed down Jen's mottled face, her swollen eyes testimony to the amount of red pepper Bree had thrown at her.

"Emogene Jena Stanton," James said, taking no pity on her condition, "you're under arrest for the murder of Hannah Rogers." He continued, listing her Miranda rights in a cold monotone.

"Emogene-sick-and-green?" whispered Liz.

"Don't you call me that! You bitch." Jen squinted at Liz through her reddened eyes. Fury contorted her red, splotchy face. "You're as guilty as she was. You were there. You encouraged them when you could have stopped them. You…you…" She uttered a foul name and spat at Liz's feet when James dragged her away.

Liz's hold on Bree softened and Bree felt herself slipping away until another arm came around her waist to hold her steady.

Matthew.

Only when he led her from the storeroom did she notice the red and blue lights flashing through the open door of the bar.

Uniformed policemen swarmed the area and patrons scattered.

In the chaos, Matthew drew her away from the crowd, into the open air, and out of danger.

CHAPTER 31

Hours later, Bree sat with both James and Matthew, drinking coffee in an all-night diner and explaining how she determined the killer's identity.

James glared at her. "You should have called me and actually talked to me with your suspicions before racing in to question her on your own."

"For once, the Boy Scout and I agree," added Matthew. "Besides, almost going in without backup, you disobeyed a direct order."

"I waited for your backup," Bree insisted. "As for disobeying orders, I hardly think asking me to do nothing all afternoon counts as an order."

"When your commanding officer tells you to relax, damn it, you relax." Matthew's mouth took on a mutinous set. Bree barely suppressed a giggle as the thought of Matthew making love to a woman and ordering her to enjoy it popped into her head.

"Much as I disagree with his methods, the Spook, here, knows how to run a covert op. At least, he should."

"All right." Bree shoved her wayward thoughts aside and held her hands up in surrender. "Next time, I won't just ask for your backup. I'll plan the entire operation with you before making a move."

"Good." Matthew gave her a nod.

"No, not good," James insisted. "There won't be a next time. You need to stop investigating crimes and focus on chemistry. All-in-all, it's the safer of the two professions."

"What about my contract to consult with the Plainville PD?"

"That was a one-time event," James shot back.

"We'll see," she replied. "Now, I've told you how I figured out who the killer was. How did you guess her identity?"

James took a sudden interest in his coffee while Matthew picked up the narrative. "I ran the new set of prints you gave me. Turns out the woman you knew as Jen Stands was born Emogene Jena Stanton. I cross checked her social and discovered she'd put in three semesters at Northwestern before getting kicked out on a cheating scandal. She also had a record for trying to steal some high-end jewelry—which was dismissed after it was revealed to be a sorority prank. Sound familiar?"

"That's the same type of prank that got Miranda Tinsdale in trouble," she said. "I put those two pieces of info together, too, when my sorority sister told me that bit of Kappa Z history."

"I still don't know how I'm going to justify your shady methods of getting and running prints," James grumbled.

"My methods saved Bree's neck."

"Thank you for that." James ran a weary hand over his face. "Anyway, after we booked her, Jen talked. And talked. And talked. All about how cruel the university and sorority were to her. For what it's worth, the cheating charges seemed to be trumped up. That's a crime I'm putting at Liz Tinsdale's feet."

He drained the rest of his coffee. "I don't know what would have happened to Jen if the circumstances had been different, but don't lose sleep over her. Jen was on a self-destructive path. Serial marriages and divorces and an obsession with finding people from her past to make them pay. I have a full couple of days ahead of me. I want to be sure she didn't commit other murders."

James rose and the others followed suit. He wrapped Bree in a friendly embrace and kissed her cheek. "You scared the hell out of me tonight. I'm just grateful you're safe. Please stop this crime fighting." His green eyes gleamed as he looked at her.

He led her a short distance away from Matthew, before asking, "What do you say we get together this weekend? There's a new restaurant in Chicago I'd love to take you to. We can talk about anything—as long as it doesn't involve murder and crime. What do you say?"

Before she could reply, a shadow fell over them.

"Break it up," Matthew muttered. "We have a few loose ends to tie up related to the drug case, then, my operative needs her sleep."

"Think about what I said." James rested his hand on her shoulder and gave her one last pleading look before turning to walk away.

Did he want her to think about his career advice? Or was he referring to his stated intentions to pursue a deeper relationship with her? Either way, she'd have plenty to think about.

James was the kind of man she'd fantasized about when she played dress-up as a child. A real-world knight in Kevlar armor.

The kind of man her family would approve of. Solid. Stable.

Everything sleuthing and spying wasn't.

But could she give up adventure to return to normal? And if not, was she willing to settle for what scarred, battle-tested Matthew could give her? Could she dare hope it might one day be real, instead of pretend?

"Come on, Watson. Time to go home. We'll finish debriefing on the way. We can pick up your car tomorrow." Matthew herded Bree into his car, all bustle and business, with none of the sweet concern James had shown.

As they rode through the darkened streets, Bree sagged against the seat, exhaustion finally taking hold. "Can we debrief about the drug investigation tomorrow? Surely nothing else needs to be handled tonight."

Matthew loosened his grip on the steering wheel and covered her hand with one of his. Warmth seeped into her cold fingers. "You received an unofficial thank you letter from Mr. DuBois."

"The Undersecretary to the Assistant, etcetera, etcetera, etcetera and so forth?"

"That would be him. Since the operation was never official, neither is the thank you. But Emily Appleton's grandfather assures me all is well. She'll be receiving her PhD, despite the omissions in her thesis. I thought you'd like to know."

"I'm glad that worked out."

"Thanks to you. And your insistence on sending the sanitized thesis draft to her advisor."

Matthew slid into a parking space on her street and walked Bree to her condo door. He paused, his hand on the knob she'd just unlocked.

"There is one more thing, Watson."

Bree turned to find him close. Close enough to … She shoved her wayward thoughts away. Her back to the solid door, and her front to a solid man, she breathed deeply. His subtle scent filled her lungs. "Yes?" she asked, a tremor in her voice.

He smiled and leaned closer, closing the tiny gap between their bodies until only a sliver remained. A deep enough breath on her part and they'd be touching.

Matthew released the doorknob and gently tucked a strand of hair behind her ear. His breath whispered along her cheekbones, past her temple.

"We never did get that date…"

EXPERIMENTS FROM BREE'S RECIPE BOOK

Bree's Piña Colada Chicken Strips

Raw Materials List (Marinade):

- 1 20 oz. (570 mL) can (~1 C) crushed pineapple
- ½ C (120 mL) brown sugar
- 1/3 C (80 mL) soy sauce
- 1T (30 mL) vegetable oil
- 2 lbs. (4.4 kg) chicken, cut into strips

Raw Materials List (Coating)

- 2 C (480 mL) crushed corn flake cereal
- 1 – 1½ C (240–360 mL) shredded, sweetened coconut
- ½ – 1 C (120–240 mL) finely ground pecans
- ½ tsp (3 mL) salt
- ½ tsp (3 mL) chili powder
- Zest of two limes

Raw Materials List (Egg wash)

- 2 egg whites
- 1 T (15 mL) sugar
- 1 tsp (5 mL) lime juice
- 1 tsp (5 mL) rum extract

Synthesis:
Prepare the Sauce (can be done a day ahead)

1. Combine the juice from the pineapple with the other ingredients for the marinade. Reserve the well-drained crushed pineapple for later.
2. Place chicken in the marinade for ~2 hours (overnight works better) and refrigerate. A zipper-style plastic bag works well for this.

Prepare the Coating (can be done a day ahead)

3. Combine corn flakes, coconut, and nuts in a food processor and pulse until the mixture is crumbled. The coarser the mix, the crunchier the chicken strips will be. (If you don't have a food processor, put the mix in a plastic bag and use your rolling pin to crush.) Makes about 4–5 C of coating.
4. Mix in the salt, chili powder and lime zest. Store the coating in a tightly sealed container.

Cooking the Chicken

5. Whisk together egg whites, sugar, lime juice, and rum extract until well-blended and airy.
6. Remove chicken from marinade. Discard marinade.
7. Lightly spray a baking sheet with non-stick coating.
8. Pat chicken dry. Dredge the chicken first in flour, then the egg wash, finally in the coating.
9. Place coated chicken strips on the baking sheet
10. Bake at 350°F (175°C) for 20 minutes or until done.
11. Serve with Piña Colada dipping sauce (recipe below)

Notes:

1. Chicken breasts or thighs work well with this recipe. Chicken can be cut into strips or, for a dinner portion the chicken cut can be kept whole.
2. The recipe also works well with shrimp. The cook time for shrimp is ~ 10 minutes.
3. This recipe calls for pecans, but any nuts will do. It all depends on your budget and your taste buds.
4. For more lime flavor, "infuse" the coating mix by adding the peel of a lime to it. Bree likes to wrap the peel in coffee filters and secure with a twist tie before dropping the filter in with the coating.
5. For the egg wash, real rum can be used in place of extract. Bree found good success using coconut rum, for an intensified flavor.
6. When coating the chicken, a pie plate is an ideal holder for the coating.

Happy Experimenting!

BREE'S PIÑA COLADA DIPPING SAUCE

Raw Materials List:

- 1 20 oz. (570 mL) can crushed pineapple, pulp only
- ½ small white onion, chopped fine
- 1 large red bell pepper, chopped fine
- Juice of ½ lime
- 2 T (30 mL) rum extract
- 1 tsp (5 mL) hot sauce
- ½ C (120 mL) honey

Synthesis:
Prepare the Chicken (can be done a day ahead)

1. Sauté pineapple, onion and bell pepper with 1T (15 mL) of rum extract and lime juice until tender.
2. Add honey and cook until thick, about 10 minutes.
3. Puree the solids using a hand-held immersion blender (or food processor) until it has the consistency of applesauce.
4. Return mixture to pan. Cook until volume is reduced to about 1/2 to 1/3 of the original volume.

5. Finish by whisking in 1T (15 mL) rum extract and 1 tsp (5 mL) hot sauce.
6. Refrigerate in tightly sealed container.

Pairs well with Piña Colada Chicken or Shrimp.

Notes:

1. Real rum can be used in place of rum extract. Try coconut rum or spiced rum for a twist on the original.
2. Adjust ingredients to individual taste.

Happy Experimenting!

Mabel May Mayfield's Macaroni Salad

Raw Materials List:
Salad Base

- 1 lb.(2.2kg) ham cut into bite-size pieces
- 1 lb. (2.2kg) cheddar cheese cut into bite-size pieces
- 1 dozen hard cooked eggs, chopped
- ¾ C (180 mL) Miracle Whip
- 1 small green, yellow, or red pepper (Bree adds one of each to "lighten" the dish)
- 3 stalks celery
- 1 small onion, chopped
- 1 lb. (2.2kg) cooked macaroni, drained

Dressing

- 2 C (480 mL) sugar
- ¼ C (60 mL) vinegar
- 2 eggs, beaten
- 2 T (30 mL) flour

Synthesis:

1. In a large bowl, stir the salad base together. In a saucepan, mix dressing ingredients and cook until thick.
2. Pour over salad base and thoroughly mix.

"Jackie's" Cheesy Chicken and Rice (Serves 6)

Raw Materials List:

- 3 C (720 mL) cooked rice
- 3 C (720 mL) chopped broccoli (frozen or fresh)
- 1/2 C (120 mL) each: sliced mushrooms, chopped green onions, and other veggies, if desired
- 2 T (30 mL) butter
- 2 C (480 mL) diced cooked chicken
- ½ tsp (3 mL) each: salt and pepper
- 1 C (240 mL) milk
- 4 eggs
- 1 can condensed cream of chicken soup
- 2 C (480 mL) cheddar cheese

Synthesis:

1. Sauté mushrooms, onions, and other fresh veggies in butter till tender
2. Combine sautéed veggies, rice, broccoli, and chicken together and spread into a lightly greased 9x13 inch baking dish.

3. Beat together eggs, milk, salt, and pepper and soup. Pour over the rice mixture.
4. Sprinkle with cheese (reserve ½ cup for garnish)
5. Bake, uncovered at 350 °F (175 °C) for 30 min or until heated through.
6. Sprinkle with remaining cheese and place under the broiler until cheese is bubbly and melted.

NOTE: Bree tried to reconstruct Jackie's recipe. The details—such as the amount and type of veggies and cheese—are easy to experiment with. (She's trying Pepper Jack cheese next.)

Feel free to put your own twist on this classic—and drop Bree a line to let her know how the experiment turns out.

Happy Experimenting!

RICCO'S MEXICAN
SPICED COCOA

Raw Materials List:

- ½ C (120 mL) sugar
- ¼ – ½ C (60 – 120 mL) cocoa powder
- ½ tsp (3 mL) cinnamon
- 1/8 tsp (½ -1 mL) each: ginger, allspice, cayenne
- Pinch salt
- 1/3 C (80 mL) warm water
- 2 C (480 mL) milk
- 2 C (480 mL) heavy cream
- 1 tsp (5 mL) vanilla

Synthesis:

1. Combine sugar, cocoa, spices, and salt in a saucepan
2. Whisk in water, stir well while heating over medium heat until the mixture begins to boil. Remove from heat.
3. Whisk in milk, cream, and vanilla.
4. Heat until it reaches desired drinking temperature (don't boil!)

Notes:

1. Ricco doesn't follow a recipe, so he couldn't give one to Bree. But that never stopped a researcher from trying something new.
2. For a lighter version, Bree sometimes uses only milk.
3. The next time she makes this, she plans to try almond milk in place of cream for a nutty, sweeter taste.
4. Adjust the amount and identity of spices to suit individual tastes. Pumpkin pie spice might make an interesting twist. A dash of chocolate or cinnamon liquor is another option.

Feel free to try your own twists on the basic recipe.

Happy Experimenting!

Fruity Oatmeal Cookies
(~2 dozen)

Raw Materials List:

- 1 C (240 mL) white sugar
- 1 C (240 mL) brown sugar, packed
- 2 eggs
- 1 tsp (5 mL) vanilla (or other flavor)
- 2 C (480 mL) all-purpose flour
- 1 tsp (5 mL) baking soda
- 1 tsp (5 mL) salt
- 1 ½ tsp (7 mL) cinnamon
- 3 C (720 mL) quick-cooking oats
- 1–2 T (15–30 mL) water (optional)
- 1–1 ½ C (240–360 mL) dried fruit, coarsely chopped*

Synthesis:

1. Cream together butter and sugars. Beat in eggs one at a time. Add vanilla.
2. In another bowl, stir together flour, baking soda, cinnamon, and salt. Slowly add to creamed mixture.
3. Mix in oats and chopped fruit. Cover, and chill dough.

4. Preheat oven to 375°F (190°C). Roll dough into walnut-sized balls. Place 2" (5 cm) apart on lightly greased (or parchment lined) cookie sheet. Flatten each cookie with a large fork dipped in sugar.
5. Bake for 8 to 10 minutes. Cool.

NOTES

1. Bree's grandmother uses raisins. Bree mixes in raisins, cranberries, apricots, pineapple, and mango.
2. Thin mixture with 1–2 T water if needed.
3. Bree doesn't always chill her dough like her grandmother does. That's why her cookies spread a bit more than Gram's when they bake.

Feel free to try your own twists on the basic recipe.

Happy Experimenting!

LIME BARS

Raw Materials List:

- 1 C butter (2 sticks or 240 mL), softened
- 1/2 C (120 mL) white sugar
- 2 C (480 mL) all-purpose flour
- 4 eggs
- 1 1/2 C (360 mL) white sugar
- ¼ C (60 mL) all-purpose flour
- 2 limes, juiced
- 1 drop green food coloring

Synthesis:

1. Preheat oven to 350°F (180°C).
2. Blend together softened butter, 2 C (480 mL) flour and 1/2 C (120 mL) sugar. Press into an ungreased 9"x13" (22.5 cm x 32.5 cm) pan.
3. Bake for 15 to 20 minutes or until firm and golden.
4. Whisk together the remaining 1 1/2 C (360 mL) sugar and 1/4 C (60 mL) flour. Whisk in the eggs, lime juice, and food coloring. Pour over the baked crust.
5. Bake for an additional 20 minutes. The bars will firm up as they cool.

<u>NOTE:</u>

The recipe also works with lemons in place of the limes. Bree is going to try it one day with oranges, but has not done so yet. Drop her a line if you try it to let her know how it comes out.

Happy Experimenting!

Basic Yellow Cake Recipe
(~2 dozen cupcakes)

Raw Materials List:

- 2½ C (600 mL) all-purpose flour
- 2½ tsp (12.5 mL) baking powder
- ¼ tsp (1.2 mL) salt
- 11/3 C (320 mL) granulated sugar
- ¾ C (180 mL) butter, softened
- 1½ tsp (7.5 mL) vanilla
- 3 eggs
- 1¼ C (300 mL) milk

Synthesis:

1. Cream together butter and sugars. Beat in eggs one at a time. Add vanilla. Beat until fluffy.
2. In another bowl, stir together flour, baking powder, and salt.
3. Alternately add dry ingredients and milk, until well mixed.
4. Preheat oven to 350°F (180°C).
5. Line a muffin tin with paper cupcake liners. Spray the inside of the liner with non-stick cooking spray.

6. Fill the wells 1/3 to 1/2 full with the cupcake mix.
7. Bake for 15–20 minutes or until a toothpick inserted in the cupcakes comes out clean. Cool.

NOTES

1. A modified version of the basic yellow cake recipe is used in both the Piña Colada and the Margarita cupcakes.
2. If you prefer, a boxed yellow cake mix can be used.

Happy Experimenting!

Piña Colada Cupcakes
(P) (~2 dozen)

Raw Materials List:

- basic yellow cake (or boxed mix)
- ¼ C (60 mL) sweetened, flaked coconut
- ¼ C (60 mL) crushed pineapple, well drained (reserve liquid for frosting)
- 2 T (30 mL) rum

Synthesis:

1. Prepare as directed in the yellow cake recipe with these modifications:
2. Add rum and vanilla at the same time.
3. Beat in pineapple before adding wet/dry ingredients.
4. Mix coconut with the dry ingredients.
5. Alternately add dry ingredients and milk, until well mixed.
6. Preheat oven to 350°F (180°C).
7. Line a muffin tin with paper cupcake liners. Spray the inside of the liner with non-stick cooking spray.

8. Fill the wells 1/3 to 1/2 full with the cupcake mix.
9. Bake for 15–20 minutes or until a toothpick inserted in the cupcakes comes out clean. (Excess liquid may take a few extra minutes of bake time.) Cool.

Frosting

Raw Materials List:

- 1 C (240 mL) butter
- 5–6 C (1200–1440 mL) powdered sugar
- ¼ C (60 mL) coconut milk
- ¼ C (60 mL) pineapple juice
- 1 tsp (5 mL) rum if desired
- 1–2 drops yellow food color
- Cherry (garnish)

Synthesis:

1. Beat the butter with the liquids until smooth. Add color.
2. Add powdered sugar slowly, with mixing, until desired consistency.
3. Add frosting to a pastry bag or a zip-close bag with a tiny corner snipped off. Pipe in a swirl pattern on top of cooled cupcakes.
4. Garnish with a cherry and a sprinkle of coconut flakes.
5. Add a tiny straw (coffee stirrer cut to 1" lengths) if desired.

<u>NOTES</u>

1. You may need to add small additional amounts of liquid and/or powdered sugar to reach the right consistency. It should hold soft peaks, but spread easily for best frosting results.

Happy Experimenting!

MARGARITA CUPCAKES (MG) (~2 DOZEN)

Raw Materials List:

- basic yellow cake (or boxed mix)
- zest of 1 lime
- juice of 1 lime
- 2 T (30 mL) tequila (optional)

Synthesis:

1. Prepare as directed in the yellow cake recipe with these modifications:
2. Add tequila, lime juice, and vanilla at the same time.
3. Add lime zest last.
4. Preheat oven to 350°F (180°C).
5. Line a muffin tin with paper cupcake liners. Spray the inside of the liner with non-stick cooking spray.
6. Fill the wells 1/3 to 1/2 full with the cupcake mix.
7. Bake for 15–20 minutes or until a toothpick inserted in the cupcakes comes out clean. (Excess liquid may take a few extra minutes of bake time.) Cool.

Frosting

Raw Materials List:

- 1 C (240 mL) butter
- 5–6 C (1200–1440 mL) powdered sugar
- ¼ C (60 mL) lime juice
- ¼ C (60 mL) tequila (or milk if you don't wish to use alcohol). Remember the alcohol in the frosting won't "bake off."
- 1–2 drops green food color
- Kosher or sea salt (garnish)

Synthesis:

1. Beat the butter with the liquids until smooth. Add color.
2. Add powdered sugar slowly, with mixing, until desired consistency.
3. Add frosting to a pastry bag or a zip-close bag with a tiny corner snipped off. Pipe in a swirl pattern on top of cooled cupcakes.
4. Garnish with a lime zest and coarse salt (or coarse sugar if you prefer)
5. Add a tiny straw (coffee stirrer cut to 1" lengths) if desired.

NOTES

1. You may need to add small additional amounts of liquid and/or powdered sugar to reach the right consistency. It should hold soft peaks, but spread easily for best frosting results.

Happy Experimenting!

For more about the Undercover Cat series of romantic mysteries, visit www.kellezriley.net where you can find tidbits such as:

- The "how-done-its" including details about how the crime was committed and a look into the killer's mind.
- The science behind the murder and how I researched it.
- Optional and/or deleted scenes.
- Links to cooking demos featuring recipes from Bree's "kitchen lab book."
- Information on upcoming releases.
- How to join Kelle's STARS (Street Team of Amazing Readers)
- And more!

And now for a peek at the next Undercover Cat Book:

Six months ago, Bree had been a confirmed dog person. Until she'd inherited a cat from her murdered boss. Now she held a tiger by the tail. Or rather, by a leash. But when it came to tigers the difference was just splitting hairs.

"This way," shouted the tour guide, his thick Australian accent a sharp contrast to the murmurings of the local Thai tiger trainers. "And stay with your tigers."

Bree was fairly certain he didn't mean for her to follow the energetic tiger cub over the dusty, rock-strewn flatlands to her right. But it tugged on the leash, intent on exploring, so she followed. Sweat trickled down her back a she scrambled over the barren, dusty terrain of the Thailand Tiger Sanctuary. Her foot caught on a rock and she stumbled as the wayward cub pulled her forward.

A strong male hand grabbed the leash and jerked the tiger back onto the path. Bree suppressed a shiver of awareness and turned to Matthew Tugood, both grateful for—and irritated by—his presence.

"Tell me again why we're here," he grumbled.

"My sorority is donating a rescued tiger cub to Terrance University for their wild animal vet clinic."

"I know that part. I cut through the red tape to make it happen, remember?" He slowed his pace, widening the gap between them and the rest of the tour group. "But why are we spending the day in a tourist trap?"

"I wanted to meet the cub's trainer and get first-hand experience."

Matthew answered with a dissatisfied grunt. His mouth firmed into a tight line as he scanned the horizon, squinting against the bright sunlight. "You're wasting time you could spend preparing for your assignment." His voice dropped low and he kept his eyes trained on the horizon. After a slow pivot, he leaned close, his breath warm on her ear despite his harsh tone. "Or have you forgotten about your mission?"

Bree disentangled the leash from his hands. "I liked you better before I knew you were a spy."

"No, you liked my cover story." His voice softened and he glanced her way. "That's not the same thing." Despite the 90-degree heat, a shiver chased down Bree's spine, as if he'd touched her rather than just looked at her.

"What I don't like is that you never stop thinking about your mission. Not for a minute. Look around you, Matthew." She gestured to landscape and the tourists in the distance, all leading tiger cubs by a leash. "We're exploring a new culture. Bottle feeding tiger cubs. Having adventures. Living. And you're missing it."

"Lower your voice. We don't want to be overheard."

Bree eyed the terrain, wondering if the clumps of scrub grass and rocks were cleverly disguised surveillance devices. She dismissed the idea with a snort. "Can't you think about something besides the mission?"

"May I remind you, that my single-minded focus on the mission saved your life on more than one occasion?"

Bree dropped the argument. For one thing, his interference had saved her life when a murderer—make that two murderers—had wanted her out of the picture. On the other hand, she hadn't found a single dead body before she met Matthew. So, in her mind, it was a toss-up.

"I helped you with your project." He glowered at the tiger cub.

"Thank—"

"You can repay me by focusing on our mission. I don't need thanks, I need you to complete your <u>assignment</u>."

"Fine. You've made yourself very clear." Bree shrugged. "Next topic." Beside her Matthew bristled. Bree hid her smile, taking secret delight in being able to needle him the same way he constantly needled her.

"Zed will be at the Royal Thai Energy Summit tomorrow night. He is convinced you're a brilliant researcher with access to cutting edge technology."

Bree stopped in her tracks so fast the tiger cub did a back flip at the end of his leash. She whirled on Matthew. "In case you've forgotten I *am* a real researcher, complete with a PhD in science. Just because my cover story involves a fictional company doesn't negate my experience." Behind her, the tiger cub let out a noise—something between a growl and a whine—as if to support Bree's statement.

"Your science degree isn't the only reason you're an asset to the Sci-Spy organization."

Another yowl, accompanied by a tug on the leash, made Bree turn back to her tiger cub. The rest of the tour group was no longer in sight. Ning, one of the young tiger trainers, hurried to them and tugged on Bree's sleeve. She chattered in Thai and gestured. "Hurry," she said, finally remembering the English word she needed.

Bree followed Ning and her tiger, moving quickly to catch up with the group. Tugood kept pace, his voice low and insistent in her ear. "Like it or not, your days as a simple researcher ended when you signed on with Sci-Spy. Your fictional energy research could be the key to thwarting a terrorist."

"The meeting isn't until tomorrow."

"You need to prep for it today."

"We've prepped for weeks. In the office. After hours at home. On the flights here." Bree stopped again, at the edge of the tour group and turned to Matthew. "Please. I need a day to do something fun. Something... normal."

As if anything about her days could be normal. Across the clearing, a large tiger roared, shaking the ground under her feet. The tour guide explained the procedure for approaching—and being photographed with—the massive, 500-pound tiger.

Bree surrendered her leash to Ning, without releasing Matthew's gaze. When he nodded in reluctant agreement, she turned to the tour group, but all thoughts of fun—and normal—had fled at Matthew's mention of the man they'd code-named Zed. Tomorrow, she'd have to confront him, while trying to find information to link him to his network of associates.

Compared to that, even the 500-pound tiger seemed docile.

76966121R00180

Made in the USA
Columbia, SC
14 September 2017